# Farspace
# 2

# Books by Authors in Farspace 2

Max Griffin
*SHADOWLANDS OF DESIRE* (loveyoudivine Alterotica, 2009)

Simon Logan
*KATJA FROM THE PUNK BAND* (Chizine Publications, 2010)
*PRETTY LITTLE THINGS TO FILL UP THE VOID* (Prime, 2008)
*ROHYPNOL BRIDES* (Prime, 2006)
*NOTHING IS INFLAMMABLE* (Prime, 2006)
*I-O* (Prime, 2002)

SoNNetWolF (as Susan Joyner-Stumpf)
*RAGDOLL CHRONICLES* (Available 2011)
*CRIMSON WHISPERS* (AuthorHouse, 2008)
*TORTURED LIGHT* (PublishAmerica, 2008)

David McGillveray
*CELERAINE* (Sam's Dot Publishing, 2008)

Timothy Masters (as Sandy Sampson)
*RED DUST AND BONES* (Purple Sword Publications, 2010)
*DEMON'S REDEMPTION* (with Anastasia Rabiyah; Purple Sword Publications, 2009). Audio version available for download from Audible.com

J. David Bell (as Joshua David Bellin)
*FRAMING MONSTERS: FANTASY FILM AND SOCIAL ALIENATION* (Southern Illinois University Press, 2005)
*MEDICINE BUNDLE: INDIAN SACRED PERFORMANCE AND AMERICAN LITERATURE* (Southern Illinois University Press, 2005)

# Farspace
## 2

Edited by
Edwin H Rydberg

Utility Fog
Press

First Published 2010 by Utility Fog Press
53 Rydal Road
Harrogate HG1 4SD
UK

*www.utilityfogpress.com*

ISBN: 978-0-9560469-3-2

A CIP catalogue record for this book is available from the British Library

Front cover image "Farspace Moons" by Carla Ralston and Lisa Cobb
Cover design by E.H. Rydberg (www.edwinhrydberg.com)

Editorial Staff

| | |
|---|---|
| Chief Editor | Edwin H. Rydberg |
| Assistant Editor | Alice Shevitz |
| Copy Editor | Sarah E. Holroyd |
| Acquisitions Editors | Stephanie Cassey |
| | Eric Fretheim |
| | Amanda Irazusta |
| | Nicole Smith |

# Contents

**INTRODUCTION**     1
     Edwin H. Rydberg

**COGITO ERGO SUM**     5
     Ben Shirar

**SYMBOL OF THE ORDER**     11
     L.D. Dailey

**WATERLOO**     23
     Calie Voorhis

**THE FAITHFUL SERVANT**     39
     Adriana Noir

**THE TALISMAN**     45
     Kate Sender

**THE GOTH MUSE**     51
     Ben A. Bell

**THE EXAMINED LIFE**     67
     Max Griffin

**NEYON DREAMS 2.0**     81
     David Snyder

**WATCH**     97
     Simon Logan

**ALIEN**     109
     SoNNetWolF

**THE SNAKE THAT BARKED**     111
     David McGillveray

**PARADOX**     127
     Lane Diamond

**FOREIGN GODS AMONG US**     137
     Timothy Masters

# Contents

**FROGSONG**      157
     J. David Bell

**ONWARD**      175
     Gregory Marshall Smith

**OUT THERE IT WILL BE DIFFERENT**      181
     Steven Lugo

**SKY FIRE**      197
     Robert Holt

**LEAVING MY HOME**      215
     K.S. Riggin

**GRANDFATHER**      221
     Eric Paul Fretheim

# Introduction

## Edwin H.Rydberg

*Farspace 2* was a lot longer in coming that I had originally planned or expected. And like humanity, it has evolved much along the way. While there was no stipulation for story content other than something "out there," be it in time, space, or mind, the stories that have found their way into the anthology paint a multifaceted picture of human endeavours. On the one hand, there is the striving forward, the human desire to know more, to discover what's beyond the known horizon, whatever the cost. On the other, there is fear of the unknown, fear of getting hurt, fear of taking risk.

*Farspace 2* feels a lot darker than *Farspace 1*, more cautionary and less care-free, and undoubtedly that's in keeping with the *zeitgeist*. As Terry Pratchet might say, these are interesting times we live in. Yet *Farspace 2* is also an anthology of hope and promise for the future, an anthology that urges us to keep moving forward despite the hardships we might find along the way.

The first group of stories, which I collectively think of as The Watchers, are about control: control by entities that want to harm or protect us—and sometimes the line between the two is invisibly thin. From Ben Shirar's opening story, "Cogito Ergo Sum", where dead minds are watched in a future theocratic crime investigation, to the noir in "Faithful Servant", and the depressingly realistic near future Orwellian voyeurisms of Max Griffin's "The Examined Life" and "Watch" by

1

industrial fiction author Simon Logan, characters have their lives dominated by others. Perhaps it's manifest desire given form, or a government meant to serve and protect that no longer does either. Whoever they are, the watchers are always there when we least desire it.

The second half of the anthology, Exploration, details off-world exploits—extra-terrestrial exploration; meeting little green men who may not be so little, or so green. These are not happy, "everything is wonderful out there and all will be great if we only go" stories. These are "yes it's dangerous out there, yes we can get killed out there, but we still need to go" stories. These are stories that explore the dangers of leaving Earth, the perils that may be waiting out there, in the cold depths of space, or on inhospitable planets when friend and foe are not always obvious—in other words, stories in the true spirit of exploration and colonization.

A spirit I feel much of our society has lost.

Most of us will be reading this from our sofas or easy-chairs, in front of our big screen LCD TVs, smack in the middle of a society that is, or has been, at the pinnacle of human civilization. Unfortunately, that also implies that most of us will be reading this from smack in the middle of a society that is now on the down side of said pinnacle; a society that no longer looks forward, striving to explore the unknown, to expand into new frontiers. Instead, we gaze fondly on past glories, hoarding what we have and what we are, desperately protecting ourselves and our ideologies from the future—that fearful unknown.

Once there was the Wild West. Now we're just the tired West. Sure, the spirit of exploration lives on. But it's more often despite, rather than because of, society. Consider that one of the largest economies in the world doesn't have a manned space program. That's the case in the UK, where it seems that any spirit of exploration has been squashed by fearful bureaucracy.

Unfortunately, what such fearful bureaucracies fail to consider is that, yes, people could get killed exploring space, yes, our species could get wiped out, but how would that be any different than if we stay Earth-bound? And the trade-offs for that risk are opportunities for discovery and knowledge beyond imagining.

As in "Leaving My Home" by K.S. Riggin, it's frightening to leave our nest, to fly or fall on our own. But, ultimately, out there are hope and the promise of new beginnings. And anyway, if Steve Lugo is right, we might even find, as much to our dismay as Commander Dan Hathers's, that out there is not that much different than here.

So, with curiosity, wonder, and a little trepidation, let's begin our journey. Onward to that Farspace!

# Cogito Ergo Sum

**Ben Shirar**

Ben Shirar hails from St. Louis, Missouri, though he can most often be found (if one is willing to search the cornfields) in Grinnell, Iowa, where he is an anthropology student at Grinnell College. When not in school, he works as a construction/ maintenance worker and plays a mean fiddle. Thanks go to friends, family, and Mr. Colston, English teacher and curmudgeon *par excellence*.

*I am Seeker. I am Finder. I am Hunter-of-Memories and slayer-of-lies. I bring justice for the victims—the same justice that has been denied me. Hah! Me. As if there is such a person. No, I grant them justice, and in return, they grant me those few fleeting moments of a life long-lost.*

~

I entered through the shattered doorframe, flanked as always by a pair of armed guardsmen. I bent over to pick up a piece of splintered wood, and the two men swung their rifles in my direction, the clicking off of safeties sounding like a thunderclap in the still room. I lifted my hands up and stared one of the men in the eyes.

"I'm wearing my gloves. I can do no harm. We must await the arrival of the Inspector."

The men lifted their guns back to port arms, glancing uneasily in my direction. I suppressed a smile. Fools. Didn't they realize that the restraining device on my hands could only be opened by an authorized Inspector?

With the heavy tread of booted feet, a squadron of the Home Guard marched down the dingy corridors. I heard the soft whisper of the Inspector's heavy cloak as he entered, and turned to face him. His cold eyes looked into my own, and I recalled all the things I've heard about Inspectors. He beckoned me forward, and gave me my instructions.

"I want a complete memory sweep of the body. Also, there is a blood-stained fragment of a wine glass. I require a memory read on that as well. There may be additional objects later, but for now, simply the victim and the glass will be sufficient."

"Did she die unshriven?"

The souls of those who are killed immediately following any of the thirty-four officially recognized atonement procedures are often too restful to yield much in the way of evidence. Fortunately, the use of the P.I.N.—parishioner identification number—and similar devices allowed the government to keep track of the spiritual state of all citizens.

"Of course. Why else would I request a memory sweep? Now, begin your work."

So saying, he drew the key from the chain around his neck, and bade me raise my hands to him. With an audible click and hum of pent-up energy, the systems that powered my gauntlets were deactivated. Now I could remove them without suffering any ill effects.

Striding further into the apartment, I glimpsed the body: a young woman with pale skin and fair hair lay dead on the kitchen floor, a pair of bullet holes in her chest bearing mute testimony to the manner of her death. I squatted down beside her and braced myself before tentatively grasping her hand.

~

*Fear. It washes over me, a tidal wave that threatens to overcome my own senses. This is not unexpected. As the initial onslaught of sheer terror subsides, I examine the detritus it has left behind. Affection. Betrayal. She knew her killer—I know because her final thoughts were tinged with shock at the treachery done to her. Ahh...here's something unusual. Resignation. Many humans expect their deaths; few have the wisdom not to struggle. When one combats death, the conflicting emotions prevent a clear reading—an unwilling soul often refuses to accept its demise. Most curious.*

~

"She knew her killer. And she wanted to die—there was no outrage, no sense that she had been wronged—shock, certainly,

7

but only because of the suddenness of the act, not the act itself."

"Do you see anything?"

"Let me look again."

~

*Once again, I am submerged. None can know the bliss that is memory diving. I attempt to access her visual memories—this is extremely difficult, as the electrical impulses to the brain are short lived, but I can trace her neural pathways back to their source.*

~

"Do we have a technician?"

A middle-aged man in a white lab coat stepped forward.

"I need ocular access. Make the incision."

The man hesitated for a moment, until the Inspector nodded his assent.

"Right away, sir."

The procedure completed, I turned to the Inspector.

"I'm requesting you remove the second barrier layer. I need complete immersion."

"Request granted."

Punching a button on his key, the man removed the electrical interference generator implanted in my skin. I knelt back over the body and plunged my hand down, brushing the surface of her brain.

~

*Fulfillment. A sense of completion long denied. This is what any Reader feels when he connects with the brain of a subject. Sensitive nerve endings react to the electricity flowing through my skin, and I bare myself to their intrusions. Like seeks like, as the residual energy in her neurons connects with my own, and supplants my own memories. Everything vanishes. It does not go black—the sensation is like nothing I can explain. It is a nothingness so palpable I could smell it, were my nose not hers, or see it, were my eyes not her own.*

~

"John!" I screamed, my voice sounding raw through my throat. "Please, I didn't mean to hurt you! It wasn't what you think! He was my brother! You have to believe me!"

A vision passed before my eyes: a tall, light-skinned man, holding an antique .45 pistol, rage and betrayal burning in his eyes. I felt an inexplicable connection to this man, confirming my initial suspicions: an estranged lover, a murder committed in the heat of passion.

"What is his name? His full name. Answer me!"

"John...John Brokaw..."

"Disconnect, Reader. Disconnect now!"

~

*I try. The disorientation that accompanies disconnection elicits a moment of absolute terror from me, the fear that I will never make it back to my own body. Briefly, some vestigial part of her soul attempts to grasp my own, and I force it back down, manipulating the electrical impulses of my body to negate her own nerves. She returns to what she was—a cold corpse, before being brought to life again.*

~

"Good work, Reader. Time to wipe you."

I struggled as the Inspector drew a scrambler from his belt. Two guardsmen held my arms while their captain began charging the device. In spite of my efforts, the hated gauntlets were forced back onto my hands, and the static generator reactivated.

~

*I must savour these moments. For only seconds more, her life shall be mine. However painful or agonizing her last moments in this world may have been, I shall treasure them.*

~

Scrambler charged, the Inspector placed the device next to my ear. A whine, a brief pulse, and nothing remained.

~

*I am Seeker. I am Finder. I am Hunter-of-Memories. And I am born anew, my mind an empty vessel. Cogito ergo Sum? Perhaps. Man is the sum of his experiences, they say. In this sense, I am both the least and the greatest. I have experienced countless lives. But none of them has been my own.*

# Symbol of the Order

**L.D. Dailey**

L.D. Dailey hails from Virginia, where he is a telecommunications engineer by day and an aspiring writer by night. This anthology marks his first publication. He keeps unpublished work at duggadugga.Writing.Com

Sitting in front of a sacked mosque, the watcher strained weary eyes against the rising sun obscuring the Temple of Solomon. A new day in the Holy Land did little to stave off the chill. The beggar-in-disguise pressed his rags, newly acquired from a deceased contributor, tighter around his slim frame.

The Byzantine cursed the name of Emperor Alexius, even while serving the man as his spymaster. "Jerusalem, the Kingdom of Heaven." A cynical snort answered his own mutters, "Nothing here but a den of thieves, murderers, and rapists. These fools pose no threat to the empire, just Christian wolves killing Muslim dogs, the whole lot of them."

Thoughts drifted to his wife and two sons back in the empire as a pilgrim strode by and tossed some coins in a cracked bowl. The spymaster lifted his face and met the eyes of the supposed benefactor, memorizing his features out of habit, giving a false smile of thankfulness, before returning to the mission.

Four men, young squires and grizzled men-at-arms— warmongers lacking social standing or political prestige in their various homelands who fancied themselves the Knights Templar—exited the temple. A tattered standard rustled against the desert wind, displaying two armoured men astride a lone horse, an all-too-true sign of their wealth.

The spy found it odd that men charged with guarding the Pilgrim Road would embark before travellers braved the roads and without patrons seeking safety from Jerusalem. A fifth exited wearing a breastplate covered with an ivory tabard dyed with the crimson cross. The watcher smiled at the unmistakable dark eyes and high cheekbones covered with an ebony beard matching shoulder-length hair. *Grand Master Hugh de Payens, why would he embark on a simple escort mission? Most curious.*

In silence and on foot, the spymaster trailed the mounted Templar Knights. He kept to the shadows of ruined husks that once housed Muslim families, shattered remnants of life before the wolves descended upon Jerusalem to capture their prize. The party exited the St. Stephen's Gate and travelled a northwestern route.

The watcher raced toward the nearby inn, tossing the morning's disguise in an alley, displaying the garments of a wealthy Byzantine trader beneath. He slowed as the inn appeared, smoothing his silks before crossing the threshold.

A slim proprietor, his angular face creased with a perpetual frown, greeted the trader with a tight smile. "Good day, Silvanus Moschus. Breakfast?"

Silvanus feigned haste. "My horse, and quickly, I have a client in the west. The fool wants to trade wool for olives— olives for God's sake!" Silvanus smiled as the blasphemy caused the dreary man to widen mahogany eyes and rush to the stable himself, ignoring a nearby stable hand in his rush. Mentally, he chided the actions that would only bring more attention upon him, making the mission harder to complete, delaying the return home. Sometimes, Silvanus could not help the antagonistic streak within. His loathing of God-fearing hypocrites ran deep.

Moments later, he mounted a chestnut gelding and raced to catch his quarry. Alone and unarmed, he kept a safe distance, following the fresh tracks churned in the dirt road by the knights' haste.

The crimson sun crested an azure horizon as he pulled rein atop a large rise, surveying a small city dominated by the ruins of a Byzantine monastery upon a large hill. Memories of the empire's history came unbidden as a map flashed in his mind. "Mons Gaudi." Even as a shell of its former glory, the church awed him. "Then this is Arimathea." Silvanus delved into his photographic memory once more, pleased that it had not failed in his advancing years. "Nothing here but peasants, so why are the Templar Knights here?"

"Because they are fools, as are you."

Turning to the voice from behind, he blinked at the Arab, stunned by his ability to speak Greek.

The man, adorned in the golden garb of the Saracen army, smiled, displaying a row of gleaming teeth through an ebony beard trimmed to the size of a man's fist. "My knowledge of your heathen tongue surprises you. I learned Greek from our Greek slaves."

Silvanus offered the soldier silent congratulations for catching him unawares. He transitioned to Arabic, hoping to return the shock. "Why are you here? You're a Saracen. You were beaten, your people slaughtered."

The fighter replied with a nod, a sad nod, hidden behind angry eyes affirming Silvanus's recollection of events. "Yes, but a man must eat." With the practiced fluidity of a trained killer, he unsheathed a scimitar and raised it high, screaming to Allah for victory as the blade rushed downward.

Silvanus leaped from his horse, sacrificing the animal to the killing stroke. The weapon struck horseflesh and the beast whinnied in pain. The animal kicked and bucked, striking the bandit in the face before fleeing.

Silvanus recovered from the brush with death and scurried over to the assailant, ready to send the Muslim to his god if need be. He surveyed the thief's snapped neck and nodded a silent thanks to his dying mount.

The naked desert before him offered no other surprises. Deeming it safe, he removed his colourful clothes, displaying a filthy cotton robe and linen pants. Without a second thought, he trekked onward to Arimathea, leaving the weapon behind. A pilgrim strayed from the Pilgrim Road was a poor disguise without the need of an Arabic weapon to heighten suspicion.

Silvanus stalked the dirt-covered streets and beheld an odd assortment of Christians, Jews, and Muslims. A lone church bell rang in the distance. An Arab sang the call to prayer from the heights of a domed mosque. Silvanus found the harmony difficult to comprehend. These peasants found some semblance of community within a province too unimportant for the new king to claim. Their society offered hope for humanity to the spy's cynical mind. *No wolves here—yet.*

Silvanus approached an old beggar working in the shade of an unremarkable building. He queried about the knights' whereabouts in German, French, and Greek before settling on Hebrew. The old man shrugged knobbed shoulders, visible through a flimsy garment of stretched linen, and looked away. With a deep sigh, Silvanus tossed a pair of coppers into a cracked bowl. The old man rubbed a clean-shaven chin, assuming a mask of deep thought that made Silvanus roll his eyes while adding a silver coin to the donation. Failing to hide surprise, the informant's thundercloud eyes grew wide as the silver rolled about the bowl. He reached for the coin but a cough from Silvanus gave him pause, and he deftly pointed to a steep hill behind Silvanus. "Tomb of Samuel."

The ruby sun reached its noonday peak before Silvanus arrived. Sparse outcroppings provided scant cover as the spy crawled up toward the tomb. He spied three men dislodging the boulder guarding the dead. *Three?* Silvanus turned about, fearing a second ambush, and found nothing.

The sound of racing hooves turned his attention once more to the grave robbers. Five riderless horses fled across the landscape. Four men gave a valiant chase before realizing the futility of it. *Madness piled on madness.*

One of the men-at-arms saw him and pointed. He turned to flee and almost impaled his neck on a sword aimed at his exposed throat.

"Why are you here?"

Silvanus understood the Frenchman and replied in German, "I don't understand you."

A shadow loomed over him and Silvanus twisted his head to see, scraping the sword's edge along his neck. He ignored the trickle of blood staining his pale tunic.

Hugh de Payens stepped from behind the rock and spat at Silvanus's feet. "A Frank." The eerie sound of unsheathed steel caused Silvanus to close his eyes in uncharacteristic fear.

Another Templar approached from the left, hard eyed and grim-faced. An arrowhead scar marred his sun-darkened cheek. "Do we kill him, my lord?"

Lord Hugh shook his head. "No, not here on holy ground. Your thoughts must be pure, Sergeant. It is the only way." Payens looked down into Silvanus's eyes, "What do I do with you, peasant? I cannot kill you and I cannot set you free." He nodded over Silvanus's shoulder.

Pain against the base of his skull buckled him over, followed by darkness.

Darkness surrounded him as Silvanus awoke with an exploding headache making the simple tasks of thinking straight and moving difficult. Silvanus recalled his training, detached himself from the pain, and focused on his plight. The darkness turned out to be a blindfold. His immobility came from bindings around his hands and feet. The spymaster refused to panic, determined to ascertain the situation with his remaining senses.

Bound hands traced the ground: cold, hard, and dry. *A cell? No. I feel rocks, dirt. There's no wind—the tomb? I'm in the damned tomb!* Panic pricked through his mental shroud, but he tamped it back down as the inklings of a plan surfaced.

Silvanus crawled along the floor, looking for anything resembling a sharp object. After minutes of searching, he found nothing. *Very well. Now it's time to panic.*

A terrified scream echoed across the tomb. The sounds of boots sprinting toward him caused Silvanus to squirm and crawl toward a perceived wall. The screamer tripped over his prone body. A sickening crack of skull against stone brought silence.

Silvanus acted without hesitation, crawling along the dead man's body, searching for a weapon. His hands soon grasped something that resembled a pommel. Silvanus clasped the sword and pulled enough of the blade to suit his purposes. An intense desperation sped him along as he severed the bonds.

Soon, Silvanus secured his freedom. Although the cave held no light, he refused to proceed where the Templar had fled. Sword before him, Silvanus stalked in the opposite direction, praying to reach the entrance, to see the sunlight streaming through, to feel the wind against his cheek. The poised sword clanked against stone and the spy sighed in defeat, running his hand along the smooth face of the boulder blocking his exit.

*Only one way to go now.* Turning about, he crept back, picking up the deceased's buckler while passing. The old fear returned, rising like bile in his throat. *Why did the fools lock themselves in?*

"Searching," a soft voice replied in the darkness, giving Silvanus notice that he'd spoken the last thought aloud. The soft sounds of weeping caused him to search for its source. He discovered a shadow in the darkness shaking as it wept.

Silvanus knelt close by and chose to speak French. "What's wrong with you?"

"My soul."

The dark musing came from the familiar voice of Hugh de Payens. "What?" Silvanus shook his head. "Why are you here, Hugh?"

"Searching for…"

"For what?"

"Salvation."

"You're—mad."

Footsteps echoed from around a sharp bend. "No, he's not mad. He just didn't like what he saw."

Silvanus looked up at the stranger, a scrawny adolescent holding a torch above freckled cheeks still fat from childhood. "You are no knight."

The boy held out his palm in greeting—and returned it to his side after the spy refused to respond. "Squire François, sir." The boy's dark eyes regarded de Payens with a hint of commiseration. "You might as well leave him be, he has to find his own way—I think. If you're looking for answers, follow me." The squire turned around, taking the precious light away.

Silvanus followed, leaving Hugh to his fate. "So why are the Templar Knights interested in Samuel's Tomb?"

"They're not," François started before shaking his head. "Sorry. I mean we're not. Watch your step, there're bones everywhere."

Silvanus glanced down and tried to leap out of his skin as corpses in various stages of decay stretched before them. A full skeleton bearing the ebony lacquered armour of a Hun sat to his right. Beside it, the mummified remains of a Roman

Legionnaire clutched an ancient standard of a black eagle on a crimson field. The golden armour of the Saracens glimmered against the flame's light as they trekked past a third. Further still, the recent dead lay, bearing the familiar marks of the empire. "Armenians, the Emperor's mercenaries. What is all this?"

The pale youth seemed to pale more as they crossed the gauntlet of dead. "I don't know."

Silvanus placed a hand on the boy's shoulder. His palpable fear reminded the spy of his own children when the Crusaders arrived at the gates of Byzantium. "Perhaps we should stop."

François shook his head. "No, you need to see this."

They walked around a curve in the tunnel and came to a square alcove with walls lined in flaming torches, their light glistening off a wide table of solid gold. Silvanus controlled his mouth-watering greed as he eyed the golden bowls, plates, and wineglasses set about it. A second teenage squire hovered above two sergeants, their lifeless forms amid the opulent scene turning the moisture in Silvanus's mouth to ash.

The ornate dinner scene intrigued the master of disguise. He strode toward it with his sword and shield poised as if expecting attack, and paused when the nameless squire gasped, as if scandalized by some perceived impetuousness. Irritated, he jerked the boy from the scene, tossing him toward François. Silvanus inspected the corpses from a distance, yet found no wounds marring their armour, no signs of a struggle. *Curious.* "How did they die?"

"Screaming," François muttered.

The second piped up, "They tested God, and He killed them."

Silvanus held back a condescending retort. In his line of work, a real answer always lay beneath the religion of the ignorant masses. His thoughts drifted back to his journey with the Crusaders through Antioch and the barbarous slaughter of defenceless Muslims in the name of the same God their enemies worshipped. *What God of peace bloodies His hands with innocents, and what do you say for the fools who die in His name?*

François clucked in irritation "Wasn't God, you buffoon. They did it to themselves. They tried to steal it."

Silvanus concealed a smile before facing the two. *One of them has hope.* "Steal what?"

François rolled his eyes. "The chalice, sir, the Holy Grail. The cup Jesus held for his last supper. It's right there in front of you, ready for the taking. That's what the Templars—what we wanted."

Silvanus stared hard at the wineglasses around the table. "They look like normal glasses to me."

François's contemporary snorted. "Well then, you try touching it."

Silvanus did not take the offer. *Only heroes die for their courage.* "Who locked us in the tomb?"

"God did."

François sighed. "He might be right about that one—the rock just tumbled on its own when we were all inside."

Frowning, Silvanus surveyed the room for signs of unnatural nooks or cracks, the telltale signs of man-made traps. "Tell me everything that happened in this room."

"Well we were looking for something Lord de Payens called 'the symbol of our order.' Lord de Payens runs to the table, grabs for the chalice, and starts babbling stuff like, 'This isn't me! I'm a knight! I'm a holy man of God!' and on and on until he starts crying like a baby. The other two tried to steal the other glasses and they just—fell."

Silvanus sat down and brooded over the problem, thankful for the blissful silence from the boys. A litany of odourless, colourless poisons loomed in his thoughts. However, none that penetrated the skin matched the hallucinogenic symptoms of de Payens. *But that does not mean that none exists.* The incapacitated men-at-arms represented another obscure puzzle with no answers. *Concentrate on what you can rationalize, Silvanus.* A slow, painful death from starvation plagued his rationales.

He stared at the table, at the golden objects adorning it, and fancied an end without the torment of famine. Thoughts of his wife and children obliterated the suicidal thoughts. Placing his face in his hands, the spy uttered a weary sigh. "I should never have followed you. I don't care about the Templar and I don't care about Jesus's damned wineglass. I just want to get out."

A small tremor interrupted his musings. The gold dinnerware melted away to nothing, leaving a single bowl placed in the table's centre. Azure flames erupted from the bowl. A scene played within the fire.

*A well-dressed Hebrew youth argued with a man with Mediterranean features, adorned in the uniform of an Urban Cohort. The Roman nodded. A sack bulging with coins exchanged hands. The Hebrew sprinted to a hill littered with a trio of crosses with a corpse nailed to each. A woman watched as he pulled a slender frame from the centre cross and carried the body to the back of a tomb. She perched a small wineglass, golden and studded with gems, atop the raised grave—*

The flames died. The rumbling ceased. Silvanus leaped to his feet, shocked by the inexplicable vision. A life grounded in the quest for secrets offered no solace, no answer for this oddity. A faint sensation caressed his cheek. "The wind. The cave is open!" He threw the borrowed weapons away. Laughing at the stunned youths, he encircled them with his arms and escorted the pair out of the cave.

Arriving at the entrance, Silvanus noticed an armoured shadow silhouetted against the setting sun.

The form beckoned them forward. "You might as well come out. You have something that belongs to me."

Shocked at the lunatic's recovery, Silvanus uttered the truth. "We don't have anything, Hugh. I swear to God."

"You have the chalice. How else could the cave open? I felt the Hand of God move. I want it. I want it!" The shadow charged, raised longsword screeching across the tomb's ceiling.

Without thought, the spy pushed the lads behind him, ushering them back to the alcove, back to—a golden table littered with bowls, plates, and wineglasses—

Without pausing to observe this new mystery, the spy tossed the squires to the sides of the opening. He picked up the sword and shield he had left behind, and turned to face the maniac, feeling overmatched and foolish as rationale sunk in. *I await a knight's charge—and for what?* He peered at François to the right, turned toward the nameless one perched against the left wall, and thought about his own children.

The screech of steel against stone heralded Hugh's entrance. He screamed and unleashed a mighty chop against Silvanus's buckler. The impact knocked the smaller man backward into the table.

Silvanus realized the futility of his situation before the attack and planned for the inevitable failure. With Hugh distracted, Silvanus screamed, "Run, boys," and watched the pair escape beneath the shelter of a dented shield.

The knight snatched Silvanus's source of defence from his grip, launching the metal across the room, and lifted the stunned Byzantine by the hair. "It will be mine!"

Fearing for his life, Silvanus strained to employ his strongest weapon, his mind. "You would kill me on hallowed ground?"

Hugh's face slackened for a moment, but only that, before a grimace of anguish and lunacy marred his features. "I am worthy."

"Then take it. It's still here."

Ebony pools widened as Hugh surveyed the magical scene. His grip slackened, and Silvanus slid to the cold floor like a lifeless sack. A gauntleted hand reached for the gem-encrusted cup and paused, surrounding the chalice but not clutching it. "No." Hugh pulled the Byzantine to his feet and turned him round toward the dinner setting. "You take it." With his sword pointed at Silvanus's back, Hugh backed away.

Silvanus faced the table, unmoving, entrenched in deep thought as his eyes glanced down at the corpses beneath it. *Either by God or by Hugh, I'm dead. I wonder if the boys escaped.* The cornered spy noticed the absence of the breeze. Although sealed within the tomb once more, he smiled. Somehow, he believed that they survived. Somehow, he knew it for truth. The spy laughed, and received a painful thrust to his spine for the outburst.

*What God of peace bloodies His hands with innocents?* The question flowed through his mind unbidden. *What do you say for the fools who die in His name?* An answer, secret until this moment, followed the query.

Unafraid, Silvanus turned and gazed up into Hugh's eyes. He laughed at the hatred within them. "I refuse." Silvanus crossed his arms. "We'll both die here."

An impotent scream, full of venom and fury, replied as the sword impaled his chest. Pain erupted within him, bringing darkness and with it—The Light.

# Waterloo

## Calie Voorhis

Calie Voorhis is a life-long fanatic of the fantastic, with over 15 short story publications, including stories in *Ray Gun Revival, Beyond Centauri, Fusion Fragment,* and *The Online Anathema Anthology*, and stories in the print anthologies *Dead Set: A Zombie Anthology* and *Space Sirens*. Upcoming stories will appear in the print anthologies *Anywhere But Earth* and *DOA—Tales of Extreme Terror,* and in *Andromeda Spaceways Inflight Magazine*. She holds a BS in Biology from UNC–Chapel Hill, an MFA in Writing Popular Fiction from Seton Hill University, and is an Odyssey workshop alumna.

It always rained on June 18, 1815. The showers poured down over the temporal shield of her chameleon suit.

The Old Bitch checked her chronometer—almost 9:00 a.m. Waterloo wouldn't start in earnest for a few more hours. She flicked her cigarette ashes against the beige stone wall of the Hougoumont house, the key to Wellington's right flank. It was a good place for her team to keep an eye out for Chronoids.

A British regiment marched by, the bright red of their jackets staining their white trousers pink. She held her breath out of habit as they passed. Not one of them looked at her.

She hoped they'd be through this sequence of Waterloos soon and on to the next assignment. The geeks in the science branch assured her each analogue was different, but damned if she could tell. It always rained, it was always muddy, and it was always loud. At least it was Friday, for her. For Napoleon and Wellington it was always Monday.

Her ear implant chimed. "Perimeter reporting clear, ma'am," Big John said. "No sign of Chronoid intrusion. Can I come in now?"

"Hell, no," she said. The mud squished under her feet as she shifted.

Big John must not have shut his internal switch off because she heard him mumble "old bitch" under his breath.

"Damn right, son. And don't you forget it."

He apologized and clicked off. She finished her cigarette and stuck the filter in her pocket. Before joining the Legion she'd had a name. But in the Legion names weren't given— they were earned. "Old Bitch" suited her.

The offensive pounded in right on time at noon, just like always. The first barrage of artillery splattered mud as cannonballs smashed to the ground. Fortunately the chameleon suits projected a temporal bubble, keeping her invisible and safe.

Gods above, this was one of her least favourite assignments. Give her a crucifixion in sunny Jerusalem any day.

"Napoleon met his Waterloo," she sang under her breath as a mortar round smashed to her right. "And like it or not it seems I'm destined, too." A step to her left and a bullet whistled overhead through the grey sky, same as every analogue. She activated her throat mike by poking her tongue at the side of a molar. "Sing it with me, everyone."

Her company's voices rang in her ears. "Ooooh, Waterloo, here in the mud at Waterloo. Wishing I had a good vindaloo, dreaming I could be with you." The company sang out of key, but made up for it with gusto.

In the midst of the chorus, Wolf's voice cut through. "Ah, crap." The voices went silent. "You see it, Little Fox?"

"I see it, Wolf. We've got an intrusion. This orb is growing fast. Must be coming from a timeline close to us. Hold on, someone's coming through." She paused. "Oh, shit."

"Little Fox?" Raindrops blew against the Old Bitch's chameleon suit, a brief bitter patter.

"Captain," Little Fox said, "they dumped a suicide bomber, looks to be from about 1990 or so. He's standing in the field, right where Wellington's going to be in about thirty seconds."

The Old Bitch marked Little Fox's position on her helmet monitor. Shit, she couldn't reach the bomber in time. But she could see Little Fox's blip heading towards the anomaly. She wanted to call her back, but knew she couldn't. They couldn't afford to lose another Earth analogue.

"Little Fox," she said into her mike. "Get a force field around the bastard and get out." She kept her voice steady.

"No time, Captain." Little Fox's voice cracked on the last word.

"Wolf?" she asked.

"I'll try." His words stuttered; she knew he was already running. Drop after drop of water rained down, each a sparkling globe.

Gunfire rang out in the distance as the light companies of the Coldstream and Third Guards advanced.

An explosion burst through the headset, ricocheted through the Old Bitch's eardrums, and Little Fox's blip faded from the screen.

"We lost her, Captain." Wolf said. "She shielded the bomber with her own field, trapping him inside. I don't think Napoleon noticed."

Explosions burst from the munitions dump in a distant field. Mud and grass hailed down and pattered harmlessly around her, just like every other day at Waterloo.

She stayed silent. The wind swirled. She stood there, the faded taste of nicotine in her mouth. It felt like the rain had seeped inside her shield. She could feel the dampness spread across her cheeks. "Sorry," she whispered. If she'd been more alert, if she hadn't been complacent. The headset voices offered no absolution.

~

Wolf found her at the altar, kneeling down in front of the centre shrine. Little Fox's holograph stood there, a smile on her face, the other dead lined up to the left and right. Each hologram on its pillar gazed into eternity. *Too many of them*, she thought. Sticks of incense wafted sandalwood fumes. The smoke drifted through Little Fox's holographic smile and shimmered in the candlelight. With the haze and the flickering light, she looked almost alive, like any minute she would toss her brown hair back over her shoulder and tell a dirty joke. The cold of the stone floor seeped into her knees and her back hurt, but the Old Bitch stayed put.

"We've got a newbie," Wolf said. He touched her shoulder with his warm hand.

"It's too soon," she said, still focused on the dimples in Little Fox's cheek.

"No, it's not," he said. "And you know it. We need to get back to full strength."

He held out a hand. She stared at it. "I'm not ready."

"Doesn't matter, Captain. You know that."

She sighed and took his hand. "I know that." She let him help her to her feet. Her knee popped. "Where is she?"

Wolf shrugged. "Guess *he's* in the barracks. Haven't had time to check on him yet."

They headed towards the door.

She turned around at the threshold and stole one last glance at Little Fox. She took a deep breath.

"That leaves you with the paperwork tonight then," she said.

"Bitch," he said, not bothering to mutter.

She twisted her mouth in an approximation of a smile. "Ah, the joy of being in command—delegation." She headed towards the barracks, still smelling sandalwood.

~

The newbie stood by the cot, a thin grey blanket clutched around his bare shoulders. Knobby knees stuck out from the folds. The barracks was a communal environment—sleeping area, recreation corner, weight section cluttered with machines, dirty grey lockers plastered with stickers and posters, and a separate bathroom. The rest of her company sat over in the corner under a funk of thick cigar smoke, seated around a green felt table.

"At ease," she said, while she looked him over. He was skinny and lean, the kind of body she liked—narrow through the hips. The Old Bitch shut down those thoughts. Damn, she needed some R&R if she was thinking about a rookie like that. She sat down on the cot facing him. Twelve other blue cots were clustered about, reflecting current sleeping arrangements. On the field, they maintained military protocols. Off the field she didn't normally care what they did, or how they paired up.

"Hi." She pulled out a cigarette and lit it, adding to the funk in the room. His face tightened as she blew smoke. Had to be from the Prude era of the early naughties, she realized. How he'd deal with a coed bunker she didn't know.

"Hi," he said. He stared at her cigarette.

"Why don't you put your uniform on?" she asked. "Not that I'm minding the view, but you might be more comfy with some clothes on."

"Uniform?"

None of the slack-asses had shown him anything, she realized, not even his locker. What absolute creeps.

"Attention!" she yelled. It gratified her how fast they jumped from the corner of the room, cards spilling on the table and cigars crushed underfoot. "Get your asses over here."

They got.

"You want to explain yourselves?"

"Well, we thought he could use some time alone," Scarlet said.

Big John and Iggy were smart enough to say nothing at all, and Bonehead and Jugs stared at the floor with a look of moronic despair on their faces.

"You just wanted to finish your game," she said. "Who was winning?"

Big John grinned. "Me, ma'am."

"Wrong." She held out her hand. Under his dark skin he flushed purple. But he dug into his pocket and handed over the money without another word. She'd buy more incense with it for the shrines, and perhaps some fresh flowers. Little Fox had liked yellow irises.

~

She left them cleaning the barracks. They might be the Legion and not under strict military law, but there was some slackness not even she could tolerate. *You took care of the team*, she thought. *Always. Even the newbies.*

Newbie already sat in the hot tub, where she'd sent him to warm up while the others found his uniform. He averted his gaze as she stripped and jumped in, splashing water over the sides to the white tile floor.

"Don't worry, son, you'll settle in," she said. He flinched away from her into the furthest curve of the large white tub. *Oh, good grief.* It wasn't like her nipples were going to leap out and bite him. She checked her body quickly. Everything was in its relative place, still reasonably firm, thighs still strong, stomach still flat.

"Yes, ma'am," he said. His bright eyes avoided her. To help him out, she leaned back further in the bubbling water, piling her hair loosely on the top of her head The water soothed her aching knees.

"Why can't I use my name?" he asked after a few moments.

"They didn't tell you much of anything, did they?" the Old Bitch said. "And what they did tell you is garbage." She snorted. "Administrative staff. Let me guess—you figured out the secret of time, got caught in a paradox, your world evaporated around you. Congratulations, by the way. We don't get many from your century."

He nodded.

"Anyway, your best friend didn't know you, your wife screamed, even your dog turned away. Then some people in bright blue uniforms showed up and gave you two choices. Join the Legion or spend the rest of your days in temporal jail."

He blushed. "It wasn't my wife. It was my husband."

Well, she could still *look* at him.

"As for names, it's an old tradition. You're one of us now—we'll name you when it comes along."

"There're a few other things I don't get. Why fight?"

"What'd you do, fall asleep in class? Or are you just dense?" The tips of his ears glowed red. "There's an infinity of timelines, but only a finite number of Earth analogues are worth living in, the ones on the middle of the curve," she said.

"I don't understand," Newbie said, still not looking at her.

She wanted to torment him further, just for fun, but she needed him to understand what he was fighting for. "When do you pick an apple?"

"In the fall, when the fruit is ripest, before the freeze," he said.

She could see the wheels turn in his head.

"Exactly," she said, stretching her sore knee. "The Earths we're saving are late summer Earths, Earths in the sweet spot. Some of the others were destroyed by wars. Some by pollution. Some by viruses. And in others the dinosaurs still rule. Every time the Chronoids succeed in altering history to their benefit we lose another to their darkness. Fortunately, only the big events alter time. None of this killing a butterfly stuff changing the world." She ran her finger through the foam, watching the bubbles collapse into each other, then pop.

"I don't see the point," he replied. "What do the Chronoids want? No one would answer me during training."

She stared for a moment at the bubbles rising from the pressure jets around the edges of the bath. They reminded her of the Chronoid orbs, growing and collapsing in on each other as they expanded. "I don't know. The end of humanity?" She poked a toe through a bubble. She brushed her foot against his and he flinched away again. "I don't hate the Chronoids for trying to change time. I hate them because they kill my people. I fight them because I hate them. And because I get paid to do it. Those reasons good enough for you to fight?"

"I've lost Dave," he said. "He was everything to me. If what we're doing will keep him safe…"

She nodded.

"Then I'll fight." He looked her in the face for the first time. "Ma'am. Captain ma'am."

"One or the other will do, son. Wolf?" she asked through her throat mike.

"Yes, Captain. Almost finished with the paperwork."

"Excellent." She relaxed even further in the tub, positioning a jet at the sore spot at the base of her neck. "Make sure to get Newbie here outfitted over the weekend. I don't see any reason he can't join in on Monday."

~

Here she stood, Monday morning, once again in the mud and the rain. Another analogue, another Waterloo, and who could tell the god-damned difference?

The Legion had assigned *her* team here, however. They must still expect trouble or they'd have been able to move on. She yearned for a cigarette. The urge twitched through her fingers, but she resisted. No more smoking during work.

She checked her sensors.

Her team covered the perimeter. She could see the red dots indicating placement and zoomed in on Newbie. He chewed on a piece of gum, chomping it with fervour. From the look of tension on his face, he was going to need some time in the hot tub once the day was over.

A scan of her surroundings revealed everything normal. Almost noon, time for the French offensive on the British garrison at the Hougoumont farm.

Her earpiece chimed. "Captain," Wolf said, "I think we have a slight problem."

Uh oh. A *problem* was no big deal. A *big problem* meant "I can take care of it with the rest of the team". A *slight* problem meant "I don't know what to do about this".

"What is it?" she asked. Her voice stayed calm through years of habit—how many years she didn't like to think.

"We've got incoming bubbles." He hesitated. "More than one." Another pause. "More than I've ever seen."

She checked her display monitor. Four within her range. "How many do you see?" she asked team-wide. "Report in."

The tallies came back, pinpointing on her monitor as the feeds linked. Even Newbie sounded calm. But ten! Holy shit. This wasn't just a raid.

She switched to a private channel. "Wolf, what do you think?"

"I think we're fucked. We can't hold off this many."

At least the bubbles were still at billiard ball stage, glowing white hot in the monitors as energy swelled. They couldn't come through in full mass; the laws of energy wouldn't permit that much through the gate.

She assigned a team member to each incoming bubble. The Old Bitch hesitated when it came to Newbie.

She directed her next comment to Newbie. "Wait for the event horizon to materialize; you can't do any damage until then. And don't touch the bubbles or even get too close to them. Your suit and their technology are violently incompatible...You hear me, Newbie?"

"Yes, ma'am, I hear you."

"You got a problem with my orders?"

"Yes, ma'am, I do."

The headset stayed silent.

"And?" She kept her eyes on the floating targets in her internal scope. She wasn't heartless—she'd give him a few seconds to change his mind or she'd…The first mortar round boomed in the distance. Noon. The garrison of British emerged from the farm house.

"I think there's another way," Newbie said.

Wolf came back online. "We need your orders," he said.

"You have them. Including you, Newbie. We'll discuss your situation in private. Later."

She clicked off. *Damn him.*

"Big John," she said on a direct channel. "Take care of Newbie. Don't let him get hurt on his first day out."

She watched her team move into position on the monitor.

"I lost him, Captain," Big John said. "He slipped right by me."

*God damn it. Son of a bitch. Stupid, mother-loving idiot.*

Newbie's blip moved on her monitor, away from his assigned position, and she took off at a run, barking orders to rearrange her team to cover Newbie's hole.

"What the hell do you think you're doing?" she yelled when she saw him. He wasn't in his chameleon suit. He carried an empty bag slung over his shoulder. Rain dripped off his brown hair. The movement sent droplets flying. "This is battlefield insubordination," she yelled as she ran to catch up with him.

Gunfire sounded in the distance and Newbie shivered. "Remember the hot tub?" he asked.

"Go get your suit and get back into position." She was going to kill him if he got hurt.

"But—"

She cut him off. "That's an order!"

Overhead a shell whistled past.

She kicked him in the back. He slammed into the mud. *Just in time*, she thought. A swarm of bullets spat over her head.

The battle was in full swing now, the French artillery in position and firing.

Shrapnel screamed past her through the air. From long experience, she knew where it headed and could almost see each shard landing in flesh.

She flung herself forward, spread-eagled. She landed on top of Newbie with a thump. He grunted as the shrapnel laced his flesh. The Old Bitch knew she hadn't been fast enough or large enough to protect him, even before she got up. The one quick gasp he had made in her ear had told her all. Her suit hadn't covered all of him.

"Aw shit," she said. "Scarlet, Jugs! I need you here now."

Blood poured over her hands as she waited for them. It was warm and sticky and faded into scarlet rivulets in the falling rain.

"Here, ma'am," Scarlet answered after an eternity, running towards her. Jugs knelt in the mud and pulled out a field compress. Half of Newbie's left arm dangled by a shred of skin; white bone glistened in the torrent of blood. Worse, red blotches of blood formed on his abdomen.

"Jugs?" she asked.

"Not good," he replied, applying stick and seal. "We've got to get him back."

"Right," she said as she straightened. "Get him home. And don't let him die—I'm going to kill him later." She wiped a lock of his brown hair off his wet, pale face. His lips stood out blue with the shock but he didn't scream. She'd give him that—under the immense amount of pain he had to be feeling, he wasn't drawing attention to himself. In fact, he was trying to speak. She bent down.

"Get them," he choked. Blood trickled from his mouth. The Old Bitch nodded. Jugs and Scarlet lifted him up.

Her knee popped as she stood up.

Newbie would be safe. Her team would see to it, but now they had an even larger hole in their defences. Why had he been babbling about the hot tub? Her mind flashed back to the bubbles, collapsing on each other, inward and popping. *Would it work?* It was worth a try; they were already knee deep in shit.

"I've got it," she said into the mike. "Flank me. We've got ten minutes, and then I want the team the hell away from here. Help me get the orbs, then get the fuck home."

"Captain," Wolf said, "I don't think—"

She cut the mike off.

She peeled the chameleon suit off and shivered as the rain drenched her one-piece. She'd never tried to touch a sphere before, didn't know if it was possible. No one in the science branch had ever said anything one way or another.

"This way," she screamed. She picked up the empty sack Newbie had held. If she could get the orbs, get them to the munitions dump in the field before it exploded, the timeline would heal. Even the Chronoids had limited resources and it looked to her like they'd blown theirs for a while.

Cold air whistled through the thin cotton of her undersuit.

The expressions of the soldiers rushing past didn't help. Although Newbie had been strange in his long johns, he was a male and thus expected on the field of battle in this era. A woman wasn't. It didn't help that her nipples had the usual reaction to chill and excitement. Her jaw hurt from clenching. She wanted a nicotine fix.

Still, hesitating got her nowhere, so she took the first step and felt the mud squash under her feet. She started a list of things to do when she got back to the barracks, to keep her mind distracted from the roar of war. One, hot bath. Two, beat the crap out of Newbie. Three, knee replacement...

The wind blew against her back as she ran to claim the first orb. The sphere, when she picked it up, was heavy and the size of a watermelon. It slid in her fingers, both warm and cold, smooth and prickled, with a shimmering rind. Stars danced in its surface and her face refracted across the gamut of her life—crying baby, spotty teenager, decrepit old woman. It burned her fingers. She shoved it in the bag and hefted it over her shoulder before it cycled around again. She'd tell the geeks about it later, if she survived.

She paused to get her bearings, bereft of her suit and its monitors. She shivered and stumbled. A bullet slammed past her ear with a crack.

The faces on the shrines got her back up. Little Fox's, and all the others she'd lost over the years of command. No more, not today.

The French offensive intensified around her, a reeling mass of horses and men. Screams of the dying filled the air with a babble of French and English. Working from memory, she made her way from orb to orb. She ignored the burning of her hands.

She snatched the last orb from under the heels of a galloping horse. The rider on top stared open-mouthed as she fell past. She landed on her bad knee and pain stabbed through the joint.

There lay the ridge though, just on the edge of vision. Beyond that the field rose up green and misty before her.

The orbs grew heavier. She slogged her way down the hill and past the Hougoumont house. Sharp needles lanced through her knee, but she kept going.

Once she felt one of her team hold her up. She shrugged them off, checking her watch. "Go home," she yelled. "I told you ten minutes." A strong hand grabbed her shoulder for a second, squeezed hard, then released. She was alone. One minute left.

Usually she made a point of avoiding this part of Waterloo. Too much French mortar winging down from the sky. Even the fiercest veterans of all sides had chickened out and run away during the onslaught, and the Old Bitch now knew why.

It was the noise, the confusion. It was the sheer terror of not knowing when the sky would fall on top of her. Even raindrops made her flinch.

Time ticked down. She struggled on. Little Fox's memory kept her going and Newbie's pinched face in the rain, with all the blood, still trying to talk. Her heart stuttered.

She swept back her grey-streaked hair and trudged on, cringing at the cannons' incessant explosions. Was it her turn to follow next into the darkness? Would the others of her command, the ones she'd lost, forgive her?

She tripped over someone's hand in the mud and glanced down. The boy's hair dripped red with blood. His eyes stared at forever.

She worked her way to the centre of the pasture and staked the bag down with a forlorn branch. The rate of expansion quickened and she backed away.

Looking back she saw the plastic bag split as the orbs reached critical mass. The spheres overlapped each other; their growth accelerated. A hidden root tripped her. She fell in the mud. Her knee buckled when she tried to stand.

Shimmering blue rim met shimmering blue rim. The bubbles joined together, tank size, house size, growing one on top of another. It looked like a sculpture of soap bubbles in the bath. Some grew inside each other, others formed like boils joined together. It should have been pretty, but it grew like a disease—a time-lapse video of multiplying bacteria.

Then the portals opened. A pity for the Chronoids. Not a good thing to materialize out of the depths of time on top of each other. Or in each other. Forms twisted and merged. Arms grabbed out of stomachs. Heads twisted into grotesque cauliflowers. Form after form piled up, one on top of another, as the time portal dumped them out of the spheres.

Then with a terrific bang, the edge of the munitions dump explosion hit her unprotected body.

~

She awoke strapped to a bed in the infirmary, her palms itching with the regrowth of new skin. To the right she could see Newbie, his arm and lower body encased in regen tanks. "Why, hello," she said.

His eyes popped open. "Hey. You look better."

She growled. "As soon as I can get up, I'm going to..." She stopped and peered over her stomach. Both her legs disappeared into sealed vats. "Hell's bells. They'd better fix my knee while they're at it." She turned towards him. "You're on cleaning duty."

"It worked," he said.

"It worked. So I'm only going to leave you on clean up for a year or so."

"Better than being court-martialed and shot."

"You're a stubborn ass and if you ever disobey me again I'm going to kill you."

"I won't," he said.

Realization hit. "Official log," she requested.

The computer voice responded from the ceiling grill. "Official log, recording."

"Name change. Note troop one four four one, currently registered as Newbie. New name, Stub. As in Stubborn Bastard. Confirm."

"Confirmed," it replied, "Old Bitch."

# The Faithful Servant

## Adriana Noir

Adriana lives in a historical Ohio town that provides inspiration for many of her stories. A self-described typical Gemini, she dabbles in a wide scope of fiction, from emotional drama, to horror, to dark, gritty tales. When she isn't writing, she's usually enjoying time with her family and friends, or experimenting with her other passion, cooking. She attributes her creative side to the support and encouragement of her parents, three children, and her loving husband, Jim.

A late summer breeze stirs, carrying her intoxicating smell across the room. Hints of orchid and vanilla infiltrate my senses. Vibrant and seductive, it stirs something within me. She moves to her dresser and turns on the radio. Haunting, melodic notes waft through the night, a serenade for the dead. My eyes drift shut for a brief moment as the music speaks to me. I resist the urge to reach out and touch her, my unwitting bride. I remain rooted, content to watch from the shadows. What is a mere moment compared to the promise of eternity? Our time approaches with swift peril.

The sound of rustling silk interrupts my fantasy as she turns the covers down. Her slender hand lingers over the mound of pillows. Delicate features twist into a mask of uncertainty. A distinct aroma fills the air: the smell of fear. My lips quirk as she searches the room with questing cerulean eyes. Her gaze sweeps the posh space, probing the shadows. I hold my breath, an exhilarating rush of excitement pulsing through my body as her eyes meet mine—a beautiful illusion, for she can't see me. I am not strong enough to manifest a physical form humans can distinguish from shadow. Not yet.

A visible shiver afflicts my mate as she turns back to the bed and shrugs out of her sheer nightie. I catch a tantalizing glimpse of pale curves before she turns off the light and slides between the sheets. She pulls the covers tight under her chin, her body stiff. Whispery words sound from crimson lips. Her honeyed voice soothes the beast in me until her words take effect. A fierce burning explodes within my core, the pain so intense I shriek in agony. The sound pierces the night and somewhere in the distance, a dog howls.

The traitor gasps, the prayer dying on her lips. She sits up and I glare from the shadows. My affection dies, turning as black and foul as the depths she freed me from. Seething, I vow she will pay, for it was she who summoned me into this putrid existence. My rage abates as a narrow beam of moonlight illuminates the tear sliding down her cheek. I yearn to lick the salty jewel from her face, to feel the certain heat radiating from her flesh. Pleasant warmth suffuses me at the thought.

I turn my attention to the wooden board near her bed, the link between her world and mine. Love and hatred war within me. I am trapped on this earthly plane, servant to her whims and slave to my own desires. Closing my eyes, I will her to rise, to speak with me again or set me free. She is weak, too pathetic to do either. A muted sniffle breaks the silence and she rolls onto her side. I remain, watching…waiting as she seeks her slumber.

I wonder if she knows I am always with her: protector, destroyer, scorned inhuman lover. She whimpers in her sleep as I draw near. Her reposed features take on a sensual allure as I caress her cheek and whisper against the dark haven of her hair.

"Anna, my darling."

My lips brush her ear; my fingers trace the firm outer curve of her breast, drawing an audible moan from her lips. She stirs at the touch. I watch with mixed emotions as she shivers and sinks deeper under the comforter. Escape is futile, for I am bound to her for eternity. As life is bound to death, she shall be mine in both. I love her and hate her, my passive, tormenting bride.

Sometimes, the conflict drives me mad and I lash out, attacking her with razor sharp talons and gnashing teeth until she screams. But not tonight; tonight I want to love her. The bed bows beneath my weight as I lay beside my precious Anna. A sleepy smile curves her honeyed lips as I massage the back of her head. Unaware of her actions, she presses into my touch. I relish the moment, knowing her joy will not last long.

Leaning over, I kiss the nape of her neck and her cheek, before claiming her lips with ardent hunger. Long, sooty lashes flutter against her cheek like the wings of a struggling butterfly before her eyes snap open. She scans the darkness, the uninvited pressure intruding on her waking conscious. I cannot resist the urge to touch her again.

"Shh. It's alright, my love."

She sits upright with a whimper and presses her back against the headboard. Her hands clutch the comforter, twisting it with nervous fingers. I drape a reassuring hand over her thigh. Anna's scream pierces my ears as she scrambles off the bed. She hits her knee on the bedside table. A glass of water spills as her hands fumble across the top of the nightstand in a blind panic. The liquid drips onto the carpet in a rapid succession of soft thuds. I can hear the frantic hammering of her heart. My lips quirk as she lights the white candle in her grip and waves it in my general direction.

"Leave me alone! Get out of my house."

Reclining against the headboard, I throw my head back and laugh at her ill-placed faith in the wives' tale. White candles have no affect on me, nor does light. I just prefer the obscure comfort darkness offers. Foolish woman. What's next, stakes and garlic? Silver bullets? I am not some imaginary monster. I am quite real, a reality she conjured the day she summoned me. She was the one who invited me in…into her home, into her life.

"Put the candle down before you hurt yourself, Anna." As I speak, I lean across the bed and extinguish the dancing flame. "Stop being foolish. Come back to bed, darling."

Anna's sobs are deafening now. She covers her ears, trying to drown out the sound of my voice. I play off her fear and run my fingers through her hair. The way the onyx curtain ripples under my ministrations mesmerizes me for a moment. I once heard her describe my touch to a friend as a slight tingling, like warm static, or the prickling unease some people feel before a storm. It makes me wonder if she can feel it approach now…our storm. The thought of such turbulent violence makes me want her that much more. Raw, aching passion consumes me. I revel in the sweet agony coursing through my being.

She kicks the Ouija board across the room. I watch it slide across the blue shag carpet and slam into the far wall.

"I hate you!"

I wonder if she speaks to me or the board. It matters little. I grow tired of toying with her and her ingratitude is starting to infuriate me. A low growl rumbles through my core. Rising to my feet, I cross the room and kick it back in her direction. I throw the planchette back onto its rightful place on the board. Anna begins to scream, ear piercing shriek upon shriek. She scrambles to get to her feet. Once she does, she runs for the door. A sigh escapes me and with a wry shake of my head, I slam it shut. The house shakes with the force. My patience is gone. I grab a fistful of her hair and drag her back to the bed.

Her sobs are deafening, broken only by the gasping pleas tumbling from her lips. I cover her mouth and she struggles, but I pin her down. Immobile, Anna's cries are muffled and she makes a snorting sound against my hand as she struggles to breathe. I release her face long enough to strike her. The blow lays open a small strip of flesh along her cheek. She is too afraid to scream, too afraid to move. The only noise coming from her is the ragged sound of her breath and a low, keening whimper. Our time has come...the time to join and become one. My bittersweet spell is about to be broken.

I love her more in this moment than I have ever loved her...enough that I almost hope she will pray. But, she doesn't. She is too afraid and her fear gives me strength, absolute power over her. I draw from it, lifting off of her. Anna's beautiful blue eyes are so wide, I can see the whites, and for a moment, I see myself in their reflection. Gone is my human appearance, the pale skin and lucid green eyes that drew her in and allowed me to mingle with her soul. I am no longer her tragic, ghostly lover but a menacing black mass swirling above her prostrate form. She opens her mouth to scream, but nothing comes out.

I take advantage of the invitation and thrust myself into the searing heat of her body. It is like nothing I have ever felt before, and I marvel at the sensation of having flesh and blood, substance to my being. I feel invigorated...alive. The first shaky breath is an exquisite paradise. Anna holds on, struggling to regain control, but we are one. I feel the heated blood pulsing through our veins, the delicious adrenaline rush heightened by her fear, and her heart beating faster and faster. It races at a fevered pace, slamming against the walls of our chest. Breathing becomes harder and harder, the pulsating mass feels like it is in my throat. Then…it stops.

I smile as her heart stops beating. It is done, and I am eager to join her in death, to show her all the things I couldn't before. I withdraw from her body, before it traps me in its hollow core. My joy is short lived as the wind stirs, bringing with it a faint whisper. I pause, straining to hear the sound. Every fibre of my being tingles with delight and my eyes drift shut. The whisper grows into a melodic lover's serenade.

Another one calls my name, her fingers trembling with excitement as she glides the planchette across smooth wood. A new lover invites me into her home…into her life. Another bittersweet spell is cast as she reaches out and summons me to her side. I cannot resist the pull. They all call in a moment of light-hearted fun and laughter. Forever ensnared by destiny, I remain a faithful servant, bound until death by words and careless whispers. Regardless, I devote myself to them all. In the end, they learn love is no game.

# The Talisman

## Kate Sender

Kate Sender began writing stories and verse when she learned the business end of a pencil. But it was decades later, with encouragement from fellow writers at Writing.Com, a community of writers and artists where she is a moderator, that she opened her eclectic world of prose and verse to the public. Her work has been published in *Falling Star Magazine* and in the anthology *Between Life and Language, Pride in Poetry Volume I* (Navworks Press, 2009), as well as a recipe in the *Zombie Cookbook* (Damnation Press, 2009). Kate lives in Ohio with her husband and two feline companions (none of whom would taste-test the above recipe). She welcomes visitors to her emerging otherworlds of words at kate2world.wordpress.com and writing.com/authors/manga_kate

Thorn hovered a wingspan from the Talisman, compelled to pause in his quest at this first sight of the pulsing cerulean blue disc. It wasn't the bolts fixing it against the wall that stopped him. With the slightest effort—a flick of his tail or touch of a sharp talon—the disc would hover or fall, free of constraints. His eyes were drawn to the mesmerizing paths of three wands, their shafts affixed to the core of the disc, propelling or chasing each other around twelve equidistant glyphs. He paused to try and hold fast the flicker of understanding that eased just beyond conscious comprehension, like the flutter of an approaching butterfly just out of sight. He shivered in the sanctuary. Its cool darkness was palpable, denying the warm summer night's breeze.

The Talisman was a subject of both myth and legend in the Glen of the Dryads. Faeries learned at a very young age of its power. Legend held that wingless biped overlords knew its secrets and, to hold their own power, selectively encouraged the mythos among their own kinsmen. They used the talisman to compel the general population to erect massive edifices, gather goods, and amass wealth out of proportion to their needs. They encroached with impunity upon the lives of other beings, destroying entire forests, along with their inhabitants, because the Talisman empowered them to do so. Toiling day and night, encased in carapaces manufactured from the waste of stripped land and dammed rivers, they were heedless of rain, sun, passing seasons. They multiplied, each generation more avaricious than its parent.

Although born with the ability to see faeries and the beauty of nature, the bipeds quickly learned to close their eyes to all but the symbols of the wealth provided by obeisance to the

Talisman. They adorned their bodies with gems and gaudy raiment earned by rote obedience, compelled by the ceaseless cycle of wands over glyphs to erect, then break, glass ceilings.

That they could break ceilings of glass without impaling themselves had to be a direct effect of the power of the Talisman. Everyone knew that glass cut and, like falling stalactites in the caves beneath the Glen, would impale and end the life even of a swift-winged faerie, much less a wingless biped.

For Thorn, however, this quest was more personal. His beloved Rose, a dryad of ethereal beauty on the outskirts of the Glen, had fallen victim to the encroachment. Her Guardian Oak had been felled to build a warehouse for the repose of gold rocks. Her Guardian murdered, Rose, as delicate as the sparrows which had called the Oak home, quickly succumbed to despair. Her feathers dried and withered until one morning she was just gone, with but a whisper of faerie dust to mark her former presence. Thorn would no longer feel her sweet caress on his muscled wings or hear her gentle voice sing the robins to sleep at sunset. A need for vengeance accompanied his flight this night, augmenting the drive to help not only his kind, but also the world.

The memory of his precious Rose shook off the Talisman's apparent somnolent spell, and Thorn flicked his wings, unsheathing his talons, which would make quick work of removing the bolts holding the Talisman to the wall. Ready to attack, he stopped. With one flap of powerful wings spinning him about, he prepared to fight whatever foe had arrived in the rush of warm air at his back as the heavy portal to the sanctuary creaked open.

"Who, uh, umm, WHAT are you?" cackled the creaking voice emanating from the figure framed in moonlight, stepping through the doorway. Thorn actually dropped his feet to the ground to keep from rolling somersaults in the air at the sight. Wattled skin drooped from a lined face nestled between hunched shoulders. But it was the weapon the creature wielded that stopped Thorn from slaying it outright. The seamed old thing was waving a large broom as though it were a sword!

"Who are you?" Thorn countered, in an effort to regain his composure.

"I'm Rumplestiltskin, the schoolhouse janitor," the wattled chin jiggled in reply.

"Then you are here also to take the Talisman?"

"I'm here to mop the floor of the schoolhouse. I once taught here, literature and history, but the Master Builder says history is superfluous and literature is a waste of time, so I was relegated to cleaning up the mess left behind by the newly illiterate students."

"So this is a schoolroom and a sanctuary?" Thorn queried. "Where the young ones learn to both worship and use the magic of the Talisman?" It made sense, explaining why fewer children called for faeries to guide them in their dreams or help with vision quests. If they were trained from an early age in the use of the Talisman, they would not need further magic.

"What Talisman?" the wingless biped asked, the map of his face furrowing even more as he lowered the broom, then leaned on it with a creak of loose bones that was audible over the sibilant wind.

"The Talisman on the wall, whereby your masters control time," Thorn flicked a wing in the direction of the Talisman.

"Ha ha ha ha," the creature named Rumplestiltskin choked. "You think they control time with that clock. It's the clock that controls them. They rush to and fro to beat the clock, to beat back time, not realizing that time always wins in the end. You don't want that for your kindred; you don't want to end up like me, watching my kind wantonly destroy true beauty, replacing it with ceaseless consumption of gain they don't allow themselves the time to enjoy." The creature's passion strengthened his voice, and Thorn could envision him as an orator of poetry or literature, holding the rapt attention of an audience of imaginative young minds.

"But will they self-destruct before they destroy our world, or even the entire world?" Thorn's question was now posed to an equal. He realized further that his quest spanning one wheel of the year was forsaken. The earlier flicker of understanding now ignited to full flame. Thorn would not be the one to introduce this instrument of ignorant avarice to his world of beauty and light and, yes, history and mystery. He realized its power and that minding the Talisman compelled ennui and vapid lives.

"Then I shall destroy it, and its minions will be compelled once more to follow natural law, rising with the sun, reaping from the Earth what they truly need, and giving back what they do not." Thorn rose with a flap of wings, preparing to shatter the orb with his spiked talons.

The old one reached up and grabbed a handful of wing in a gnarled hand, a smaller copy of the disc on its wrist. "But it's only a marker, reminding the wearers and observers of the passing of time, and all they still do not have."

"The rising sun and the shimmering moon are markers of time, and they remind all creatures of the bounty they do have," Thorn whispered, a tear trailing down his cheek as he realized the magnitude of the loss in quality of life for these poor creatures. "Is there nothing that can be done to make them once again see?"

"I can think of but one way," Rumplestiltskin replied, straightening his spine and locking his shining eyes on Thorn's. "You have to keep showing us the way. Come to the children as you do in their dreams. Lead them to your forest and let them taste of the cool spring waters of your Glen. And, do not forget the rest. Cast some faerie dust on the grown ones as well. We are all as children when we dream, innocent seekers of truth, beauty, and light."

"Rumplestiltskin, you are still a great teacher. I will take your lesson to heart, and return with others of my kind to do as you bid. Perhaps we can make a difference."

"Yes, with love and vision, we can learn to live freely once again."

"I'll see you in your dreams," Thorn smiled, soaring swiftly through the starlit summer sky. The orb, its mystery revealed, was no longer a compelling force. The image of the old one's face, however, a smile now easing the lines of age, held fast his heart. He would return time and again to share the joy, beauty, and magic of nature with the innocent heart that beat in every dream. Time may always win in the end, but living it, not rushing through it, makes life the champion!

# The Goth Muse

**Ben A. Bell**

Ben A. Bell was born in Boston, Massachusetts, but now lives overseas, working as a freelance writer. His published stories include "Mascaren" in *Emerald Tales*, "Marlene and Earl" in *Literal Translations*, and "The Happy Frog" in *Moondrenched Fables*.

Kevin Barry swiped a forearm across his dripping forehead and glared at the air conditioner. Electricity was too friggin' expensive, and he couldn't afford to run the darn thing even when the July temperature teetered into the high nineties. He scratched at his face, fingers chafing against ten days' worth of scraggly growth.

Remnants of half-eaten food, empty bags of chips, and sticky soda cans marked a trail from the kitchen to the dining room, spilled off the coffee table, passed the TV, and led to Kevin's cluttered empire at the computer. Hunched over the keyboard in a way guaranteed to make his absent mother "Tsk, tsk" about posture, Kevin pounded the keys in a fervent attempt to write something good. All the ingenious ideas he concocted somehow lost their appeal when translated into mere ciphers on the computer screen.

The cramped apartment sweltered with heat. The heat spoiled the food and attracted ants. The little free-loaders did not even pitch in on the rent, which was overdue. During his most recent visit, the angry landlord spied the ants that ate the food spoiled by the heat because the air conditioner was off, and got even angrier, threatening to return with bug spray. Whether the spray was for the ants or for Kevin wasn't quite clear.

Kevin scratched at his beard again. Then at his nose. He itched all over, and it wasn't on account of the ants. Something was wrong. Something bothered him, making it impossible to focus on his book. He arched his stiff back, stretched out his arms, and—*clink*—knocked over his soda can. "Damn!" A stream of Coke raced toward his keyboard.

He wasted precious seconds looking for the Kleenex box, and the headwaters of the flood reached the corner of the keyboard and disappeared beneath.

"Damn, damn, damn!" His language became filthier and louder as he ripped his T-shirt over his head, snatched the keyboard off the ledge, and staunched the flow. After wadding up the shirt and throwing it into a corner, he sat, pale-skinned and pitiful, wondering how it had all gone wrong.

His phone thrummed against the table. Caller ID displayed *Jean*, his editor.

"And the laughs just keep on coming." He pressed the button. "Hi, Jean. How are you?" his voice rang with false joviality.

"Hello, Kevin. I haven't heard from you in a week, and you're now two months overdue on the book deadline."

*Thanks for asking, Jean. I'm fine.* He sagged in his chair. "I've been meaning to call. I've been making progress."

"When am I going to see something?" Jean growled.

"Um…I think…well," Kevin stammered, surprised at her abruptness. Last year she'd been so nice, almost obsequious in her attention. But last year he'd been on top of the world after publishing a novel about a magic eel. It hadn't sold well initially, but experienced a jump in sales when a horror novel about giant killer eels became a best-seller. His book resurfaced, carried along on the riptide of the other book's success. A new contract floated his way without any effort on his part. However, now that he'd spent all the advance money, the dark waters of destitution were closing over his head, and there wasn't a lifeboat in sight.

"Now, Jean, don't be impatient. You're going to love the new characters in the magic shop scenes!" His new manuscript about Lola and her magic shop totally didn't work. "I've written a great comic sidekick." Not even the talking cat sidekick could save his stinkeroo book.

"A *comic* sidekick? Try something darker. Horror is selling better than fantasy now."

"But I can't…Uh, you know? You're absolutely right. I've been working on an evil landlord."

"Landlord?" She sounded bored.

"Huh? No, I meant dragon. An evil dragon." He made up lie after lie to get Jean off the phone.

When he finally got rid of her, he wondered how he could think up so much B.S. and yet draw a blank when it came to the actual book.

"Comic sidekick cat. Ha!" He'd actually created the cat to please his girlfriend, Yvonne; he named it after her cat, Bugsy, to curry favor. Yvonne hadn't shown him any of her favors in more than a month.

He glanced around with the strangest feeling that he had forgotten to do something.

*Hurry...hurry...*Urgent words prodded him. He studied the chaos on the desktop, hoping something would jog his memory. Nothing.

A musical alarm from his phone interrupted his befuddled thoughts. Trebly, counterfeit music played the Stars Wars theme until he shut it off and unwound his stiff body from the chair.

It was time for "Heartbeats of the Fallen." He clicked on the TV and plopped down on the sofa. "Heartbeats of the Fallen" was a daytime soap with little to recommend it except one very important thing: Yvonne played Ginger Fallen's BFF, Angela. Since it was only a bit part, Yvonne wasn't on every day, but Kevin always tuned in anyway so he would have something to say when she called. She liked to chat about her "delivery" and her "wardrobe," so he had to be prepared.

A funny feeling distracted him from the show.

*Come...come...*

Kevin stood halfway up before realizing what he was doing. He sank back down, wondering, *Come where?* and looked around the room searching for the source of the odd magnetic pull. Just then, Yvonne appeared onscreen in a party scene. He concentrated on her performance, and the color of her skimpy dress, and shut out everything else.

During a commercial, he ducked into the kitchen to grab a Coke and watched with chagrin as a long line of ants ferried crumbs off the countertop, down the wall, and out a crack in the plaster. For a moment, he envied the ants. They always knew where they were going and why.

When the soap was over, Kevin called Yvonne, but got her voice mail. He forced himself to leave a cheerful message about her performance and asked her to call. He'd left a lot of messages lately. As a matter of fact, she hadn't returned his calls for almost a week.

*She must be busy, going to the "right" places and seeing all the "right" people*, he mused, thinking about how much she loved her career. When they were together, she talked of nothing else.

"Back to the slave pits," he grumbled, resettling himself in front of the computer.

Hours later the sun set, and a headache rose in its place. Wrestling with the descriptions of Lola's Magic Shop trapped him in a never-ending loop of write, re-write, and delete. The growling in his stomach intertwined with a nagging unease. There was something more important he had to do.

He struggled to concentrate on what a certain flowerpot shaped like a dragon could magically do, when the roaring in his stomach finally won out over literary progress.

Take-out menus were close at hand, of course, and he leafed through them. The menu from Golden Palace Chinese Food made him pause. A red dragon curled through its logo, just like his flowerpot. He believed in signs and portents and decided to order. *Maybe Chinese food is just what I need to inspire me.*

Twenty minutes later, the doorbell summoned Kevin, and he accepted the food delivery from a young Chinese man. The man's face grew as sour as the dumplings when Kevin revealed he only had two twenties, while the bill was just twenty-two dollars.

"No change, Missah Bally, no change," the man complained in a heavy accent.

"Why don't you go to the bar downstairs and ask for change. They're nice," Kevin suggested.

The Chinese man looked at Kevin as if he'd grown bat wings. "Bar downstairs no good!" He spat on the ground. "Bad place! Velly bad place! *You* bring change."

The Chinese guy looked all weirded-out about the bar, so Kevin decided not to argue. Sighing, he put the food cartons on the dining table, hoping the ants were preoccupied elsewhere, grabbed his key chain, and stepped into the hall. The man followed him downstairs and stood well away from the bar's entrance.

Kevin entered the Black Sea Bar and paused for a moment to savor the air-conditioning. This was why he spent every night here. Well, that and the beer.

The bar's standard house music, howling, electric-guitar blues, whined from the sound system. He approached Luc, the bartender, with a familiar "Hiya!" and asked him to change a twenty. While Luc went to the register, Kevin glanced around the darkened room to see who was there.

Bob and Gary sprawled at the first table, a half empty pitcher of beer between them. Bob waved at Kevin, and Gary nodded, half-chewed ketchup-covered fries sticking out of his mouth. Kevin smiled. Gary ate too much and always complained about his cholesterol, but never correlated the two.

Thrace lounged at his regular table, stretched back in his chair with his feet stuck out, arms crossed over his chest, eyes closed. A double scotch he could nurse all night sat before him. He regularly spurned Kevin's attempts at conversation with monosyllabic grunts. He had the oldest eyes Kevin had ever seen.

Kevin peered through the darkness to the back pool tables. In the dim light cast by an overhead Tiffany-style fixture, a group of players parted ranks to reveal a woman with a pool cue. She leaned forward, showing a massive amount of cleavage, and took her shot.

The click of the pool balls and the electricity that jumped through Kevin's at the sight of her were simultaneous. Like a child at the circus, he ogled her big top and leaned forward to better catalog her main attractions.

She was a Goth. Streams of shiny black hair flowed around her pale face as she studied the table, setting up her next shot. Her eye liner, lips, and nail polish were all the same cemetery-in-the-dead-of-night shade of ebony. Kevin salivated. Her tight—*Oh, so delectably tight*—black leather pants and vest hugged every curve.

She glanced up from the table and locked eyes with him.

The patrons froze. All sound faded. Through a haze of tickling whispers, Kevin saw only the woman. Fragments of laughs and the music of a calliope floated around him.

*She's incredible!*

She smiled as if she could hear him. Her image bent and distorted into fun-house mirror shapes. She glided up to him. She came closer and closer, her lips parted in a glistening—

"Hey, Kev!"

Kevin blinked.

The Goth woman finished making her shot at the table and the bartender, Luc, stood at his elbow.

"You dreamin'? Here's your change."

Kevin looked at the money in Luc's hand and then up into his angular face. "Uh...sorry...thanks." He took the money, but his eyes drifted back down the bar toward the beautiful woman. She wasn't looking at him; she was just playing pool. *What a weird daydream.*

He emerged from the bar into stark streetlights. The Chinese deliveryman watched him warily, as if he'd come out of the bar a different, less trustworthy person. After he paid what he owed, and returned to his apartment, Kevin ate his dumplings and moo shu pork at the computer.

The Chinese food did not help him find the magic in his story. Kevin found himself thoroughly bored by Lola, her cat, and her magic shop. The red dragon flowerpot, though, that was still interesting. He imagined a new character.

He set down his carton of dumplings and began to write.

During the next week, he forged ahead with a new story about an old Chinese man who owned a botanical nursery where he cultivated strange, mystical plants. The Chinese man knew just what his customers needed. Even if they'd come to buy something else, the customers went home with the plant chosen for them by the old man, and then experienced wonderful, inexplicable changes in their lives as they cared for their new plants and watched them grow.

With a start, Kevin realized he'd missed the entire week's episodes of "Heartbeats of the Fallen." Yvonne had never even called to find out why he hadn't left any messages. She had obviously tired of him. *I'll show her. My new book's going to be great—a best seller!* The Chinese character was a modern metaphor for the enlightening experience of following a new life path that you didn't know you wanted, or needed, until you were on it.

*There are going to be T-shirts with my name on them!* he thought with swelling confidence.

Satisfied with his progress, Kevin turned off his computer and headed down to the bar. *Time for a little rest and relaxation.*

At the bar, he belched behind his hand as Luc cleared away the remnants of his burger. A TV at the side of the bar showed a game. Fuzzy, silent players pursued their own brand of immortality. He thought about expanding on the characters in his book and absently carried peanuts to his mouth.

After he gave Luc the sign to bring him the bar tab, his skin prickled. A cold breeze that had nothing to do with air conditioning blew across the back of his neck. He looked over his shoulder.

In the entrance, the Goth woman stood, silhouetted against the streetlights. She was taller than he remembered, taller and more commanding.

Her eyes brushed over him, swept the room, then returned to caress his face with a gaze that sucked him into a dizzying vortex. His breath left his body in a deep exhaust as feelings of loneliness, desperation, and hunger bubbled up from a profound chasm within him. Her dark eyes grew larger in his vision until everything else vanished. Something cold touched his cheek.

He jumped as she withdrew her hand from his face. She slid onto the stool next to him. Her black lips parted, and he wanted to—

"I drink Armagnac."

She pronounced it "ar-mah-nyak" with the emphasis on the last syllable. He furrowed his brow in concentration, but couldn't recall the word. Nevertheless, he gallantly signaled Luc and repeated the word to him.

Luc studied the woman for a moment, and then rattled off some words that sounded like French or Greek. Kevin was lousy at languages and it could've been Russian, for all he knew.

The mysterious woman frowned at the bartender before giving a delicate moue. She lifted her hands in a genteel shrug and replied to him in the same language.

Luc's brows descended over his eyes like crows landing on carrion. A muscle in his cheek twitched. He turned and stalked away.

Her onyx eyes swiveled to rest on Kevin.

Too vulnerable to speak and terrified that if he opened his mouth, she would disappear like a fantastic mirage, Kevin remained silent and drank in her image.

Chains of a tarnished metal hung from her neck. Random glimmers sparkled off them. He swayed, mesmerized, wondering what caused the unusual reflections. They dangled into the darkness of her cleavage.

"You like my necklaces?"

He looked up, blushing, a child with his hand in the cookie jar. Before he could frame a response, she continued.

"They are verrry old." Her peculiar accent rolled the "r", making it purr like a cat.

He almost asked where she was from, but stopped, trying to think up something more original, something clever and unforgettable. As he considered and discarded alternatives, her drink arrived. *Some writer I am. Can't even think of a decent pick-up line.*

She lifted the glass. In the small brandy snifter, the liquor gleamed dusky red. Raising it to her mouth, she drank, the liquid staining her lips the color of blood.

Kevin shivered. He glanced up at the air conditioner, thinking that was the culprit. A movement at the corner of his eye startled him. Directly across from them, a long baroque-framed mirror covered the back of the bar's serving area. Her reflection appeared totally black as if he sat next to a shadow, except for her eyes, which glowed. After a sharp inhale, he blinked, and their images returned to normal. The light of the bar made her silver earrings flicker when she tilted her head. That was what he'd seen in the mirror, he told himself.

She lowered her empty glass to the counter and placed her icy hand on his. She spoke to him in a foreign language full of sexy vowels and wet consonants.

The room spun. His vision blurred.

She squeezed his fingers. His gaze dropped to her hand. Her fingers elongated into feral claws. Black-tipped nails became pointed and deadly. His heart stuttered, and his breath came in quick gasps. A moment before, the air seemed too cold. Now, it smothered him: hot, humid, and oppressive.

The echoes of her imprecation slithered through his mind. Saliva filled the back of his throat. The air, thick with strange phantasms, stole the breath from his lungs. He fought nausea, but it overwhelmed him.

Kevin jerked his hand from under hers and dashed to the bathroom.

His insides rolled as he lunged at an open stall. Beer and food came spewing out before he could get to the toilet bowl. He heaved and gagged, then heaved again. When his stomach had purged its contents, he knelt on the floor, leaning against frigid porcelain.

Gradually, his breathing slowed and his heart rate returned to normal. His nose and eyes ran from the force of vomiting. Rubbing his hand across his sweaty forehead, he paused and studied it in disgust. It was the same hand she had held. The memory of her hand's horrifying transformation came back. He retched, but there was nothing left to come up.

After several minutes, Kevin recovered enough to hoist himself up. He walked on unsteady feet to a sink. Looking at his pale, sweaty reflection in the mirror, he began to be ashamed. He'd imagined everything. Of course her hand hadn't changed.

*What an idiot! What a colossal dope! I eat a bad burger and get all weirded-out in front of this beautiful girl. She must think I'm an escaped psycho.* He splashed cold water on his face. *What am I gonna say to her? I ran out like I was being chased by demons. Congratulations, Kev.* He glared at his dripping countenance. *You've managed to lose two girls in one week. Some new friggin' record. Maybe if I wash a little harder, I can get the big "L" off my forehead.*

Kevin dried off, cleaned most of the traces of puke from his clothes, and got himself under control. Obsequious apologies hovered on his lips as he re-entered the bar.

However, the beautiful Goth woman was gone. He squinted and peered around. Everyone was gone except old Thrace, who slept in his chair.

*How long was I in that stupid bathroom? And I didn't even get her name.* Kevin's shoulders drooped.

Kevin spotted Luc behind the bar, washing up. He charged over and grilled Luc. Where was she from? What did she do? What was her name? Luc, usually cheerful and forthcoming, shifted around as if his shoes were too tight and shot a nervous glance over at Thrace before he answered.

"She's an old customer." He dropped his voice. "She used to be married to Thrace. But they had one heck of a falling out after their son died—"

The scrape of a chair brought Luc up short, his eyes bulging. Kevin looked around and saw Thrace reposition himself. The man scratched his ear, settled back into his chair, and was silent. A few seconds later, a rasping snore issued from his mouth.

Luc touched Kevin's sleeve and gestured at the entrance. "You'd better go now."

Kevin glanced at Thrace as he walked cat-like out the door.

In his apartment, Kevin sat unmoving in front of his computer screen. Something had drawn him to the computer, but he couldn't think of one word to write about his Chinese horticulturalist. His eyes wandered from the screen and focused on a moth lying on the nearby windowsill. The ants had found it. They worked in determined coordination to dissect its head and wings. Already, squads of ants were carrying off the severed legs. Nausea and disgust sloshed around his guts.

*The world is carnivorous.* The thought depressed him.

He shut the computer down and went to bed, pulling the covers over his head. But his sleep became a realm of nightmares. Scenes came in terrifying glimpses and macabre vignettes. His novel's botanical nursery used the bodies of dead babies for fertilizer. The old Chinese man was actually a demon who consumed hopes and dreams. The customers' new plants, grown on a diet of blood and gore, became savage monstrosities. They attacked their owners, burrowed through flesh, and drained their blood.

The next morning, memories of the images so overwhelmed Kevin that he couldn't even recollect his original ideas for the book. In an attempt to exorcise the hypnotic dreams, he went to the computer and worked madly, day and night.

New ideas consumed him. He rarely slept, and when he did, visions of horror dominated his dreams. Blood-starved plants thrust tendrils into the rooms of sleeping children, choking them in their beds. Gruesome vines plunged into open mouths and erupted from oozing eye sockets. Lurid red-tinged leaves shook with monstrous fervor at their newfound food supply. Terrorized victims, unable to avoid the grasp of sucking stalks, cowered in corners before being devoured.

An image of a half-plant, half-human hand, clawing its way from the rubble of a house in a last desperate attempt to escape its fate, was too much for Kevin. He woke up screaming in tangled sheets.

With his face twisted in revulsion, he staggered to his computer and wrote as if possessed to purge the sickening scenes. He wrote for hours until he could no longer focus. Twilight loomed outside his windows. He trudged into the kitchen to get a soda. Just as he removed it and closed the refrigerator door, he heard something from inside.

*Crooshhh...crooshhh...*

He jerked the door open again. Among take-out leftovers and a few plates which held barely recognizable food substances, he heard a slow rustle-crinkle of food wrappers. Something moved within the graveyard of foodstuffs. His eyes widened. Something evil crawled toward him from the decay. Something voracious was coming to get him. His heart skipped a beat, the soda can crashed to the floor, and he slammed the door shut.

*I have to get out of this apartment. I'm going crazy!*

He escaped into the Black Sea Bar. In the feeble lighting, he saw the Goth woman at the bar.

Kevin cursed himself. He wished he'd washed his face, or shaved, or at least found a shirt that didn't stink.

He shuffled toward her, but didn't take a seat. His mouth formed the first words of—he hesitated—what? Should he apologize? Greet her as if nothing had happened? As if he'd never bolted to the bathroom like a dork?

The chiaroscuro tableau melted as she turned to him. She solved his problem by piercing him with moist black eyes and saying, "Kevin. How nice. Sit down."

*She knows my name!* He stopped himself from dancing with glee and seated himself with what he hoped was nonchalance.

Maybe the exhaustion of the past days finally caught up with him, or maybe her intoxicating influence clouded his senses, but whatever the explanation, the next hour passed in a surreal trance from which he comprehended only bits and pieces.

His pulse quickened when her hand slipped along his thigh. She tossed her hair, laughing at witticisms he didn't remember saying. Her necklace sparkled in animated counterpoint to her breathless flirtation. Her cold hand clasped his and she led him out the side door of the bar into the alley. She murmured soft questions in the darkness, asking about his new book, but fastened her lips on his before he could reply.

He closed his eyes as she pressed him against the damp bricks of the building opposite. Her kisses pulled the breath from his body along with all coherent thought. His ears filled with a harmonic buzzing. At the same time he thought he must die from suffocation, he wished her delicious touch would never end.

The metal door of the bar burst open and clanged back against the wall.

A figure appeared in the doorway. In a voice that shook the heavens came the cry, "Calliope!"

Dust and pieces of mortar fell off the walls of the alley and cascaded around the couple. Kevin's seducer gently extricated herself from their embrace, put a hand on her hip, and turned insolent eyes upon the intruder. "What?"

Thrace stepped into the alley. Long sumptuous robes swirled around him. His hand fingered the hilt of an old-fashioned broadsword at his side. "You get away from that boy."

"I was only trying to help him—setting him on the path toward his true destiny."

Winds ripped through the alley. Loose papers and wrappers from trashcans whirled in the air. Thrace stepped further away from the bar into a dim pool of light. A crown on his head gleamed dull gold. As his robes flailed in the squall, he shouted, "Destiny! Pha!" He spat the words. "Was it destiny that took our Orpheus from us? Did destiny inspire your besotted affection for Apollo? I can forgive you for your betrayal, but I cannot forgive you for going on as if nothing occurred." Strands of hair blew in his face, and he shook his leonine head. "You bring back memories best forgotten. I do not desire to look upon you any longer." He tore his sword from its scabbard and brandished it above his head. "Begone from my sight!"

Calliope crossed her arms, her wind-blown locks lashing Kevin's face. She looked at Thrace with narrowed eyes. "I remember, too. It was not Apollo's fault. It was Dionysis and his silly women. Blame him!" She flung her defense like a gauntlet into the turbulent tempest.

Thrace glowered.

Kevin watched them, his heart thumping. They stood, staring at each other for an eternity as the wild storm swept around them, testifying to their battle of wills. Thrace appeared to grow older as his rage burned him to a husk, leaving him wrinkled and pale. He continued to hold the sword high, but his arm trembled.

Sympathy softened the planes of Calliope's face. She dropped her gaze and bowed her head. "Very well. I will go."

She pivoted smoothly away. Unaffected by the great gale, she strode out the end of the alleyway. At the last moment, she seemed to take flight on silvery wings.

The airborne debris settled back to the earth, and Thrace sat down heavily on the doorstep.

Kevin pushed himself off the wall and stumbled over. There were no robes, no sword, and no crown. They had disappeared with the wind and the dust and the beautiful woman, Calliope.

Thrace looked up at Kevin and grunted. "Women! They get your juices flowing, but they suck the life right out of you."

Kevin helped Thrace up, and they studied each other as whispers of music spilled out of the bar. Kevin opened his mouth to speak, but Thrace silenced him with a sharp hand gesture. "I can see she was right about you. You'll go on to do great things. But take care. Money and power are fleeting." He dropped his head and went on in a lower voice. "There's only one thing a man truly needs in this life." He turned and shambled through the open door.

Kevin laid his hand on Thrace's shoulder, stopping him. "What? What does a man need?"

Thrace looked over his shoulder, crooked an eyebrow, and snorted. "When you're my age—a good bowel movement!" His raucous laughter slashed the night before he disappeared inside.

Kevin stood for a moment. Beside the door, a little line of ants, buffeted by the storm, resumed their trek across the dusty wall and continued on. Although Calliope had finished her work, theirs was never done.

~

Epilogue –

*It's been many years since I thought about the events of that night. I've written many horror novels since then. My books continue to be well received, and I've had more than my share of best sellers. As I stand on the deck of my home, listening to my laughing wife tease my children about whose turn it is to set the table, I can't help hearing Thrace's voice in my head. I know what words were really in his heart that night. It's all about love and family.*

*On a clear day, I can see almost to Venture Avenue where I had that little apartment. I wonder if I walked into the bar on the ground floor right now, would I find Luc still behind the bar and Thrace sprawled out in a chair dreaming of happier times?*

*Calliope? Who knows what corner of the world she's visiting. Who knows who she's inspiring to find their true destiny.*

# The Examined Life

## Max Griffin

Max Griffin writes horror and science fiction stories, often with a dark twist. Authors as diverse as John Updike, Richard Matheson, and Lawrence Block inspire and inform his literary style.

Max Griffin is the pen name of an academic and professional mathematician, who is the author of a graduate textbook in real analysis and numerous research articles. When he is not writing fiction, his days are filled with teaching mathematics and statistics, research, and administrative work at a major comprehensive university in the Southwest United States. He is the proud parent of a daughter who is a librarian. He is blessed to be in a long-term relationship with his life partner, Mr. Gene, who is an expert knitter.

The two humans in Max's household are the pets of an Abyssinian cat named Mr. Dinger, short for Erwin Schrodinger the Cat. Mr. Dinger graciously lets them live in his home in return for food and occasional petting. Oh, and there's that litter box thing they do for him, too.

You can visit Max online at: members.cox.net/maxgriffin/

That day started like every other, just another in an endless string of sterile days.

Constance woke to the caress of an easy melody from her alarm clock. The impassive walls watched as she stretched and yawned. "Oliver, please turn off the alarm." Her voice bore the flat tone of command that one assumed with servants. "Oliver, please start my bath." Even though Oliver was just a computer program, she never failed to be polite.

"Yes, ma'am." Oliver's soft baritone, programmed to be warm and comforting, filled the room. She had given him a faint accent, as though he were from a lower class neighbour-hood in London. In her daydreams, she replaced the real world of their Dallas condo with the fantasy world of an English country estate. "Shall I start breakfast, ma'am?"

"Yes, thank you, Oliver." She stood and slipped off her nightgown. She stretched again while the water splashed in her bathroom. "Do you think I'm putting on weight, Oliver?" Her mirror gazed back at her as she posed sideways, lifted one leg, and held her tummy.

Of course, Oliver was programmed to be polite. "You are as lovely as ever, ma'am." He was also programmed to be truthful. "But you have put on four pounds since last week, ma'am." Oliver monitored Constance's health with mechanical care: weight, respiration, heartbeat, urine and stool samples. He even took a blood sample with her weekly pedicure.

Her expression soured. "I think I'll just have fruit and tea this morning, Oliver."

"Yes, ma'am. I'll fix the usual for Master Clifford."

"Thank you, Oliver. Please wake my husband while I bathe, will you?" She tested her tub with a toe before immersing herself.

"Of course, ma'am."

Constance lounged in the steamy water and longed for a book to read. She had finished her romance novel the night before, and now frowned, contemplating the annoying task of finding another to while away the time. Before the accident, before Clifford became bound to his chair, reading had been but a diversion. Now fiction provided an escape for her uneasy mind, a surcease from the perils of daily life.

Not that Constance's daily life was particularly perilous. She had arranged their lives to eschew peril above all else.

Their first-floor condo rested inside a gated community, secure and exclusive. Private guardsmen stood in steady vigil to protect the tenants from criminals and all other social deviants. Outside, security cameras hid in the trees while bushes and flower beds marched in geometric arrays, manicured to precise specifications. Inside, cybernetic controls preserved a placid tranquillity.

There was never any reason for either of them to leave the condo, let alone venture into the chaos outside the gates. Constance purchased everything online and had it delivered straight to their door. Food for their table, medicines for Clifford, movies for their viewing, books for her nightstand, clothing for their backs: it was all available online. Constance had even found Clifford's physical therapist online. An endless stream of smiling delivery people brought all of their worldly needs to their front door. Their only callers were servants arriving with goods or services, wearing distinctive uniforms that marked their function. Yet somehow those very uniforms erased all distinctions with a bland efficiency.

After her bath, Constance sat in the kitchen sipping her second cup of tea. Her brown hair, cut in a blunt bob, clung in wet clumps to her skull. She only half-listened to the news programme on the television. The picture showed young people in handcuffs, under arrest for reading something called *Ulysses*. The voice-over prattled about the dangers of reading terrorist propaganda. When Clifford rolled into the room, she turned off the sound. The video panned over other subversive books the students had been reading against the backdrop of a burning city. She read the titles—*Women in Love, 1984, The Catcher in the Rye*—but she didn't recognize any of them. "Good morning, Clifford. Did you sleep well?"

He grimaced. "Well enough, after I took a pill. Damned nightmares again."

"Um-hm." Constance stood and set the table for Clifford, pulling his meal from the microwave oven. "Here you are, dear. Pancakes and an omelette, your favourite!"

"Thanks." Clifford ran his fingers through his tousled hair. "Can we go out today? I could get a haircut and we could maybe eat at a restaurant? Like we used to?"

She tipped her head and frowned as her eyes raked over her spouse. "We could have that nice lady come and trim your hair. You know, the one from Designing Women?"

"You mean Faitha. I like Faitha. But let's go to her shop instead of having her come here. She makes the people there sound so interesting. I'd like to meet them."

"Now, now, Clifford. You know how much trouble it is for you to go out. We'll just have her come here, like usual." Her voice rose slightly. "Oliver, would you please call Faitha and arrange to have her come to trim Master Clifford's hair today?"

"No!" Clifford's eyes flashed at her. "Oliver, cancel that." His voice snapped across the table at her. "I don't want her to come here. I want to go out. I'm sick of staying inside all of the time."

Constance pursed her lips. "My, aren't we cranky today." She tapped her fingernail on the table, stood and clutched at her housecoat. "We'll see, dear. Just let me finish getting dressed." She poured Clifford some tea. "You eat your breakfast and then we'll talk, OK?"

Clifford frowned. "I mean it, Constance. I'll go out without you if I must."

"Uh-huh, yes, dear." She patted his shoulder. "Oliver, be a dear and fix some more tea, will you?"

"Oliver!" He scowled and his eyes threw daggers at her. "I swear, he's more your lover than I am. A machine!" Clifford's fork clanked against his plate. The pancake slewed around and slapped onto the floor.

"Now look what you've done, Clifford." Her voice was flat and held no emotion. She knelt and scooped up the sticky mess. "Oliver, be sure to clean in here today. And fix another meal for Clifford, please." She stood and rinsed her hands at the sink. "You know that sex doesn't matter to me, Clifford. We're intimate spiritually."

Clifford stared at the table and ignored her. His spoon clinked in his tea.

She peered at his face for a moment, hands on her hips. Silence grew like a cancer between them before a sigh gusted from her lips and she stalked off to her room.

She yanked clothes from her closet and tossed them on the bed. "Oliver! What is this?" She pulled lacy under-things from her drawer, adding them to the growing pile of garments.

"Those are your underwear, ma'am." Like all machines, Oliver was literal.

"Of course these are my underwear, you idiot!" She jerked up her panties and snatched at her bra. "I meant what is with Clifford? Is he taking his antidepressants?" She pulled on a blouse. Her fingers tore at the buttons, taking several tries each before she fastened them.

"I'm sorry, ma'am. Master Clifford has asked for a privacy shield on his medical records."

"What? He can't do that. Doctor Lawrence specifically gave me permission to monitor his meds."

"I'm sorry, ma'am. When Doctor Lawrence was here last week Master Clifford asked for the privacy block. The doctor himself put it on."

"They locked me out? We'll see about that!" Constance wrapped a skirt about her narrow waist and knotted the belt. "We'll just see about that. Oliver, get me Doctor Lawrence on the phone, right now!"

"Yes, ma'am."

The conversation between Oliver and Lawrence's avatar buzzed in the background. She kicked around in her closet and picked out a pair of sensible patent leather pumps.

"Lawrence here." The physician spoke with his usual clipped efficiency.

"Doctor Lawrence." Constance took a deep breath and steadied herself on the bedstead. "I'm calling about Clifford. I think he's not taking his antidepressants!"

"What makes you think that? I have this morning's blood work on him right here. It looks fine to me." Clifford's chair constantly monitored his medical status and transmitted it to Lawrence's office.

"Doctor! He wants to go outside. And what's this about blocking me from viewing the records in his chair?"

"Please. Clifford and I discussed this last week and we decided it was time for him to take more control of his life. And really, Constance, I think it would be healthy for both of you to get out."

She scowled. "Doctor Lawrence." She put slight emphasis on the "doctor". She thought he was rude to use her first name. "I'm the best judge of what Clifford needs, don't you think?" Her voice was sweet, but with a poisonous edge.

"Frankly, Constance, Clifford is the best judge of what is good for Clifford. If he wants to go out, there's nothing you can do."

She flushed but said nothing. Her chest heaved.

"Now, if there is nothing else, I'll see you next month."

Constance lay on her bed and fumed. Bumps and grunts thudded from Clifford's room as Oliver's mechanical minions helped him prepare for his excursion. His chair whirred down the hallway and stopped at her door.

"Constance, I'm ready."

She said nothing. The walls watched, the lamps listened, but they, too, were silent.

"I'd like for you to go with me. Like we used to." The door sucked the life from Clifford's voice.

Silence.

"Constance, I need to do this. I'll do it by myself if I must." He waited, and then his chair whirred away. The swish of hydraulics opened the front door, oozed it closed, and the latch clacked shut. The house was silent again.

She wandered on aimless feet through the condo. She tried Clifford's door, but it was locked. She ran her fingers along the top of the mantle above the false fireplace. "Oliver. Dust! This place is filthy!"

"I'm sorry ma'am. Shall I order the cleaning service?"

"No! I want to be left alone."

She returned to her bedroom. The book on her nightstand was closed; there was no escape there. She sat on the chaise and sulked.

Oliver's soft voice broke her reverie. "Ma'am, the UPS delivery man is at the door. He says you have to sign for the package."

She snapped, "I didn't order anything!"

"Shall I tell him to go away, ma'am?"

Constance stood and straightened her skirt. "No. No, I'll see him." She rummaged in a drawer and stuffed a thick roll of bills into her pocket. The delivery person would expect a tip.

He wore a smile and the brown UPS uniform. "Please sign here, ma'am." He offered an electronic clipboard while holding a small package under his arm. He waited with a fixed smile on his face while Constance scrawled her name. "How is Clifford, ma'am?"

She stared at him. "Excuse me?" Her expression was the same as it would have been if a cockroach had suddenly asked her for the time of day.

"Er, Clifford, ma'am. He's always so nice when I make deliveries. Hope he's feelin' all right." The delivery man's smile had a nervous edge now.

Constance's eyes narrowed. "Clifford has gone out," she snapped. Her mouth was hard and displeasure fouled her lips. She handed the clipboard back.

The man flushed and avoided her eyes. "Sorry, ma'am," he murmured. He handed her the package. "I meant no offense."

She snatched the parcel from his hands and fumbled in her pocket for a tip. The entire roll of bills sprayed out onto the immaculate tile of the entryway. The delivery man's eyes widened. "That's a lot of money, ma'am. You should be careful!"

She dropped to her knees and scrabbled the bills into a wad in her fist. She shoved a random banknote at the delivery person. "Here. Go away."

The delivery man squatted down. "Do you need help, ma'am?" His fingers trembled before he hid them behind his back.

"No!" Constance clutched at the money and glared at him. "Just go away. I've got my package. You've got your tip. Now leave!"

The man stood. "Yes, ma'am, thank you." He hesitated. "I just meant to be of assistance, ma'am."

She flushed. "I don't need your help. I don't need anyone's help." She looked at his shoes, worn and brown and scuffed. A stray hair had fallen across her eyes. A tremor shuddered through her hand as she tucked it back into place. She raised her gaze to his face and snarled, "Get out! Just take your money and go!" The force of her words propelled tiny droplets of spittle across his slacks.

He retreated a step before her fury. "I'm sorry, ma'am." They stood frozen in a silent tableau for a heartbeat before he tipped his hat and was gone.

Constance staggered into the kitchen clutching the package and the wad of bills. She sat at the table and pressed each bill flat, one after another, stacking them so that the portrait side was up and facing the same way on each one.

Next, she turned the package over in her hands. There was no return address, but she recognized the handwriting on the front. Only her mother would hand-address mail in this day and age. Brown wrapping paper slathered with transparent tape covered the parcel, as though her mother feared prying eyes would penetrate the contents. She sighed in frustration. She would need to get her scissors. She hoped that the contents would be worth the trouble, but she doubted it. Later, when she was calmer, then she would open it. Now was time for tea. "Oliver, shall we have tea together?"

"Of course, ma'am." Oliver was ever the perfect companion.

Constance sat in the dining room, stared out the window, and sipped her tea. She ignored the package on the table and the scissors gleaming in the sunlight. Outdoors, heat beat onto the manicured gardens where happy flowers marched in rigid, pastel arrays between concrete pathways. A guardsman in a creased, black uniform swaggered across her view, his weapon at his hip and his ebony helmet flashing in the sunlight, but she didn't notice him. Here and there uniformed workers tended the plants, and the guardsman strode with stolid purpose through the geometric pathways. Her eyes passed over the people as though they were part of the landscaping. In the shadows, a man in a brown uniform stared at her, but their gazes never met. Her eyes saw his feet shift and the sweat gleam on his brow, but he may as well have been on another planet for all the impression he made on her soul. She didn't consider the bees that buzzed about the flowers or the worms that burrowed in the earth either. The bushes and the walls and the roofs and the guardsmen looked on, ever vigilant, ever silent, guardians and wardens alike for those on the inside.

Her glance returned to the table. The sun glimmered off the transparent tape on the package. Constance seized her scissors and sliced at the edges, peeling back layers of wrapping. The packing cloaked a book, ancient, worn, and dog-eared, along with a note from her mother. The note, of course, was handwritten in her mother's angular script. Constance flattened the paper on the table, peering at the cursive characters.

"Dearest Constance," she read. She scowled. Endearments from her mother at this point in her life were too little and too late. The note continued. "I read this book when I was in college. It helped me understand the duality of our spirits: mind and body transcended through shared intimacy. I stumbled across my copy when I was cleaning out needless things and I thought of you. I hope you enjoy it as I did. All my best to poor Clifford. Love, Mother."

"Hmmph. Duality of our spirits. Transcendence!" She didn't realize she was speaking out loud. "Intimacy is overrated anyway."

"Did you require something, ma'am?" Oliver, ever at the ready, didn't understand intimacy either. He was indeed the perfect companion for Constance.

"No, no, just mumbling, Oliver." She considered the worn cover. Since she had finished her book last night, she had nothing else to do. She may as well read this.

She lounged on her bed, devouring the book, lost to time. Hours later, Oliver spoke again. "Ma'am, it's past your usual time for dinner. Would you care for anything?"

She laid the book down and stared at the clock. Where had the day gone? "Oliver, is Clifford back?"

"No, ma'am."

"No?" What could have happened to him? "Oliver, please call him." It would be awful if she had to go out to rescue him.

Moments later Clifford's voice filled the room. "Hello Constance. How are you?"

"I'm fine. Where are you? You have worried me so!"

"I'm fine, Constance. How was your day? Did anything happen?"

"No, nothing. Oh, the UPS man came. My mother sent me a book. I've spent the day reading."

"The UPS man. You mean Ed. How is he? His little girl is ill. I know he's worried about her medical bills."

"How should I know how he is? He's a delivery man, Clifford! Where are you? Where have you been all day?"

"I went into town and stopped to have my hair trimmed. I gossiped with the customers, just like a normal person. I went to a restaurant at the Anatole." He paused, as if for courage. "I've rented a room for the night, Constance. I'd like for you to join me."

"A room? At the Anatole? What in heaven's name were you thinking?"

"I was thinking a night away from our condo might do us some good, Constance. It feels like a prison, sometimes, like my chair. A night of romance would be good for both of us, don't you think? Won't you join me?"

"Of course I won't join you. Why should I leave my perfectly good bedroom and go to an unseemly hotel room? You come home, you hear me?"

"Yes, Constance, I'll come home. But not tonight. Tonight I need something different. I wish we could share it, but I'll understand if you cannot."

"Indeed, I will not." She scowled at the watchful walls. "You won't come home, then?"

"Tomorrow, Constance. I'll be home for breakfast tomorrow, I promise."

She glanced at her book and her fingers lingered on the cover; she longed to return to the strange world within those pages. "Well then, see that you do. Call me if you need anything, dear." Her voice held dismissal.

"I'll be fine, my love. Tomorrow, then." The condo again fell silent. "Oliver, I'll have dinner now, after all. Something light, please?"

"Yes, ma'am. Perhaps a salad and a feta sandwich?"

"I don't know. Surprise me."

"Very good, ma'am." A random selection was easy for Oliver.

After dinner Constance sat in the dining room and gazed at the dying sunset. She didn't notice the man in the brown uniform still hulking under the tree. If she had noticed him, she would have thought nothing of it. After all, it was perfectly safe here, under the vigilant eyes of the cameras in the trees and the walls and the roofs. The guardsmen stood watch to assure her life remained safe and trouble free. She strode to her bedroom. "Oliver, please turn on my nightstand lamp."

She picked up the strangely alluring book her mother had sent. It was a wonder that such books were permitted! This was so different from the happy romances she usually devoured. It was at once seductive and repellent. She could not stop reading even as she was revolted by the deeds of the characters. They were so physical, not spiritual at all. They behaved like she imagined beasts must, yet somehow they seemed whole and real. They filled her with longing and with revulsion.

The chapters flew by and, at last, Constance's eyes grew heavy. The book slipped from her fingers and her breathing became slow and regular. Oliver dimmed the lights without disturbing her sleep.

Constance woke to a thumping sound at her window. "What?" It was loud and persistent, right by her bedside. "Oliver! What's that sound?" Abruptly, the thuds stopped, replaced by the sounds of a scuffle and the muffled tone of voices.

"It was an intruder, ma'am. The guardsmen have captured him already. The Sergeant of the Guard is in the condo now, to make sure you are safe. He asks you to not worry."

Feet clomped down her hallway and a fist rapped at her door. Constance lurched up and clutched her covers to her chin. "Who is it?"

"Everything is all right, ma'am. I'm Sergeant of the Watch Raul Gonzales. We've caught a prowler trying to break into your condo."

"A prowler?"

"Yes, ma'am. May I come in, ma'am." It wasn't a question. "I need to make sure you're all right." The door was already opening.

"Yes, yes of course!" She tossed her hair from her face and tugged at the sheets. The book, lying face down on her bed, drew her fingers; she stroked at its cover as if it cloaked her lover.

A burly man in a black uniform peered at her from the shadows of the doorway. He eased into the room and looked left and right before he relaxed. He tipped his head toward the microphone clipped to his shoulder and murmured. "All clear." His gaze returned to Constance. "Are you all right, ma'am? We've got the prowler under arrest. Good thing you've got security glass at the windows. He tried to break in with a rock." The officer snorted.

"Yes, yes, I'm fine." Her words came in short, electric bursts.

The officer's eyes scanned the room like radar. "Apparently he got into the complex earlier today. He was wearing a delivery man's uniform."

Adrenalin rushed down Constance's limbs and out her fingers and toes. "He was here all day, in the compound? Was I in danger?"

"Oh, no, ma'am. You were never in danger. We're always on the lookout for deviants. Your condo is under constant surveillance."

Constance relaxed. Yes, of course; that was why she chose this place to live. Her fingers ran through her hair, pushing the unkempt locks back from her brow. "Well, thank God for that."

"Yes, ma'am. Criminals don't have any chance. Don't know why they even bother, the way we watch everything."

"Yes, well, he must have been insane then."

"Yes, ma'am, insane or desperate." The officer's watchful eyes scanned the bedroom and rested on her book. "Do you mind, ma'am?" Without waiting for her permission, he picked it up and read the title. He stared at her with no expression and tilted his head to whisper something into his microphone.

"Do you mind my asking where you got this book, ma'am?" His eyes bore into her. She thought no one should have eyes so blue.

"It came today, from the UPS delivery man. Say, do you suppose that was him? The prowler, I mean."

"Could be, ma'am. So you just got this book today?" More guardsmen slipped into the room, weapons drawn.

"Yes, today. I must have fallen asleep reading it. Why?"

"So, you admit to reading this book, ma'am?" The officer's voice was flat. His eyes, those crystalline windows to his soul, drilled into her. She noticed for the first time how empty those eyes were and a chill ran through her.

"Why yes, of course I read it. It's a book. What else would one do with it?" She put on her best haughty expression, although unease clutched at her heart. "Why do you ask?"

The Sergeant of the Guard nodded at the others, who approached Constance with handcuffs clanking. "I'm afraid you'll have to come with us, ma'am." His voice, harsh and no longer polite, rasped at her ears. "You're under arrest. It's a serious crime to read this book."

The officers grabbed Constance by the arms and lifted her from the bed. She shrieked and pushed them away. "What is this? I've done nothing wrong. You're supposed to protect *me*." She flailed at the brutal arms that gripped her before one of the officers reached out and touched her throat. She didn't feel the hypodermic. The effect of the narcotic was instantaneous. She collapsed on her bed, silent and still, and the guardsmen cuffed her. Two of them dragged her from the room. Her head hit the floor with a dull thud and her limp legs slapped against the polished tile. Cameras flashed as other officers photographed her bedroom, now a crime scene.

~

"Two perps in one night." Gonzales shrugged. "I guess these friggin' criminals will never learn we're always watching." He poked at Constance's book, worn, scuffed, and dog-eared. The title, *Lady Chatterley's Lover*, was barely legible. "Been years since I've seen a copy of this piece of filth. Be sure to photograph it before you burn it."

# Neyon Dreams 2.0

## David Snyder

David Snyder lives in Boston. He received his BA from New York University and is currently pursuing an MFA in creative writing from Emerson College. His work has appeared in *Coal City Review*, *Meeting House, Defenestration,* and *Crash.*

"Neyon Dreams 2.0" has previously appeared online in the July 4, 2010 issue of Meeting House (http://meetinghousemag.com).

### Friday, Morning

The stars are gone. Sunlight fills the apartment. Too bright. I throw off the covers.

She's still asleep but wakes when I stand. She blinks a couple times and rubs her eyes. Then she smiles. "That was great," she says. "So strong."

I nod, put on my TravPants. My shoes are by the door. "Where's my shirt?" I say.

"Bathroom."

Right. Forgot about that. I get mad again as I remem her spilling her drink on me, on my BlaiseShirt. It's hanging, dry but still covered with red. My fave shirt.

I carry it back to the bedroom, looking at the new stain. As I'm putting it on, thinking about people seeing me like this, she says to me, "Where'd you get it?"

Did she really say that? I look at her, then down at my shirt, then her again. So ridic. She thinks I'll leak my source to *her*? After *this*?

I grab the pouch with the Neyon off her table. The two vials clang. Not a lot left. And it *is* good stuff. Too good for her. "I don't even like you," I say.

Right as I turn to leave, I hear her say, "What's your name again?"

I'm gone.

### Friday, Afternoon

Merlin's place is small and dirty. Not a pharm I'd go to for most scripts. Just the one.

He's behind the counter, huge white hair all over. He's short and thin, shiny skin and crazy eyes that go so fast it's hard to tell when he sees me. Then he says, "How goes it, Cyl?"

"It goes."

He scans the doorway, then turns for the back door. As he walks he says, "Follow the election?"

"Neg," I say, annoyed that I forgot. Blaise was running. "Blaise win?"

As he stands in front of the door, getting read, Merlin says, "Cira."

Damn. Really wanted Blaise to win. Been watching his vids from the beginning. He's so much better, how could anyone click Cira? Sometimes I don't get people. "Was it Treasury?" I ask.

The door beeps. Merlin whispers something I can't hear and it clicks open. Over his shoulder, he says, "Defence." Then he walks through. I follow.

The back's a small room with a table and chairs in the mid and a fridge in the corner. It's lined with shelves holding mostly unmarked containers. Merlin grabs one and puts it on the table. "Beer?" he asks.

"Neg," I say. "Not staying long."

He grabs one and we sit.

"I'm surprised you didn't click Blaise," says Merlin. "He's your fave, isn't he?"

"Can't vote yet," I say.

Merlin chuckles. "Of course. I always think you're older than you are. Another year?"

I nod.

"My oh my." He takes a drink.

The pack catches me. It looks dif than usual. Nicer, maybe. My eye twitches.

Merlin notices. "I have a treat for you," he says.

I blink a few times and look away, back to Merlin. "Yeah?"

He grabs the container and unzips. Inside is a small glass bottle of clear liquid, a vial of bright green pills, and an eye dropper. The pills are def a dif shade. They almost glow. My arm flexes and I feel the table move. I make myself lean back.

"New batch. New formula." Merlin picks up the pills and looks at them. "A more intense experience, and no downside."

He puts the vial down on the table between us. I stare. I reach for it. As I grab, Merlin says, "You ever see stars while on Neyon?"

Many times. I squint at the mem. "Yeah," I say.

"Not like this. Now you'll *feel* them."

My skin vibes with the thought. But I'm worried. "How much more?" I ask.

Merlin holds out his palm. I slowly give him the pills. He takes them and the vial and the eye dropper and zips it all back up in the pack. Then he says, "I'm going to give you a special offer: normal price."

"Yeah?" Merlin's sold me upgraded Neyon twice before. Both times the price went up with the qual. I don't wanna sound ungrateful, but I gotta know. "Why's that?"

He shrugs. "I suppose I just like you, Cyl."

I don't get what he's going for. "And why's that?" I ask.

"Cyl," he says. He picks up his beer. "Such a sad question."

He takes a swig. I think I get what he means and it gets to me. Feels like I missed a breath. I look down, away from him, cough. Then I take out my wallet. "A thou?"

Merlin confirms and keeps drinking.

After the thou, I only have three left. Hope my parents left more. Haven't checked in a few days.

I give Merlin the money and he gives me the container. Prob I'm just imagining but it feels heavier than the last. I put it in my bag and then I remem I'm out of condoms. I take out a twenty and ask if he's got any.

"Only Trav," says Merlin. "Ran out of the BlaiseCondoms."

"Fine."

He takes the money and we walk out to the main part of the pharm. He goes behind the counter and grabs a pack of TravCondoms and tosses. I catch and pocket. Merlin says, "Didn't you buy a pack last time you picked up?"

Yeah. "Maybe," I say.

"One special girl, or several?"

I like Merlin fine, but don't wanna get too personal. "Does it make a dif?" I say.

Merlin smiles, shakes his head. "I shouldn't have asked. Answer's always the same with you kids. The freedom of youth."

I don't know what to say. I shift my weight and feel the pack against my side and try to think about tonight. Think about going home, sleeping, figuring out what I'm gonna wear. But instead I keep focusing on what Merlin said before. The sad question. Dunno why it bothers me so much, him saying that, but it does. The way he said it. Like there's something wrong with me.

"Don't worry," says Merlin, bringing me back. "You'll find someone."

Merlin's acting strange. He's never talked like this before. I'm feeling more and more uncomfortable. "I'm not looking," I say.

He doesn't say anything. His dancing eyes are kinda focused for once but not on anything I can see and when he speaks his voice sounds kinda far away. "To be young again," he says. "What's that like?"

Time to leave. As I walk towards the door I say, "Like you'd figure."

I push open the door and step through, and right before it closes I hear Merlin say to either me or himself, "I doubt that very much."

**Friday, Night**

I'm half a block from Astrolab when I reach the barrier. There's six bouncers making a wall in front, plus two cops. I walk up to the closest bouncer. He scans me through his shades. "BlaiseShirt?" he asks.

"Yeah," I say. It's maroon, with Blaise's logo in white. It was my second fave, but I had to promote. I've also got TealPants and TravShoes on, plus my bag. It hangs to my side, not hidden.

The bouncer nods and moves aside. I nod back and head into the tube between the barricades, towards Astrolab.

I can feel the music before I enter, and soon as I'm in I'm hit by the sound, my skin vibing with the force. I take a few steps

85

and then get banged into by a body. I feel my bag to make sure it's okay. It is. I move toward the back.

The place is crowded. Bodies everywhere, walking and dancing. It's dark but I can tell that everyone's young, good looking, and wearing top Celeb clothes. They wouldn't be in here if they weren't. Above us, the sky's made of stars. Small, bright bulbs cover the ceiling, scattered and in clusters. There's slices of colour mixed in, faint but there. Nice touch.

As I walk to the lockroom I pass the main dance floor and then the lounge. It's only 11 so the dancing's not too intense, but the floor's still filled and strong. The lounge is the same— crowded but not packed. I slow a little as I go by. Seems like most are talking and drinking. Not too many are just lying there. That'll change, too.

In the back's a big stairway. I go down and then head right, away from the bathrooms and labs. One of the good things about Astrolab is they got plenty of both, so there's no waits. I don't use the labs, though. I can't get into it when I'm thinking about how much time we have. And the beds don't get cleaned much. Why waste a trip like that? But not waiting for the bathroom's good.

I reach the lockroom's heavy black door and swing it. There's more light in here, enough to see the lockers and their nums clear. There's hunds, but most are in use. Takes me a min to find an open one. It takes my five and I type in a pass when it asks. The door swings open and in goes my pack. I pocket a couple hund from my wallet and throw that in, too. Then I lock it up and head to the bar.

There's six tenders, all wearing black and all working fast. The bar's maybe forty feet long with no open spaces. I squeeze in anyway. A couple min pass before a tender comes.

"Yeah?"

I think for a sec. "Whiskey and cola," I decide to try.

"Teal or Pria?"

"Teal."

She grabs a glass and the bottle and pours. "Twenty-five."

I hand her a hund. "Seventy back."

She goes to get the change. I take a sip. Not bad but not great. Just another drink. Nothing special. I take another.

As I drink I look over at the girl next to me. Her shirt's white and got a lotta small holes all over, so I'm thinking it's prob a KariShirt, and she's wearing tight black LanaPants. Strong combo, she looks good in it. Can't see her face but she's got short black hair and dark skin. I like her enough.

"Nice night," I say.

The girl turns and looks me over for a sec before she says, "Nice night."

Good start. I point at her glass. "What's your drink?"

She picks it up. Looks clear. "Martini," she says.

"Strong?" I ask.

A sip, then she says, "Could be stronger."

I'm pretty pos now, but still need to be sure. I lean forward, look right at her, and say, "Your eyes are pretty."

With a grin, she says, "Thanks."

A little closer, a little more of a whisper, I ask, "How do they feel?"

Now she leans. For a short sec I see her eyes up close and they *are* pretty. Shape, anyway. Too dark to tell the colour, though. Then her face is past mine, her lips just brushing my ear. She breathes and says, "Dry."

All set. Good. "Dance?" I hold out my hand. She takes it.

"I'm Cyl," I say.

"Dani."

We move away from the bar, through the bodies, to the dance floor.

The music's strong tonight. Chori, I think. Someone I like. And it's loud in a good way. We pick a spot. I put my hands on her waist, her back. She leans into me. We dance.

I know I'm okay, but Dani's way strong. She's moving better than I can. I don't wanna look bad, so I talk to slow her. "This Chori?" I ask.

She opens her eyes some. "Yeah," she says, not caring.

"Strong," I say. Nothing else to add.

The music keeps beating and we keep moving. Dani looks like she's about to close her eyes again so I say, "Who's your fave Celeb?"

Instantly she says, "Cira."

I slow, stand still. "Cira?" I say, not liking the sound.

Dani slows too and smiles at me. "Our new Sec of Defense."

"I know." I look closer at her shirt. Not Kari. "This a CiraShirt?"

"Yeah," she says.

My hands slide off her waist.

She must notice something's off cause she stops swaying and gives me a confused look.

"Blaise is my fave," I say.

Five secs pass without us moving or talking, the music filling in between us. We don't look at each other's eyes. That's that. "I gotta go to the lockroom," I say. I take a step away.

"Bye," she says. I think she sounds kinda sad, but prob I'm just imagining. I give a weak smile, she gives one back. I'm gone.

I'm feeling hot and almost sick as I walk back to the bar. Seemed like a good match. I imagine how the night could've gone if I hadn't asked who her fave Celeb is, if I hadn't noticed it was a CiraShirt. It would have gone smooth like last night. Like most nights. And I have this strange sec where I dunno if I'm glad or not that it didn't. Shame we didn't match, relieved I didn't find out after, but still off somehow. Dunno what. But there's still time and other girls, and the new batch to try, so maybe the night can still end strong.

I'm at the bar, waiting, trying to get a tender, thinking about what drink to get, and then my eye catches on a girl. Her face is pretty, with oval eyes and deep colour and dark hair curving around her. But it's her smile that gets me. It's dif than the other girls'. I can see her teeth, and they're bright white, glowing in the dark. Like stars. I move towards her.

Her smile stops for a sec when she sees me squeeze in next to her, then comes back. "Hello," she says, before I can say anything.

"Hey." I feel her eyes scanning me, like I'm being read. It feels even hotter now. "Nice night," I say.

She looks around the room, at the ceiling, back to me. "Always a nice night here."

Not sure if that's a good answer. Sounds pos, but it's dif. Least she didn't say it wasn't. "Yeah," I say. "Def a strong place."

"I come for guidance."

I stare, not getting what she's saying. She points at the ceiling. "There," she says. "Polaris. The north star."

I look up. There's one bulb that's kinda brighter. Seems like she means that one. "Where does it guide you?"

"It can lead you back." She glances at the lounge, then back at me. "After journeys with another sort of guide."

I give her a look, but she doesn't react at all. I decide to go along with whatever she's doing. "What other sort of guide?"

Her smile and her stare get sharper. "I think you know what kind of guide I mean."

Do I? Thoughts flash. I think maybe she means Neyon, but maybe she's just messing with me.

"Why do you come here?" she asks.

I'm about to answer, then stop. Seems simple, but I dunno what to say. Music and talk float around us as one sec and then another passes, and she just looks right at me the whole time. I say, "To meet people."

"Really?" The way she says it, and the way she's smiling, I know she's playing with me, but I dunno in what way. Can't tell if she's interested or not. Throwing me off. I look down the bar, scanning for a tender. Need a drink to calm.

"Aren't you gonna ask what I'm drinking?" she says.

I look back at her. "What?"

She holds up her glass. "Isn't that how these things go?"

I don't get what she's doing. Doesn't feel like she's being mean, but not nice, either. My face must look out. I try to smile, collect. "They can," I say. "What are you drinking?"

"Brandy."

Never heard that before. "Strong?"

"No," she says. "But good brandy is never too strong." She sips.

Now I'm really lost. Is she into Neyon? Is she into *me*? The feel I'm getting isn't norm, and usually I'd go and find

\

someone else, but I don't wanna now. I wanna stay. Something about her. Her smile, maybe. So big, so bright. Strong.

"Your smile's pretty," I say.

"Why, thanks." She moves her head a little closer to me and says, "So is yours, now."

"Now?"

She nods as she sips her drink. "It didn't look real before. But now it does."

I dunno what to say, but I can feel the smile on my face.

"Even better," she says.

And again, I wanna speak but dunno what I should say. I feel like I'm just floating along, like I can't find any ground. I'm okay, though. It feels okay.

Neither of us speaks. She keeps looking at me, like it's my turn, so I say, "Who's your fave Celeb?"

Her face changes a little and in a weird voice she says, "Sandra Taylor."

Dunno who that is. Name's strange. I squint, trying to remem anything about her.

"I'm not surprised you don't know her," she says. "Not too many do." She sounds like she's tired of saying that, like it happens a lot. Makes me wanna pretend like I *do* remem her, that she's my fave Celeb, too. But I know she'd know I don't. A sec passes and it's like she used up all her happiness before. I wanna bring it back. "Wanna tell me who she is?" I ask.

The way she looks at me, for a sec I think she's gonna explain. But then she says, "It's not important." She finishes her drink and sets her glass on the bar. "It was nice talking to you," she says, "but I gotta go."

"You're leaving?" I say. My voice sounds so weak it's hard to believe, but there it is.

"Yes," she says. "But maybe I'll see you here again. Another time."

"Another time?" I'm lost, but I'm still trying to follow. "Like tom?"

"Maybe."

She steps away from the bar, away from me. Seeing her leave, it feels off somehow. I have no idea why. I don't even know what that means. Over the music and the people I yell to her, "What's your name?"

Then she stops and turns, faces me. Somehow, no one steps into the path she's made and so there's an empty space, like there's a barrier surrounding us, separating us from all of Astrolab. It feels like a few secs pass without anything but our staring. Then she says, "Stella."

Stella. "I'm Cyl."

She smiles. I smile back.

And then she's gone. And right then I start thinking about coming back tom and trying to find her. Even as I'm planning, I wonder why I care enough to bother. But I do care. And I will.

"Nice night."

I turn. A girl's appeared next to me. I look at her. Can't tell what she's wearing. Looks pretty enough. Fine. But I decide that if she's holding then we're using hers, and if she's not then we're using my old batch. Not using the new Neyon tonight. Save it. Another time.

I try to smile at her, but I don't think it comes through. Doubt it matters.

"Nice night," I say.

## Saturday, Morning

Cold this morning. Sun's hitting me but it's weak. 'Cept in my eyes. They feel dry and bruised. Like raisins in my head. I'm about to go back under the covers when I see the girl, still asleep. I have no idea what her name is. Can't remem if I asked. I feel off, like I gotta do something but dunno what. Energy but no aim. I get up.

As I'm pulling on my TealPants I hear, "Hi."

She's sitting up in bed, still under the covers. With the light she's still pretty. Norm that'd make me happy. But I don't care, and that makes me feel even more off.

"Hi," I say.

I keep dressing. She lies there, watching for a min. Then she says, "Last night was good."

"Yeah," I say. "It was."

But I feel like last night didn't go right. I don't usually feel real happy in the mornings, but I feel something. Relief, maybe. Like a loss of pressure. I don't feel that now. I feel stiff, weak. I feel like an outline. I dunno what's with me.

"I gotta go," I say to the girl.

"Okay." She stands up and slides some clothes on. She walks to me. "I'm glad we met," she says.

"Me, too," I say.

She kisses me on the cheek and I grin. Friendly. Standard. But I feel like I'm not there.

"Bye," she says. She smiles some. Can't see her teeth.

"Bye."

I grab my bag. I head home.

### Saturday, Night

I wanted to get to Astrolab after 11, but it's 10:45 and I'm here. My bag's locked and I already have a drink—rum and TealCola. Right after I get it, I wish I hadn't. Not 'cause I don't like it, even though I don't. It's 'cause I feel off, standing at the bar but not wanting to talk to anyone. I know I should look for a girl to maybe be with later, just in case, but I don't wanna yet. I wanna wait. Ridic, I know.

Once I'm done I set the glass down and move to the lounge. I find a spot and sit. A few people around are def not really there, just staring at the sky and whatever they see, but most are talking, or want to. I just look around, at the dancers, the loungers, the bar. Every five min I check my watch and every time only two min have gone. And I can feel my just-cleaned BlaiseShirt pulling sweat off me.

A girl comes by and sits down next to me. She's got on a dark yellow ChoriShirt and shiny PriaPants and looks real good. "Nice night," she says.

"Nice night," I say back, wishing I could mean it more.

"What's your drink?" she asks, looking for my glass.

"Don't have one," I say. "Might later."

She nods, stands up. "Maybe I'll see you." She walks away, and I can't believe I let her go. What am I doing?

And then I see her. Coming here, to the lounge. Dressed in dark clothes I don't recognize but like. Holding her drink, prob brandy again. Smiling so bright.

Can't decide if I should stand and head to her or not, so I stay, just watching. When she sees me she stops, then moves right at me. She stands above me for a sec, then another. Then she sits.

"Hello again," she says.

"Hey," I say.

"Have you been waiting for me?"

Already I dunno what to say. "Just lounging."

Her smile goes crooked and I know she knows I was. "How was your night?" she asks.

"Nothing special."

"No?" Her face drops and her smile goes. Takes a sec, but I get why.

"I meant after—"

"I know," she says, sitting up and smiling again. "Just playing with you."

This girl. I dunno what to think when I'm talking to her, but I still want to. And her smile, it's so strong. Makes it look like every other girl's smiles aren't trying.

"How was yours?" I ask.

She shrugs. "Nothing special either. Just met a friend. You know."

"Sure," I say. "Def." I look away a little, just scan the place.

I feel her leaning toward me. "Where's your drink?" she asks.

"Don't have one."

"No? Here." She hands me her glass. "Try mine."

I take. "Brandy?"

She nods. I look at it a sec, then drink. And it's good. Sweet. Another sip and I wanna take another. I stop, though, and return it. "Thanks," I say.

"Like it?"

I nod.

"I'm glad to have introduced you two."

I laugh a little. Then I realize I've never laughed in Astrolab before. I haven't laughed in a while.

While Stella drinks, I look closer at her clothes. They're real plain. Black shirt, black pants, no designs. I don't recognize them. Can't think of any Celebs with clothes like that. Then I remem what she said yesterday about her fave Celeb. Then I get it. I realize she didn't name a Celeb at all.

"Stella," I say, careful, not wanting to offend if I'm wrong, "are you pro-Reg?"

She slowly sets her drink down. "Would that be a prob for you?" she asks.

I wanna say it's not, that it's fine with me, and then I realize it is. I don't care. Hard to believe, but I think it's true. I shake my head. "But why?"

Stella looks at me a sec, then looks at the ceiling. I look too, see the stars. She says, "'Cause we all think we're friends with the Celebs, that we know them, but we don't. We'll never even meet them."

I kinda nod and then look around the lounge, at the guys and girls laid out, staring at the ceiling. I know it's crazy to think like the pro-Regs do, but I get what Stella's saying. I get why she feels that. We'll never meet them. And I think about what I told Stella last night, that I come to Astrolab to meet people. I remem some names and faces, girls I've gone home with, but I don't know any of them. And I can't remem ever meeting a girl in a place like this that I wanted to meet again. But I wanted to meet Stella again. Even without Neyon, I'd wanna see her again. I start to think about that, but then I remem that I *do* have the new batch. Dunno how to say it to her, so I just do.

"Stella," I say, "do you dig Neyon?"

For the first time, she's the one with no words. Then she says, "Yes."

"I have some," I say. "New batch. Real strong. I've never tried it. I…" My mouth hangs open. I stop, look away. Can't squeeze out the last, the question. She doesn't say anything at first, and in the gap I hear the music. And it's Blaise. Blaise, and it's been playing. Been going for a while. I didn't notice, though. I think maybe it's a sign. That it's time to leave this place.

I look back at her. She says, kinda slowly, "Are you trying to ask me to go to a lab with you?"

I shake my head. "I don't dig the labs. But my place is weak. I thought, maybe…" She keeps looking at me. Not really smiling. It's hard, but I say, "Maybe your place." I say it too loud. I wanna look away, but I don't.

And her smile comes back, all the way, strong as ever. "I like your style, Cyl," she says. She stands. "Let's go."

As we leave the lounge, Astrolab, everything, I think about that. My style. Something to like. And I can't wait to see the stars, and feel them, with Stella.

### Sunday, Morning

It's dark when I wake, but I'm not tired. I feel like my skin's still vibing. My eyes are foggy and strained and overused. But they don't wanna close.

She only has a sheet on. I smooth it out over her shape. She shifts and stretches, then opens her eyes. Even in the dark I see the red there.

And then she smiles. She lights the room. I know I saw stars last night, but her smile's what I remem. It flashing as her head moved. It pulling me in when I was too far gone. Here it is.

I bend and kiss her lightly. I taste the brandy on her lips. I re-feel the electric of the stars from last night. Like she's got that in her. When I lean back, her face hasn't changed at all.

"So strong," she says. Her eyes are unfocused. "So strong."

"Yeah," I say. "Yeah it was."

I feel relief, but it's dif. Not like a weight lifted. More like warmth. Something I want, not wanted to lose. Looking at her there, I don't wanna leave.

And I say, "Remem when you asked why I go to Astrolab?"

She turns her head towards me.

"Everyone I've met there, I don't…they aren't…" I stop. I dunno how to say what I mean. Don't really know what I mean. But I know what I want. I'm nervous though, even now. I feel my heart going too fast. I lick my dry lips and with a scratchy voice say, "Do you maybe wanna do something with me?" She doesn't react, so I clarify, say, "Something else, I mean. Somewhere, another time."

She sits up. Her face comes alive, then freezes. Her eyes look right into me. She opens her mouth, closes it. Then she looks over. I follow and see: she's staring at the Neyon on the table. Five secs pass and I feel each one like a drop. Then she speaks.

"I…would like to see you again," she says. "Some night." Something's off with her voice. It sounds dif. Like she's not having fun.

She turns to me. She bites her lip. And she says, "I like you, Cyl, but I don't want anything beyond this." She glances at the Neyon. When she turns back, her eyes won't meet mine. And her smile's gone. She says, "Not more than this."

I watch her a sec. I know I should say something. "This," I manage.

She doesn't respond. I slide out of bed. I put on my pants and look for my BlaiseShirt. I find it under the bed. As I'm grabbing it, I hear her say, "I'll prob be at Astrolab next weekend."

My shirt's rumpled. "Yeah?" I say while smoothing it.

"Will you be there?" she asks.

I almost say no, but I know I will. Where else would I be?

"Yeah," I say, "prob."

She just sits there. I dunno what I want her to do, but she just sits there. The way she's staring. Like I did something wrong. Like there's something wrong with me.

My eyes really itch. I turn, scratch them. My hand's wet.

I open the door. I say, "Meet you there."

I'm gone.

# Watch

## Simon Logan

Simon Logan is the author of *Katja From The Punk Band* (ChiZine Publications, 2010), *Pretty Little Things To Fill Up The Void* (Prime Books, 2007), *Nothing Is Inflammable* (Prime Books, 2006), and *Rohypnol Brides* (Prime Books, 2006), and *I-O* (Prime Books, 2002). He lives and works in Edinburgh, Scotland, and has just completed the final revision of his latest novel, *Guerra*. You can find out more about him at his official website www.coldandalone.com

A blonde in a black cocktail dress walks in front of him, glazed eyes briefly meeting his own, and he hears the whirr of several wall-mounted cameras as they follow her across the bar to the ladies' toilets. His attention then returns once more to the man he's been watching for over an hour now, the two people who had been talking to the man finally getting up and leaving. He takes his drink with him and walks across to the man.

"Do those things actually work?"

The man is short with a quickly receding hairline; his thick arms are spread out in front of him with a line of upturned shot glasses between them. His name is Warek Zmuda and he is part of the wave of Polish immigrants that flooded into the country after it joined the EU. He takes the Pseudorette from his mouth, shrugs.

"I've been trying to give up myself. You mind if I join you?"

Zmuda leans back in his chair, gestures for the other man to sit.

"My name is Dev. I collect home movies."

One of Zmuda's eyebrows kinks. "Yeah?"

Dev nods. "But I have a few gaps in the collection, some items that I've not been able to find so far. I've heard that you might be able to help?"

"I think you must have wrong person."

"I don't think I do," Dev says, holding Zmuda's gaze.

Zmuda takes a drag on the Pseudorette. "Maybe depend on exactly what you looking for."

"Her name is Lola," Dev says.

"It always a woman," Zmuda replies, smiling. "So, you together or...?"

He notices Dev's confusion, leans in over the table. "It not unusual, you know—people wanting to watch those they still with. See guy over there by bar? His name John, he a regular. He been married to wife for 35 years now and they barely speak yet he pay for footage of her every week. Maybe I giving their relationship new life, you know?"

"Does she know he's watching her?"

Zmuda shrugs. "That not of my business. Parents wanting to see what their children are doing out of house. People obsessing about workmates that they too frightened to speak to. Businessmen want to check up on their competitors. Bored housewifes tired of reality TV. I just give them what they ask for, you know?"

Dev licks his lips, glances around, notices that Zmuda's table seems to be nestled in the middle of a weak spot for the CCTV cameras and knows that it is no coincidence. "We broke up six months ago. Her decision."

"And you want to know who she fucking now?"

Dev stiffens, suppresses a brief rush of anger. "It's not like that. I just miss her, that's all."

"Well I first to admit I a sucker for romantics amongst us. So what exactly you looking for?"

"Everything you can get."

Zmuda leans in conspiratorially. "Maybe I can get big lot. Exterior, interior, full tracking...High Access."

"High Access? You can really do that? I'd heard rumours but..."

"You heard of woman walking into bar?" Zmuda asks.

"I'm sorry...?"

"Woman walks into bar. Man sits next to her, says 'You sleep with me I give you two million pounds?' She looks at him, she says, 'Yeah'. He says to her 'You sleep with me I give you five pounds?' She says 'What the hell you take me for?' Man says, 'I think we already establish that—now we just haggle over price.'" A smile momentarily flickers across the man's face. "People long ago decide it ok to watch, to be watch—now we just haggling, yes? I can get. At a price."

"I have the money," Dev says.

Zmuda looks at the other man—the worn jeans, the ratty jumper and ill-fitting hooded jacket, the four-day stubble. "No offence but it not look like from here."

"I don't need clothes or food. I need her."

Dev reaches into his pocket and takes out a sheet of folded A4, unfolds it and pushes it across the table. "This is her home address. This is her sister's address where she sometimes stays. And this is her work address."

Zmuda looks it all over, lingering on the final one. "You shit me? This the home of Jack Gillies."

"She's a maid," Dev explains. "She's only worked there a few months."

"I not care what she is, you ask me to get footage from home of fucking *cabinet minister*?"

"Yes."

"Then costs just doubled. Fuck it, *tripled*."

"I don't care who she works for."

"Not make it any easier to get into feed. So—you want footage or not?"

And the answer is always the same.

~

The room is on the top floor of a bed and breakfast on the south side of Edinburgh with a view of Arthur's Seat that is slightly obscured by the surrounding buildings, but Dev has instead spent the entire evening so far staring at the little television mounted on a wall bracket next to a security camera.

The remote in his hand, his fingers roll across the buttons as he skips from channel to channel. He settles on BBC One, the news anchor just starting an interview with a visiting movie star. The first question is about makeup.

"Fucking hell."

He flips the channel onto Sky News and the text banner superimposed over the images reads *The National Protection Act—Security or Surveillance?* A Government minister is in the middle of a scripted, quietly condescending response to the host's question.

"...has been running for over a year and it is now clear that people's initial concerns about the Act have been shown to be completely unfounded."

The camera cuts to a woman in her early thirties, dark hair tied back from her face. "I'm sorry but that is just not true and the minister knows it. It's still far too early to judge the programme and every day at Amnesty we receive several hundred reports of invasion of privacy, the vast majority of which have yet to even be acknowledged by the Government."

"Most of which have been proven to be complete fabrications or the result of the hysteria created by organisations such as yours who seem to have a vested interest in painting any government as being a brutal dictatorship."

"Your words, not mine, minister," the woman responds. "And how do you respond to the stories we've heard about the system being hacked into by..."

"If I could just stop you there, Ms. Pieterson." The camera cuts to the program's host, in his fifties but with the silver-haired and roughly handsome look of someone from a shaving advert about him. "You have to admit, Ms. Pieterson, that the minister is right—the Government *is* doing more to address these concerns."

"The minister's government has set up a system of over 43 million surveillance cameras including 25 million in private residences—how can he possibly assure us that there are no abuses going on?"

The minister rebuts. "The National Protection Act itself has many, many protections built into it and you must know that as well as anyone otherwise you really have no place being here tonight, my dear. In addition to these measures we brought in the High Access Act several months ago which gave every citizen of this country, citizens that these Acts exist to protect might I remind you, the right to apply for any camera within their home to be deactivated should they wish it to be."

"And thereby invalidating their home insurance, their private medical insurance, and their life insurance?"

"The insurance companies have deemed it an essential part of proving or disproving any claim to be able to view footage of the claimant should it be necessary to do so, thus enabling them to bring down the cost of premiums for all their customers."

"But the cameras can be re-activated at any time *without* homeowner consent if the Government deems it in the interest of the State, correct?"

"Of course!" the minister says, exasperated.

"So you're comfortable with the fact that a camera in *your* home, in *your* bathroom, can be trained on your teenage daughter should the State deem it necessary?"

"Would you rather we turned a blind eye to another possible terrorist plot when we have the means with which to stop it? I don't understand why people like you seem more interested in protecting criminals and terrorists than you are innocent people!"

"But the cameras are in *everyone's* home, minister, not just criminals and terrorists."

"And I think the vast majority of people in the country will agree that we're better off for it…"

Dev hits the power button and the TV fades into darkness in time for him to hear the knock at the door being repeated. He goes to the door and opens it a few inches, keeping one foot wedged behind it. A teenage boy stands on the other side, holds up a bag of food with a receipt stapled to it.

"Twenty quid," the boy says.

Dev takes a thick wad of notes from his pocket and gives it to him then takes the bag inside. He removes plastic cartons of lemon chicken, spare ribs, rice, and beef in black bean sauce, and tips them out into the room's tiny sink one by one until a shrink-wrapped Blu-Ray disc drops out. He slides it into the portable player he's hooked up to the TV, switches the set back on, then sits down on the edge of the bed to watch.

The screen flickers for a few moments, then a woman lying in her bed appears. The shot is from high up enough to give a view of the entire room as she slips out from under the sheets, stretches, then walks into another room. The shot jumps to a bathroom which the woman walks into. She switches on the shower then sits on the toilet and urinates, talking quietly to herself, then gets up and steps into the shower. She puts on a dressing gown that Dev had bought for her a year ago. She dries herself off and gets dressed. Then another shot, this one from high up on a street, panning across to follow the woman as she walks into a Starbucks. Cuts to another shot of inside the shop. She buys a large skinny cappuccino.

Dev had told her that there was no point in buying a skinny if she was going to get a large but she had never listened.

The footage continues, a scrappy stream of varying quality that occasionally overlaps, as she walks to a large house in the exclusive Grange area of the city. Cuts to a shot which looks like it's coming from the house next door, then darkness for a while. Dev sits forward, tensing at the idea that that was the end of it, then more shots follow from outside the house peering into the windows as she walks backwards and forwards in front of them. Then tracking her walking home again, headphones looping from her ears as she cycles through songs on her mobile phone. Cooking a microwave meal. Opening a bottle of wine. Watching TV. Going to bed.

The screen goes black.

~

The next night Dev is three pints in by the time he finally walks across to Zmuda's table, ignoring the tear-stained woman sitting across from the man.

"I want to talk to you," Dev says.

"I busy," Zmuda says matter-of-factly.

"Sorry," Dev says to the woman this time. "We have business."

Nobody says anything, then the woman stands, hands shaking as she clutches a framed picture of a teenage boy. Dev ignores her, staring past her to Zmuda until she is gone, then sits in her place.

"Her son missing six months," Zmuda says. "She hope I..."

Dev flicks the Blu-Ray at the man. It bounces off his chest and onto the table, spinning around several times before settling.

"This isn't what I paid for," Dev says. "She spends eight hours a day at work and at best there are eight minutes there."

Zmuda's face twitches and Dev can tell he's fighting back the urge to grab him and slam his head into the table. "It not easy getting into HA feed."

"I said I wanted everything and I meant it. I'll go to another dealer if I have to."

"Okay, okay, I see what I can do, yes?" Zmuda says, shoving a fresh Pseudorette into his mouth.

Dev nods and gets up. "I'll wait to hear from you," he says, then walks out of the bar.

Cameras click and swivel to follow him.

~

Over the next few days meals are brought to him—pizzas, curries, Thai stir-fries—and with each meal another disc, this time with footage that follows her throughout the entire day. He watches each of them obsessively, scribbling notes on pieces of scrap paper—time codes and descriptions of what she is doing, of where and when.

She laughs and drinks wine with her sister as a small girl runs around in the background. She goes to a club—grainy footage of her dancing and rejecting the advances of a drunken male and Dev feels jealously flaring up within him. She staggers into a taxi. Undresses and falls into bed. Night vision footage of her sleeping, her body bathed in an eerie green light as she twists and turns, sweat beading across her back and shoulders. Goes for coffee. Talks with two little boys in the big house as she hoovers. Drags clothes from hampers and shoves them into a row of three washing machines. Removes the clothes and hangs them up. Empties out-of-date food from the cupboards and fridge. Cautiously fingers through jewellery boxes. Watches movies and more reality TV alone on the couch. Shops for a book. Surfs the internet.

He selects the latest disc and skips forwards to a shot of Lola at work, folding sheets in the master bedroom, mumbling to herself, and her employer just visible in the hallway talking on the phone. He hits PLAY, turns the volume up, and continues to watch.

~

Sitting in a bus shelter further up the street he watches Lola leaving her flat, wearing a short tartan skirt and knee-high boots. He keeps his head down as she walks past him then waits until she is a block or so away before following her along the footway that winds alongside Arthur's Seat and towards Studio 24, a grotty club off the bottom of the Royal Mile. Cameras whirr and move to follow them and the others on the dark streets, a thousand dark eyes.

He pays the club's entry fee, pushing past rivetheads and teenagers in ludicrous makeup and fetish clothing. Thundering, bass-heavy music vibrates through him, strobe lights making it seem as if everything around him were flashing into and out of existence. He watches her buying a bottle of beer then slipping past the crowds to a less congested area where she perches on one of several benches bolted to the graffiti-scarred wall. An underage girl asks for a light for her Pseudorette. A tall goth whispers something to her but Lola shakes her head, smiles gently as she walks back into the crowd.

Dev follows her, shoving his way through and drawing some dirty looks, walks straight up behind her and grabs her by the waist, pushes her towards the edge of the room and into the doorway of a store room. She spins around and looks ready to lash out but Dev leans in towards her, wraps a hand around her neck, and pulls her close enough to hear each other over the music.

"Where the fuck have you been?" she shouts into his ear.

"Watching you," Dev says. "Getting used to it, I guess."

"I always knew you were the type," she says.

He glances up at a camera mounted on the wall next to them then pulls her back in again, tilting his head to one side so that they wrap around one another like kissing lovers. "I think we all are."

She smiles to herself. "So…?"

"I got it," he tells her. "I'll need to get Adam to clean it up but it's what we need."

"You hear him saying he got us fired?"

"As close as. You did good. What about the others?"

"Already done. Jake got the smoking gun earlier today— archive footage of Gillies threatening Mark Thompson to revoke the Beeb's charter if they didn't fall in line and destroy everything from our investigation. That was *not* easy to get but we have it."

"So all we need to do is cut it and get it ready for upload then…"

"Then wait for it to go viral," Lola finishes for him.

He nods. "You know, it wasn't that long ago that this would have been the lead story on the 10 o'clock news, not just another clip stuffed in amongst other ones of piano-playing dogs and sports bloopers."

Lola smiles and pulls him close enough that he can smell the leftover perfume on her top from the last time she wore it. "Yeah, but what do you think is more likely—that the people in here will tune into the 10 o'clock news or log onto YouTube? We can still do what we've always done, Dev—BBC or no BBC. The difference is that now there's nothing they can do to stop it from spreading."

And she moves away from him, swigging at her beer then vanishing into the leather and piercings.

~

Dev slows as he approaches the door to his room, noticing the pizza box set down before it. He picks it up and enters the room, flipping open the lid and pushing aside the spicy chicken pizza to reveal the shrink-wrapped Blu-Ray beneath it. Despite the fact that they already have what they need, he puts it into the player and opens the single remaining can of lager from a six-pack he'd bought a few days earlier.

As before there are shots of Lola reading magazines in her flat and washing dishes but also painting her toenails and waxing her legs and he thinks about how she had always been reluctant to let him see her do such things when they had lived together. It cuts to her blow-drying her hair then stepping into a tartan skirt. Pulling on a pair of knee-high boots.

Dev sits forwards.

Putting on her coat and leaving the flat, walking down the street. A figure emerges from a bus shelter once she has walked past and can be seen in the background all the way to a nightclub. Then inside the club, the footage grainy and any sound distorted beyond recognition but the camera moves away from Lola to the man coming through the crowd behind her. Dev watches himself leaning into her against the wall. Cuts to her leaving the club, handing the unfinished beer to a punk girl with liberty spikes and platform boots, then walking further along the street. Cuts to another camera and a van is visible behind her. It slows alongside her, then stops. The door slides open and she is pulled inside. The van speeds off.

Cuts to a small bed and breakfast.

To a corridor.

To a door.

There is a knock at the door.

Dev's hands are locked around the can of lager. Before he can do anything the door swings open and Marek Zmuda steps inside, closes the door behind him.

"You get square eyes if you look at that thing too much," he says.

"What have you done to her?"

"I not done anything," Zmuda says. "But he has."

He nods over Dev's shoulder to the TV and a shot of the corridor outside. A man leans up towards the camera but it's not Zmuda. This time it's Gillies. He smiles, then draws his expensive woollen coat around himself and walks off.

"After a while you forget cameras there. You stop care because you think 'they not watching me—they watching everyone else'. Make my job hell of lot easier."

"How long has Gillies known?"

"He power-hungry asshole but he not stupid. You not fire bulk of the BBC investigative journalists and expect them to just go off and work for McDonalds, yes? Maybe few sell their souls to Sky or go to US networks but those that don't? Well, you got to keep close eye on them. You never know what they might do. Some might say they maybe even threat to the country."

"To the country or to the government?"

Before Zmuda can reply there is the sound of sirens and the room is suddenly bathed in the blue flicker of police lights as three cars pull up outside.

Dev's mind is in overdrive trying to find a way out of the room but he knows that Zmuda won't be alone. And even if he could manage to get away, he knows that he couldn't stay hidden for long. Everywhere he went there would be mechanical eyes trained upon him, following him. There was no such thing as hiding any more.

And perhaps somewhere a disc would be getting delivered to another grubby hotel room or executive suite to someone else who had paid their money and this time it would be Dev who was being watched as he slept rough on park benches and crept through the haunted closes of the Royal Mile like just one more ghost.

# Alien

## SoNNetWolF

SoNNetWolF has been writing since she was a young child. Coming up abused as she did, writing literally saved her. Through writing, she was transported to another world free from the cruelty that followed her on a daily basis. When either reading or writing her own stuff, she was safe in the wings of words that cupped her in a world that wanted only to crush that little girl. So, to this day she looks upon writing as a mortal lifeline. It must flow like some fish in the sea must swim, or die...she chooses to live in the embrace of poetry.

She can be found online at rainbowwalkers.tripod.com

You exist between fractal winds;
lines of linear degree that never
interweave my dimensional space

You bleed through Aurora light;
the dawn of pain I could not suffer
transparent tears of ice across your face

Arithmetic folds encompass thought;
finite conclusions incomprehensible
to our Newtonian philosophies

Creation's edges you've fingered
along the way; witnessed Orion's Belt
begin its debut as pearly stars' debris

You experience time as osmotic
moments in eternal loops; never
separate, linking like my day-to-day

Memories like programmed chips
resurface for learning value;
no lips for words to ever say

We are to you as blips of light
in Moon shadow tinted
across eons of infinite nuclei

Having never touched Earth,
you scrape along the Rings of Saturn
with sad familiarity when even you,
reluctantly, die

# The Snake That Barked

## David McGillveray

David McGillveray was born in Edinburgh but now works and lives in London. His short fiction has appeared in *Futurismic*, *Space and Time*, *Neo-Opsis*, and many other venues. His anthology of interplanetary sci-fi, *Celeraine*, was published as an e-book by Sam's Dot Publishing in 2008.

"These startling pictures are coming to you LIVE from the ESA Mars probe Vixen, currently in orbit around the red planet. Equipped with new technology, they left Earth orbit only nine days ago and in less than two hours you will see the first manned expedition to reach Mars, I'm sure, a triumphant conclusion. As the lander detaches from the mother ship…"

Switch.

"OK, unfortunately that's all we've got time for today on Problem Call, where we've been talking to the Nation's Youngest Grandmothers. Remember, if you've been affected by any of the issues discussed in today's programme or would like to bring to our attention any other issues affecting your community, contact me, Clive Noble, on the number appearing on your screens now. Calls cost 75 pence per minute and may be recorded…"

Velteen turned off the TV and reached for the rum bottle. A couple of centimetres of dark liquid sloshed in the bottom when she shook it. She drank its contents straight down without needing to swallow and then placed it back on the table by the armchair. Velteen frowned, tongue flickering over thin grey lips. She had built up an unwanted resistance to alcohol all too quickly.

"You could be homeless soon, my lovelies," she said to the contented forms of Alfie, Bets, and Gam. They were lying in front of the TV wondering where the nice pictures had gone. On Velteen's lap was a letter from the Department for Work and Pensions informing her of the cessation of her Jobseeker's Allowance and another one containing an outstanding invoice for the rent. There were other red bills hiding behind the chipped ornament on the mantelpiece. Was it her fault she couldn't even get an interview, never mind a job?

At the sound of her voice the dogs got up and looked at her. Alfie and Bets came to lick affectionately at her long fingers while Gam, the smallest, began to wind himself in a figure of eight round Velteen's legs. All three were former strays, mongrels of one sort or another—you were unlikely to find a dog with a pedigree on this estate—but their coats were clean and glossy now, their eyes bright.

"What to do, eh? Still, look on the bright side. You can find somewhere better to stay than this." It was lucky that the mongrels weren't fussy. There was more floor than carpet showing under their feet. The single chair that sat in front of the TV was lumpy with escaping springs and geriatric upholstery. The cheap plasma TV itself sat on the box it had come in, a long time ago. A decrepit kitchenette sulked in the corner. Brown and yellow stains covered the walls and the air smelled of damp. Somewhere, someone was shouting and the trembling bass of accelerated dub seeped up through the floor.

Velteen whistled a series of high notes to her friends and they scampered off towards the single bedroom, reappearing with her shoes and hat. She took the gifts, running a grateful finger along the top of each of the dog's skulls and down their spines, enjoying their little growls of pleasure.

"I'll try not to be too long," she said, pulling the woolly hat over her naked scalp and putting on the winter coat that hung behind the door. As she pulled the door closed behind her, she could still make out the graffiti beneath the scorch marks where the local kids had thrown petrol on the door: "There ain't no grey in the Union Jack" and "Snakehead shit fuck off".

~

The sky above South London seemed to reflect the drab concrete architecture of the estate. It was November, and Velteen shivered in her coat. She hurried along the covered walkway that skirted around each level of the tower block, past closed doors she hoped would not open. Razmus's flat was round the corner, the third one along. The lock on the door had been kicked in months ago and the glass in the small window broken so Razmus had nailed a sheet of plywood over it. The wood was covered in kids' tags and declarations of teenage love.

Velteen thumped on the door twice with the side of her fist and then pushed it open. A radio chattered from above the cistern in the toilet and the place smelled of dope smoke and burnt toast.

"Razmus? You home?" Velteen called. She hoped he was. She needed to talk to somebody and Razmus was about the only one round here that would give her the time of day.

There was no answer so she headed further into the squat. Razmus was in the front room sitting on the floor with his back against a wall, head lolling forward on to his chest. A girl Velteen had not seen before was asleep on the mattress that filled one corner of the room.

"Anybody in today?"

Razmus lifted his head and opened his eyes. His afro had wilted comically into two greasy shrubs parted down the middle. He smiled when he saw her, showing a missing front tooth, and spread his arms.

"Hey! It's my favourite alien lady. How are you, babes?"

"Okay, I suppose. Well, not okay, really. My benefits have been cut."

Razmus nodded as if he had foreseen it, a confirmation of a vision. "That's tough, man. You want a smoke? There's half a spliff in the ash tray."

"No thanks. You coming down today?" There was nowhere to sit so Velteen stood where she was.

"You know me far too well," Razmus said sheepishly. "Me and Lizzie have been having a few smokes to take the edge off, you know?" He shouted over at the girl on the mattress. "Hey Lizzie, wake up, Velteen's here."

Lizzie was pale and thin, with deep circles under her eyes and dirty black hair caught up in knots. She wore woolly tights with black and white horizontal stripes, a black skirt, and a man's business shirt. Pretty, possibly. Velteen wasn't sure. The girl stirred and opened her eyes, blinking until they focussed.

114

"Jesus Christ," she yelped and bolted upright, pushing herself back against the wall. "What the fuck's *that* doing in here?" Her moneyed Home Counties accent seemed ill equipped for her circumstances.

"This is my friend Velteen. Did I not tell you about her? She's dropped in to say hello," said Razmus, catching Velteen's eye. *It's cool.*

"You've got some weird friends," said the girl, crossing her arms beneath her breasts and staring.

"Yeah, well she's not the strangest. There's a hell of a lot weirder on this estate than Velteen. Velteen, Lizzie, Lizzie, Velteen."

"Hello," Velteen said.

"Anyway, it's good to see you, babes," continued Razmus. Then, for Lizzie's benefit, "We've been pals a couple of years now, yeah? Ever since they placed you here."

"That's right. Since the end of processing."

"We've shared some intimate moments together," Razmus said, poker faced.

"Jesus, Razmus, you haven't fucked her, have you?" demanded Lizzie, looking from Velteen to Razmus and back with a sudden expression of unbalanced jealousy. A little colour appeared on her cheeks. Razmus laughed uproariously, shaking his head and trying to speak at the same time.

"I was sterilised as part of the processing programme," Velteen said. "The Solablum only mate to reproduce, so even if I had any such perverted urges it couldn't happen. I've learned to live with the disappointment."

Razmus, almost recovered, burst into fresh laughter. "Perverted urges?" he gasped. "Oh, that's nice, that's nice. Seriously, they did some vicious shit to Velteen in those processing labs. Show Lizzie your scars, man."

"I'd rather not." Velteen shifted uncomfortably on her feet. That was a part of her life that she had tried to put behind her. Nearly two years after she had finally been allowed to enter the community she still spent far too much time thinking about those days.

Razmus had lit the stub of the joint he had offered her and was looking up at Velteen thoughtfully. "You're upset about this money thing, aren't you?"

Velteen sighed, a whistle of air between her teeth. "I get the feeling it's just the start. I've heard all sorts of stories about councils refusing any sort of help to us in Manchester and Birmingham and other places. If they cut my Housing Benefit next, I'll be out on the street and it's nearly winter already. You know I can't deal with the cold."

"Let's hope it doesn't come to that. Hey, you could always stay with me. As you know, my door is always open." He passed the joint to Lizzie, who took it and gazed at Velteen with a mixture of revulsion and sympathy that probably surprised herself.

"I hope so too. Listen, Razmus, I hate to ask. I know things are tough for you too, but you couldn't lend me a tenner, could you? I need to feed the dogs and I really could do without having to rummage in the bins for them again, you know?"

Razmus's expression hardened for a moment, and then he laughed, hair bouncing on his head like a jellyfish. Giddy from the weed. "You have to be the only straight person who ever tried to borrow money off a junkie. Tell you what, why don't you drop by some other time and we'll catch a bite together? Best I can do."

Velteen nodded. "Sure. I'm sorry. I just didn't know who else to ask. Thanks, Razmus, I appreciate it. I'll see you later. Bye, Lizzie."

"Bye."

Velteen headed back onto the walkway, feeling disappointed with herself. Sure, Razmus was a mess. His addictions made him unpredictable, at times even deceitful, but when he was straight he had always showed her what kindness he could. She felt bad about having to ask him for money, but it was a sign of how desperate she had become. She wouldn't survive a winter on the streets, and if it came to that, it probably wouldn't be the cold that finished her. She was going to have to talk to Siskres.

~

The estate had been built over fifty years ago in the 70s, had been lambasted and condemned, but remained standing because it was just too damn difficult and expensive to tear it down. It had grown into one of the ghettos for the poor, the criminal, and the plain unlucky that persisted among the regeneration areas and new developments that dotted London. It was also one of the dumping grounds for the latest generation of immigrants.

Velteen made her way across the concrete countryside, huddled against a light English drizzle. Four identical blocks of flats faced on to a central square that contained rows of boarded-up shops and desolate playgrounds where broken swings and merry-go-rounds rusted in the rain. She passed a sealed post box, robbed one too many times, and rubbish piled against walls. The architects had originally designed a series of shallow ponds crossed with concrete walkways that were meant to add colour and life, but the money had never been found to stock them with fish. Now they were dark and polluted, populated with abandoned shopping trolleys, plastic bottles, and used condoms. Two young kids threw pieces of broken concrete into the water and tried to sink an old car tire.

A figure approached her as she crossed a bridge over one of the ponds. It was someone she had seen periodically round the estate and had taken pains to avoid. She put her head down and stared at the ground, trying to disappear inside her coat.

"Look, Vader, we've found ourselves a snake," said the man, stepping into her path. Velteen looked up fearfully from under her hat. She called him the Cartoon Nazi, and it was a wonder that the really dangerous elements on the estate had not yet seen him off. His type tended not to last long. He was escorted by a large bulldog on a chain. Velteen speculated that some form of genetic tinkering must have taken place, such was the resemblance of the man to his dog. He wore Doc Martens and jeans and a green T-shirt despite the cold, revealing amateurish tattoos on his forearms. He had a shaved head and a beer belly and was perhaps two feet taller than Velteen.

"It seems everywhere I go these days I find shit like you under my feet, crawling round the place. Makes me sick. Out of all the places you could go, you had to come here, didn't you? Scaring the kids and the old ladies. Why don't you fuck off back where you came from?" He encouraged the dog forward with a yank on its chain but the creature didn't move. "Ain't that right, Vader?"

"I would if I could," whispered Velteen. She tried to step around the man but he moved in front of her again.

"It's all them fuckin' wogs and bed wetters on the council that I blame," continued the Cartoon Nazi. "We should have nuked the lot of you when we had the chance. God knows what you're really up to. Plannin' an invasion, laying fucking eggs all over the shop. There's got to be something done."

Summoning her courage, Velteen said, "Look, let me past. I haven't bothered you. I don't want to have to use my mental powers on you."

"What?" There was confusion in the man's eyes.

"I could make your head explode by just thinking it. All the Solablum can do it." Velteen leaned forward conspiratorially. "The government just don't know about it yet."

The Cartoon Nazi took a step backwards. "You stay out of my head, freak!" he shouted. "Get it, Vader. Kill!" He let go of the bulldog's leash and urged it towards Velteen with a slap on the rump. "Kill!"

Vader trotted forward and began to lick at Velteen's outstretched hand, making soft contented noises in the back of his throat. Velteen squatted before the dog and whistled silently in its ear, gently scratching its wrinkled head.

"You leave my fucking dog alone!" yelled the Cartoon Nazi. "What have you done to him? Vader!"

Vader turned and snarled at his owner, lifting a black lip and showing his teeth. The dog made sure the man was pressed up against the metal railings on the side of the bridge until Velteen had walked away. When she looked back from the other side, Vader was pissing on the Nazi's boots.

~

Music filtered up the steps from the basement of the high rise opposite where Velteen lived, the angry sounds of the French hip-hop that Siskres favoured. The huge space under the tower had served as a community centre until the Solablum were given permission to use it, but even they had drifted away when Siskres and his mob had moved in. He had set himself up as some sort of community leader, but in reality he was a thug and, it was rumoured, a significant distributor of heroin derivatives around the estate and beyond.

Two Solablum, both males, played pool in the centre of the room. Siskres sat on a table, legs dangling, and nodded his head to the music. He wore expensive trainers and a shiny black tracksuit with two yellow stripes down the arms and legs. A pair of shades were pushed up on his head, partially obscuring the splashes of yellow-green colour that decorated his scalp. Big almond-shaped eyes the colour of rust followed Velteen as she entered, sharp teeth showing when he opened his mouth.

"Velteen, you light up my day," he said in their own language, a complicated series of yelps and hisses and whistles across a broad range of frequencies. Siskres motioned for one of the others to turn down the stereo.

"Happiness to you," she replied, loitering by the door.

"Come in, come closer. You'll look more beautiful out of the shadows." Siskres lit a cigarette and blew two tight jets of smoke at her through his nose holes. "We're very privileged. You've been so…aloof lately. You must want something."

Velteen looked around the room to avoid meeting his gaze. An Alsatian and a Rottweiler slept by a radiator. The ceiling was a web of piping. Plastic chairs and tables were stacked against the walls and a low stage filled one end of the room. Sad and wrinkled bunting waved forlornly in the air conditioning.

"I didn't know who else to talk to. There's no money. They're stopping my money. The flat's cold. I'm hungry, more hungry the colder it gets. They're squeezing us out; I know it. It's murder by bureaucracy. What happens next to us?" The words tumbled from her, autonomous things she had not shared with anyone else. She looked at Siskres bobbing his head in a mixture of amusement and mock sympathy and knew this was not the right place for them, but still she felt unburdened. At least temporarily.

"Only hard choices left for snakeheads," Siskres said.

"Please don't use that word, Siskres," she replied sharply.

He smiled. "We're reclaiming it for our people, taking the power out of it for ourselves. You should spend more time with your people. You are not alone, Velteen, although you act like it. Hard times for all of us." He smiled again. "You could always join the protesters." He reached into a pocket and pulled out a crumpled piece of paper. He threw it at her.

It was a flier giving the date and time of a protest some of the Solablum were organising in Westminster. "Fair treatment for your friends. Fair treatment for the Solablum. We all can have a voice!" Velteen could almost hear the desperation coming off the page.

"No one will come," said Siskres. "We're too scattered, all across the country, all across the planet. They were clever when they split us up. There is a saying that they have, 'divide and conquer'. Ugly, isn't it? But you know as well as I that most of us were already conquered when we came out of the processing labs. Many yet will drown in their own weakness." He shrugged, a human gesture he had absorbed as if to say, *It's not my problem.*

"What about the High Caste? Can't they do something for us?" Now Velteen listened to her own desperation.

Siskres laughed, a sibilant sound. The two pool players stopped to laugh with him. "You're still clinging to that? They are all either flayed open on clandestine operating tables in the Nevada desert or helping the humans build spaceships. The Low Caste are on their own. Why do you think so many of us are in the state we are now? Never used to thinking for themselves, always waiting for a fucking Highborn to point a finger. I don't feel sorry for any of them at all. I had hoped for better from you, though, Velteen. I thought you had a bit of fight in you.

"This is an opportunity for us. You just have to stop looking at the universe through the eyes of your Caste. We don't have to take orders anymore; we can do what we want. All it takes is the will to adapt. Did you know that I've got humans working for me now? For *me*." Siskres stubbed out his cigarette and blew out the last of the smoke appreciatively. He looked closely at Velteen. "Hard choices for the Solablum," he said again, smiled. "And brave ones too, for those with the guts."

"I know how you've adapted," Velteen accused. "I've seen what your choices do to other people."

"Why do you care? They don't care about you. They're all the same, all of them. But I can play in the game, that's the difference. I know the rules. Why don't you let me teach you? Maybe I could get those scars of yours fixed up. Who knows, you might even be very grateful."

"I'm not working for *you*," Velteen hissed. "There are better ways to live than that. Look at you, sitting there playing the gangster. You're a fool if you think there's any dignity in that, and I was a fool to come and see you." She made to go.

"It'll be a cold winter," Siskres called from behind her. She turned. Siskres was holding a twenty-pound note in his hand. After a moment, she ran forward and snatched it from him and left without a word.

The stereo was turned up again and the beats followed her out of the building.

She went back to her flat and sat for a while, scratching at her dogs' coats and letting the helplessness eat at her, contemplating this latest in a long list of little humiliations. Then she picked up the phone and dialled, wincing at the cost.

~

"Who can forget history when it is made in our own lifetimes?" said Clive Noble.

The studio monitors showed the vast strutted spear of the Solablum ship limp into high Earth orbit, radiation shield crippled by a meteor strike beyond the Oort Cloud. The tiny slivers of reflected sunlight that buzzed around its forward sections resolved themselves into human shuttles, come to meet the visitors. The scene shifted to pictures of world leaders meeting the first Solablum delegation for carefully staged photo opportunities.

"The moments there when the people of Earth reached out a hand of friendship across the light years to a people in need of our help. But there's a problem. According to some, our planet hasn't lived up to the expectations of our guests. These people, who without us would have been stranded homeless in the galaxy, now find cause for complaint about their standards of living! Ingratitude or discrimination? Misplaced expectations or culture shock? That's the topic for today on Problem Call."

Velteen remembered little of what she saw as she watched the montage on the screen. The Low Caste had only ever been frozen cargo on the ship, packed in containers. She still felt as if she had stepped into a dream, and everything around her was unreal. The studio lights were blinding. She was joined on the studio panel by a (very) junior government minister, a social worker, and Kandinz, a jittery female from the Solablum community in Birmingham who wore a smart skirt and spoke English with a thick Midlands accent. Clive Noble, an unsurprisingly self-important, handsome-by-numbers man in his early fifties had on so much makeup that it made him look like a grotesque caricature of his TV self.

Velteen had already decided this was a mistake. The audience sat like vultures. The presenter himself had a predatory gleam in his eye, in anticipation of a controversial—but not too controversial—ratings-winning coup. Not for the first time, she felt the tide of hopelessness washing inexorably towards her.

"The issue is not one of ingratitude," Kandinz was saying. Velteen could see she was already highly agitated. Few of the Solablum females had emerged from the processing camps completely unscathed. Some had not emerged at all. "All of us are grateful for Earth's intervention and help. The issue is the on-going lives of those who have settled here. We are seeing systematic, often institutionalised prejudice in our com-munities. There have been several cases of police inaction when our people have been attacked, cases of withholding benefits, many cases of job exclusion—"

"With respect, your situation is not an isolated one," said the government minister. "We are all working hard to ensure that the newer ethnic communities in this country enjoy all the benefits of a free society. You cannot point the finger on the basis of a few isolated incidents."

"They're not isolated!" said Kandinz, raising her voice. "They're endemic. Our people are still detained, we live in divided communities—"

"Many people think the Solablum should work to escape poverty," Noble interjected, "yet all we see are pictures of Solablum waiting outside benefits offices and complaining about their lot. Many find it difficult to sympathise, especially after the resources we have spent resettling you. You should be grateful for our charity." There was a round of applause from the audience.

"Charity! It's nothing like charity. Do you think you've not been paid? Look at the news! Look at Mars!" Kandinz shouted. Velteen placed a restraining hand on her arm and she seemed to crumple in her chair, as if all the air had been let out of a balloon.

"All Kandinz is saying is that if we are truly accepted as citizens of this country, then we should expect the same rights as everyone else," said Velteen. "No more than that. We are desperate to work, but there are no jobs for us."

"Thank you, Miss Velteen," smiled Noble patronisingly. "I think it's time to open things out and invite questions and comments from the studio audience."

"I think they should be kept away from public places. They scare my kids."

"I've always said they were spies for an invasion fleet."

"Is it true that you're immortal and live on human flesh?"

"I think they should stop whingeing and get on with it." A big cheer for that.

"One of them sold my son drugs!"

Noble stepped forward. "Now that's a serious point, isn't it?" He looked concerned for the cameras. "There have been increasing reports of the Solablum becoming involved in criminal activity. Doesn't that concern you, Miss Kandinz?"

Velteen sat forward. "There are bad elements in any community, Mr. Noble, but no more with the Solablum than any other. Much crime is born out of desperation—"

"I'll tell you about criminal activity!" screamed Kandinz. Suddenly, she sprung out of her chair and pulled up the front of her skirt. "This is criminal!" Before the social worker could move to stop her, Kandinz exposed her mutilated genitals to the nearest camera, demonstrating what butchery had taken place to ensure the Solablum could not breed.

The audience was in an uproar. People shouting. But Noble would not let them shut off the cameras just yet. Before Problem Call was replaced by some light music, Velteen managed to look closely into one of the broadcasting cameras and whistle soundlessly to Clive Noble's audience at home.

~

They walked across Westminster Bridge from Waterloo Station. Lizzie, who had decided that Velteen was her personal project, had persuaded Razmus that they should come. They had both stayed clean for a week in solidarity, so they said. The water of the Thames was grey-brown beneath the winter sky and Velteen was cold under her coat. Her dogs, Alfie, Bets, and Gam, scampered about her feet, their breath fogging in the air.

To the right lay the big wheel that was the London Eye, over twenty years old and in need of a paint job but still turning. The skyline opposite was punctured by the latest generation of prestige offices, ever more indulgent in their construction. But across the water and to the left lay the Houses of Parliament, scrubbed clean by a recent makeover. They had a feeling of permanence about them that even Velteen could feel: intricate spires topped with flags, a hundred tall windows, and Big Ben's four faces, covered in gold, watching benevolently over the city.

Rush hour had passed, but the pavement was still thick with people. Cars, backed up bumper to bumper, tooted their horns impatiently. The three of them threaded their way through the crowd and discovered what was causing the obstruction. A line of mounted police had closed off one of the lanes heading north. Spilling from the pavement on to the road was a crowd of around a hundred Solablum, together with a smattering of taller human supporters, waving placards in the general direction of the government buildings across the river.

TOLERANCE AND FRIENDSHIP
FREEDOM AND JOBS

The police separated the Solablum from a small band of vocal counter-protestors who had somehow managed to find out about the demonstration.

"There are a lot more here than I had expected," said Velteen. Lizzie gave her an encouraging smile.

"They must watch afternoon television," commented Razmus. "That show caused a shitload of trouble." It was true. Velteen had more or less had to hide in Razmus's flat since her appearance on Problem Call. Questions had been asked in Parliament about the scandal. Concerned politicians had appeared everywhere, as long as it was in front of a camera. The government had naturally insisted that nothing had been hidden from the press and public, and this was essentially true. It had just been buried under spin, bureaucracy, and indifference.

Several of the Solablum shouted to Velteen when they saw her, greetings in two languages. She bobbed her head nervously back at them. Someone thrust a placard into her hand.

"So what now?" Razmus asked, stamping his feet to get the circulation going. His eyes were bloodshot and he hadn't slept in days, although his hair had staged a recovery. "I'm dying for a smoke." Lizzie hit him hard on the bicep.

"We protest, we wait," said Velteen firmly. She was nervous. She wasn't sure if it would work, if any of them would come at all. Maybe the message was too complicated, or was not transmitted at all. Still, she had tried. It was all that she could ever hope to do, and she would keep trying for as long as she lasted. When there was nowhere to go, all there was left was to turn round and shout right back until someone listened. It was better than trying to drown in rum. It was better than taking handouts from the likes of Siskres.

There was a shout from one of the policemen. He was pointing over the heads of the crowd and across the Thames. From Whitehall and down the Embankment, through Westminster and along Victoria Street, came the sound of dogs barking. All the dogs who sat and watched TV with their masters and mistresses in front rooms across London came running towards the Houses of Parliament. They came in their thousands: gundogs and terriers and hounds, red setters and golden retrievers, spaniels, poodles, and Dalmatians—all the breeds in the city. And all of them went peacefully through the legs of the other pedestrians. A magnificent Afghan hound found its way onto the statue of one of Queen Boadicea's horses, paws on the metal shoulders, and looked down on the proceedings like a two-headed sphinx. Others overran the bridge and stopped the traffic completely. Still more began to appear on the fenced-off lawns around Parliament, forced there by an incessant canine osmosis.

Velteen laughed and began to cheer along with the rest of the watching crowd. Razmus hoisted her up on to his shoulders. As if in answer, the dogs put back their heads and howled up at the ancient buildings of government, drowning out all the human sounds of London, until there was nothing else to be heard.

# Paradox

## Lane Diamond

Lane Diamond is the pen name for a writer living in Hartford, Wisconsin. His writings cross over many genres and focus on diverse subjects, ranging from the mysteries of the human mind, with its fragile psychological and emotional states, to the everyday joy and anguish of life on Earth.

Lane Diamond has done his tours in both the U.S. Air Force and the business world, where he's been everything from a forklift operator to the lead singer of a rock 'n' roll band. These days, when not writing, he's a professional editor who works with several published and aspiring authors.

Watch for Lane Diamond's debut novel, *Forgive Me, Alex*, a psychological thriller, sometime in early 2011, and its sequel, *The Devil's Bane*, in 2012.

I see only shadows. Everywhere shadows! I yearn only to see substance, some screaming indication that more exists than just an infinite veil of black, pierced here and there by millions of pinholes of light. Oh, how I long for a smiling face, a pleasant voice or, at the very least, terra firma on a sunny day. I think I'm entitled. After more than thirty years of streaking through space in a temporary coffin, I deserve at least that much. Yet my eyes, fixed upon the windows as they probe for some faint glimmer of hope, some unanticipated harbinger of recognition in an endless exploration of nothing, do not lie. There is simply nothing out there.

The chronometer on the main computer shows the date as September 16, 2084.

"Dear God in Heaven, what has happened?"

It's the right month, even the right day of the month, but I'm thirty years off target. I was due at Mars Station on September 16, 2054. All data was double-checked, then checked again and then, just for good measure, checked yet again. I can't imagine how such a terrible mistake, one with such drastic consequences, slipped past all those technicians and all the safeguards.

Then again, it seems to make little difference at this point. Even in this age of wondrous new technology, simple human error anchors human progress. I wonder if we will ever outgrow that.

"Don't worry about a thing," Rocky said before the launch. "The computer will control everything."

He was the lead systems analyst on the mission. The idea of stasis—suspended animation—bothered me, but he said the system was foolproof.

"Hey man!" He played the sixty-year-old adolescent to perfection. "It doesn't take a rocket scientist to figure this stuff out, dude."

Yet this dude now drifts in space toward the outer edge of the solar system, with no real notion of how I might get back. I am utterly helpless—lost in space.

*Danger! Danger! Warning, Will Robinson!* I actually muster a hearty laugh despite the ominous circumstances—or perhaps because of them.

I still remember that stupid robot from the *Lost in Space* reruns. Cutting-edge when filmed, a century later the show was only ridiculous. Funny that we've progressed so far since then, yet here I drift helplessly into the endless chasm.

When I'm able to set aside the terror and the realization of what a horrible predicament I face, I have so many questions. Why didn't Space Command abort the trip and stop the ship remotely? Couldn't they see that something was wrong? They must have, as telemetry for remote control was one of their precious safeguards. Did that fail, too? We have ourselves a regular comedy of errors, it seems, though I find it not even remotely funny. It could be worse, I suppose; I could be dead.

"Think about it, Ted." I might as well talk to myself since there's nothing else to do. "What do you think is going to happen now?"

Yes, death seems rather inevitable at this point, and in the not-too-distant future. There are simply inadequate resources such as oxygen, water, and food—the little things—to get me back to Earth or even to Mars. Perhaps I should just open the hatch and step outside. At least that would be quick and easy. That doesn't sound so bad given the situation.

~

I've been out of stasis for four weeks. I sleep, mostly, to conserve resources and to stave off this maddening mix of boredom, frustration, anger, and fear. Unable to contact Space Command or Mars Station, I still have no explanations for what happened. Even from this distance, they should have received my signal and replied by now. Perhaps it is just another in a long line of failures. Yet as futile as it appears, I keep trying. The nothingness, the complete absence of both sight and sound, threatens to swallow me whole. Reminiscent of my dives off the Florida Keys, one critical element is absent: the surface. There is no escape. There is no freedom lying in wait above me. There is nothing.

"Ladies and gentlemen, this is your captain speaking. We are currently travelling at a speed of twelve thousand three hundred miles per hour and an altitude of over three billion miles. For your listening and viewing pleasure, we now offer…absolutely nothing! Please enjoy the remainder of flight 101 to oblivion." I cling to humour as the sole lifeline to my sanity.

The computer informs me, through a continually updated three-dimensional visual display on one of the monitors, that I now approach the orbital path of Pluto. That frozen sphere, the solar system's runt of the litter that the world once considered a planet, currently resides on the far side of the sun.

"That's a shame. I hear Pluto is just *lovely* this time of year."

The computer also informs me that I will exhaust the oxygen supply in twelve weeks. The ship contains enough water for that time but food for only nine weeks, and then only if I stretch it out and suck up the old gut. I get to starve for the last three weeks of my life.

*Wonderful! Is there any more good news?*

"You're finally going to get rid of those love-handles, Ted."

The computer spews all manner of output, a regular font of information. There's just one problem: it won't accept any of my input. My authorization codes have expired—another one of their safeguards.

"A safeguard against what, damn it? Of course they've expired. I've been drifting in space for over thirty years! Rocky, if I ever get my hands on that hairy ass you call a face, I'm gonna…oh, what's the use?"

~

It's week number seven. I count down the weeks like some morbid spectator at an execution—my execution! Sixteen is the magic number, for in that week I will use the last remaining oxygen—I will go bye-bye. My radio signals, my screams for help, remain unanswered. The computer indicates that the radio is working fine, yet still I hear nothing.

It's as if no one is home at the other end, which leads to even more questions. Is it possible? Is that why I drifted into deep space without their intervention? What might have happened? Did someone finally release the nukes? Did some insane scientist finally create the incurable airborne disease? Did the four deadly horsemen of the apocalypse decide to take a ride?

"That's just great, Ted, a nice pleasant thought to cheer you up."

~

As week number eleven arrives, I fade in and out of fuzzy dreams that leave me disoriented, but I suppose that's not terribly relevant given that I continue to drift through space in perpetuity. I wonder if some species far off in the galaxy, perhaps in a billion years or so, will find the vacuum-preserved shell of my former self. I also wonder whose idea it was to make this a solo mission.

"I'd like to wring that idiot's neck!"

Although a second person would use resources and cut my time in half, I can hardly imagine what possible difference that would make. At least we could converse, play some cards, whatever. Better yet, the second person could be a woman and we could end our days by...well, that wouldn't be such a bad way to go.

"Honey, I think we should make love until we die."

"Certainly, dear, that's a lovely idea."

"We've got plenty of time, though, so no need to hurry. Would foreplay for, say, six days be adequate?"

"Ooh, that sounds positively yummy!"

As it is, I must talk to myself to create the illusion of conversation, and I'm getting rather good at it. It's actually quite startling to discover that what I miss most is conversation, simple communication with another human being. I've always been such a loner, one who revels in my solitude and wears my loneliness as if it were some damned badge of honour. That certainly made it easier to volunteer for this mission—no ties. Ironically, the company and typically inane conversation of others is what I now miss most. Well, the touch of a beautiful woman, her lovely scent, and her delicious mouth at least run a close second. I have a rather significant list of things missed greatly, including some smoking-hot Thai food.

"Oh man, don't even think about food. I'm freakin' starving here!"

~

Week number thirteen is appropriately unlucky, though no more so than all the rest. I have no good news to report. I continue to sleep as much as I possibly can, the only method by which I escape the devastating loneliness, the only method by which I avoid myself. I focus on the morbid now, the imminent end of my personal journey. I've already exhausted all of my reminiscences, the journey through my life that was. My life that will be is all that remains, such as it is.

Time weighs upon me like some great, cosmic hand; it clutches me and squeezes me into nothingness. That weight lifts only in sleep, where I launch myself into the endless adventures and myriad worlds of the dreaming mind. It seems rather harmless enough, surely a better way to pass the time than the gruesome reality.

"What's the point of staying awake, Ted? It's not as though there's anything you can do."

The computer will alert me if a signal finally arrives, though it seems painfully clear *that* won't happen. Thus, I sleep. The only danger I perceive in this strategy is the vanishing line between reality and dreams, a line that grows fuzzier with each passing day.

"So what if my mind is fuzzy? How dangerous can that be now? You'll be dead soon, anyway, so who gives a rip about a little mental fog?"

~

With fourteen weeks down and two to go, the clock now ticks rapidly and—I swear that it's true—gathers momentum. I exhausted the food several days ago and I now live only on water. It's difficult to remember why I'm here, what led me to these circumstances.

The lights came on today, though I've no idea why. I must assume the computer did it for some reason. The bright lights are as spears in my eyes after many weeks in the shadow of perpetual night. I can't turn off the blinding distraction; the computer still won't accept my input.

*Whose idea was it to give the computer that velvety, seductive woman's voice? I've never even considered hitting a woman, but this one could use a serious knock upside the head. The head? Is that right, or is it the drive, or monitor, or data panel?*

"Whatever. I just want to smack the temperamental witch!"

Sleep avoids me mercilessly. I must laugh at the irony, as until recently sleep completely dominated my time and effort. Hungry for the comfort that dreams provide, my starving mind now demands sleep, yet desperate fury prevents it. Oh, the fury—over the comically tragic circumstances, over my impending death, over how I might cheat fate or destiny or whatever the hell you want to call it.

So many meaningless thoughts attack me relentlessly, eyes opened or closed, as though I'm in some reckless hypnotic state. These are not dreams, not exactly. This is just more mental fuzziness wrapped in a blanket of anxiety, smothered under a haze of desperate fear, invisible to all but God in this infinite abyss. If there is a God.

~

Week sixteen is upon me—show time! A mere few ounces of water remain to tease me from a nearby cup, like the impetuous child who says, "Na-na-na-na-na-na." No matter, since the oxygen supply is close to zero. The end draws near and, just in case I didn't already know that, the computer has started a countdown. I might enjoy that velvety voice under different circumstances, if it didn't remind me every few seconds of my impending doom. I've tried to get my head on straight and review once more the memories of my life—my way of saying bon voyage—but my mind just won't cooperate.

"I'm thinking that I thought about thoughts that I thought I didn't want to think about the last time I thought about thinking about all of those thoughts. I think!"

"I think, therefore I am...out of my freakin' mind!"

Perhaps I should have been a philosopher. They don't find themselves drifting aimlessly through space—well, not physically, at least. If only I could sleep. I might if it weren't so damned bright in here. The lights are absolutely blinding.

*Who turned on the lights? Did I already ask that?*

Sleep seems like something from a dream to me. More irony—just what I need. My emotional desperation for sleep is extraordinary, exceeded only by my physical need for it.

*Who raised the bubble on the cocoon, the stasis chamber? Did I do that?*

I can't recall.

*Why would it come up now? How long have I been awake?*

I can't recall.

*Am I asleep? Am I dreaming?*

I can't recall.

"Who the devil turned on the damned lights?"

*Did I already ask that?*

I can't recall. If only I were outside in the endless night, perhaps I could sleep. I could wrap myself in a warm blanket of starlight. I would only last an instant, but it hardly matters; I'll die shortly, anyway.

A huge ball hangs outside the window like a giant red moon. I have no idea where it came from.

*Is that what it is, a moon? Is it a planet? It can't be. I must be seeing things. Let's see, I've had no food for three weeks and no sleep for several days. Is it any wonder that I hallucinate? I think not. Whose voices do I hear? Are they outside as well, calling to me from space?*

"Don't be ridiculous, Ted. Here's a crazy idea: let's try to die with a little dignity. What do you say, buddy-boy?"

The voices are mere hallucinations, of course.

*Why do they want me to go to the Doc? Am I sick? I think I must be. Who turned on the lights? Did I already ask that?*

I can't recall. All I can recall is recalling there's something I can't recall, at least as far as I can recall. I'm not sure that's right.

"Geez, Ted, try to keep it together for just a while longer."

What a way to go: asphyxia, like drifting into a slow dream. That actually sounds all right, except for the slow part. Maybe outside would be better. Outside I can sleep under the stars in the perpetual night, out of this blazing light. When I awake, perhaps I can talk to the people calling from the dock.

*Do they wait for me to dock? Do they want me to see the Doc? Where do the voices come from? It makes no sense. They're hallucinations, right? Am I still dreaming? It must be the asphyxia taking hold. What else can it be?*

*Outside: that's the key. I must get outside so I can sleep. Maybe I'll stop hearing those wretched voices that yell at me. It's not as though going to the Doc will help me at this point. It's too late. There is no more help.*

The computer with the sultry voice still counts down.

"FIFTY SECONDS TO DOCK...FORTY-FIVE SECONDS TO DOCK...FORTY SECONDS TO DOCK."

*I simply must get out of here. If I must die, I want to do it outside in the infinite, deep vacuum of space.*

"Let's see, to open the door, just press this button and..."

*Why do the voices scream at me?*

"THIRTY SECONDS TO DOCK."

"...then pull this latch and..."

# foreign Gods Among Us

**Timothy Masters**

Timothy Masters, AKA Sandy Samson, lives in the mountains of northeast Pennsylvania. Five dogs and a delightful wife brighten his life. Marauding deer, woodchucks, and the occasional bear keep him from falling into the trap of excess happiness. When he's not writing computer programs to pay the bills, he writes fantasy, science fiction, and paranormal romance. Please visit him at www.SandySamson.com

Awareness crept into Jackson's mind, and he shivered. Years of sluggish secretions glued his eyes shut, so he focused on breathing. A pungent tang laced the air, additives to make tears flow and kick-start any other body parts that needed persuasion. As soon as his fingers and toes worked, he tried his eyes again. Sticky lashes parted, and the pale blue light of the stasis bay flooded his vision.

Before opening the pod to escape its confines, he checked the computer readouts projected overhead. Ship integrity, perfect. Health of his three crewmates, perfect. Status of the frozen embryos, perfect. Suitability of the planet for human habitation, excellent. Probability of advanced civilization, negligible. Time in flight, six-point-nine years. Average real velocity, forty-six times lightspeed. *Not the frontier, but pretty damn far.* He took one last, deep breath of the drug-laced air, released the pod lid, and sat up.

He crawled out and tugged at his flimsy one-piece stasis gown, pulling it free from the places where seven years of contact had plastered it to his skin. The other three pods were still closed. He shuffled to the nearest, lifting his weakened legs just enough on each step to break his slipper magnets free from the deck. Talia looked up at him through the transparent lid and winked. He forced a smile, wondering how she could be cheerful this soon after awakening. His head still hurt, and his mouth felt like a colony of spiders had built a nest inside.

The pod beyond hers opened and Karik sat up. The heavy black stubble that covered his swarthy face, coupled with neck muscles so tense that they stood out like taut cords, made him into a grim creature emerging from hibernation, hungry and cranky. Knowing all too well that this wasn't far from the truth,

Jackson gave the man a polite nod before turning his attention to the last pod.

Its lid rose. Elana raised her head enough to look around, and without pausing flung her legs over the side. At the same time, she pushed away from the pod and glided through the air, spinning in a weightless pirouette. Karik grabbed her arm as she passed overhead, and pulled her down until her slipper magnets clicked on the deck.

"Careful," he grumbled.

"Well, aren't we the grouch?" She pecked him on the cheek and turned to Jackson. "Okay, boss, what's the story?" She ran her fingers through the mass of tight black curls that adorned her head and waited for an answer.

Talia slipped up behind him and threaded her arm around his waist. "I could go for a juice."

"Sounds good." Jackson pulled free and crossed the deck to the food unit, where he requested four pouches. He tossed three of them to the rest of the crew, and pierced the seal on his own. "Shipboard scanners say no sign of advanced civilization, but I want to do sixteen revolutions of low-level spiral sweeps anyway. I don't want any surprises."

"Come on!" Elana skated her massive form across the deck with mind-boggling grace, stopping beside Jackson. "Surprises are what make life worth living. If you wanted a boring and predictable existence, you signed the wrong contract."

Despite the pounding in his temples, he couldn't help but smile at this rare soul. Six foot ten, and with hormone-enhanced muscles so huge they distended her stasis gown, she cast an imposing figure, borderline frightening. Yet she had never lost the playful exuberance of youth. Looking up now at her twinkling eyes, set far apart in a round face so black that it shined, he wondered how much Karik appreciated this magnificent woman. That man-of-few-words couldn't have been the only one who asked her to be his expeditionary life-mate.

Talia slurped the last dregs of her juice pack and squeezed Jackson's shoulder. "I'm going to change. Join me?"

"I'll be right there. I want to take a quick look at the scan logs, and set the computer to start descent."

"Oh, my silly, impatient little boy. Don't you want to get out of that smelly gown and put some real clothes on? The planet's waited seven years for us to arrive; it can wait a few minutes more. If the computer had picked up anything important in the scan, it would have told us by now."

"You know me." He got up and passed through the safety hatch to the control room, where he sat in front of the primary console. Orbital records scrolled down the screen, and he appraised each as it passed. They'd circled at high altitude 147 times since arrival, and when the computer had decided the planet was suitable, it had taken fifty hours to ease them out of stasis. Sensors had found no unnatural electromagnetic radiation that would indicate communication, no clusters of light or heat from cities, and no large objects moving with appreciable speed. He issued the order to descend to the upper atmosphere and commence a high-resolution spiral scan of the surface.

He stood and got as far as the hatch before he changed his mind and sat back down. Scrolling until he found the yellow text that he'd shrugged off before, he pondered its significance. Nothing else in the report even remotely indicated civilization, yet the tight-beam resonance scan had picked up a concentrated mass of titanium and ferrous alloys. The computer gave it a ninety-seven percent probability of being natural, the remnants of a primaeval volcanic eruption that had burped up a blob of molten metal from the depths of the planet. He wondered, though, if the computer had ignored one fact when it estimated that probability. The ratio of ferrous to non-ferrous metal was about what it would be in a spaceship. An Earth-model space-ship, anyway. *Did an early explorer stumble on the planet? Doubtful, this far out. Plus, it's not in the records database. An alien explorer? Damn, I won't go there. Nobody's found any aliens yet, dead or alive.*

He adjusted the programmed descent to pass over that spot first. Hoping Elana wouldn't get her wish for a surprise, he stood and strode to the hatch, in a hurry to talk to Talia. As their resident genius and jack-of-all-sciences, trained in everything from astrophysics to zoology, she could tell him in an instant if such a mix of metals might arise in nature.

Karik and Elana had vanished from the common room, and Talia was waiting for him when he entered their tiny private cabin. She sat cross-legged on the bottom bunk, naked, picking a fingernail.

She glanced up, a mischievous grin on her face. "It's been seven years, you know."

His mind shifted gears with a painful jolt. "Has it? Seems like only yesterday."

"My counsellor said it's good luck for settlers to start their new life with a bang."

He groaned. "Silly superstition."

"The manual says sex is good after awakening. Washes out toxins and gets the blood flowing. Nice bonding exercise, too."

"Hmm. Now you're talking sense." He sat beside her and tickled his fingers down her spine, taking a close look at his mate for the first time since they'd arrived. She'd lost weight in stasis, something that wasn't supposed to happen, but often did, especially to people who already had nothing to spare. Her ribs protruded, and the flesh under her jawbone had sunk into dark hollows, making her long, narrow face look even thinner. The fact that she'd followed recommendations and shaved her head before taking the infusion didn't help get him in the mood. Still, her cheeks glowed a healthy pink, and the eager light in her eyes left no doubt about what she wanted from him. He wouldn't deny his life-mate that, or feed the insecurities she harboured over her body. Successful living was all about setting the right priorities.

He kissed her cheek and whispered, "I love you." Doing his best to shove the sensor reading into a distant corner of his brain, he stood and unfastened his gown. As it dropped to the floor, one more nagging thought intruded, the one that surely plagued all new colonists as they celebrated their arrival in the traditional way. *Will this be our last time?* So many things could go wrong.

~

141

Jackson peered over Talia's shoulder as she adjusted the display settings. "What do you think it is?"

She shrugged. "It could be natural. You'd never find titanium and ferrous alloys mixed like that on Earth, but we don't know much about the geology here. You can't finagle a visual?"

"No. There's total vegetative cover. It's in the middle of a forest."

"So we land there and take a look." Karik's rumbling bass voice reverberated in the control room. He leaned back against the bulkhead, his massive arms folded across his chest.

Talia turned away from the monitor to face the rest of the crew and shook her head. "We have no idea what lives in that forest, or even what the anomaly is. We could run into trouble and jeopardize everything. We should set up the colony site first, and do a flora and fauna survey. Maybe do some remote analysis of the artefact, taking our time. When we've learned enough to feel safe, then a couple of us can go inspect it." She locked eyes with Jackson in a conspicuous plea for support.

He stalled for time. "Maybe the thing is a hazard to the colony. Failing to investigate first might be irresponsible."

"That's baloney, and you know it."

He smiled. She understood him too well. "Elana. Opinion?"

"You know what I want. Besides, if it turns out to be an alien artefact, we need to invoke the Return Prerogative and go back. Having the colony set up will complicate things, and if we've taken the embryos out of the ship's cold storage..." She let the words hang in the air.

"Good point. Karik?"

"I don't see what the big deal is. We land as close as we can, take weapons, hike over, see what it is, and hike back. I don't like weird things hanging over my head."

Jackson hazarded a glance at Talia. She knew she'd lost, and showed it by turning her back and fussing with the display controls again. The jungle image zoomed larger until foliage patterns came into focus. She put her finger on the screen, and a red cross-hair appeared.

She leaned back in the chair. "That's the closest break in the canopy, maybe a twenty minute walk if you're lucky." Without waiting for an answer, she stood up so Jackson could take over.

He leaned forward to squint at the orbital indicator and typed out a command. "We'll be on a glide path in a little over an hour. I'll let the computer take it in most of the way, and then I'll set us down manually." He faced the other three and raised his hand, holding an imaginary glass. "Ladies and gentlemen, welcome to humanity's newest outpost. Eat, drink, and be merry."

Talia smirked at him. "For tomorrow we die?"

~

Jackson twisted the display's joystick to do a sweep of the forest surrounding the ship, with the other three clustered around him. After three passes, he stopped, leaving the outside camera pointed in the direction of the artefact.

"Looks pretty open," Elana said. "I was expecting a jungle, with vines and all that nice stuff."

Talia shook her head. "You need lots of water for that kind of growth, and high temperatures don't hurt. This place has neither, plus the canopy cover discourages scrub. We're looking at a forest not much different from old growth in a temperate area of Earth. The problem is…" She stepped back away from the monitor, forcing them all to turn around to face her. "What lives in that forest? If this were Earth, bears would feel right at home. And cats, maybe big ones. Snakes. The air analysis ruled out biohazards, but there are all kinds of other perils to consider."

Karik laughed, a deep rumble that sounded perilously close to a growl. "You sure you signed up for the right outfit? I think the Girl Explorers were in the next line over."

"Laugh all you want. Put me down in the logs as saying this is irresponsible. We have no idea what's out there. We should…"

Jackson held up his hand. "We've had this discussion. Talia, we'll be in danger no matter where we put down. That's part of the job description. We might pick a nice, safe-looking plain, and discover it's overflowing with scorpions. This may be a forest, but it's open, with good visibility. I also think we need to find out what that object is *before* we set up a colony, and the only way we'll do that is by hiking to it." He crossed the deck to a row of storage bins built into the wall. Opening one, he pulled out three ear-bud communicators, and from another he extracted a trio of small sidearms.

"Karik and Talia, you come with me. The more eyes we have out there, the safer we'll all be. Elana, you stay with the ship."

Elana raised her eyebrows and looked like she was about to say something, but she nodded and sat in the command chair while the others pressed the communicators into their ears and strapped on the sidearms. Jackson led the way out through the airlock. "Karik, you watch left and behind. Talia, you've got right."

He held them back for a minute outside the ship, studying the area. "Elana, you hear me?"

"Yup. Mosquitoes found you yet?"

"No, but there are some insects buzzing around. Little things, not too interested in human blood so far. No wildlife that I see on the ground or in the trees, but I hear branches rustling, and sounds like bird calls. The noise from our landing probably scared most critters away." He glanced at his companions before checking the direction finder strapped to his wrist. "Let's go."

The tall, broad-canopied trees grew so far apart that he could see a hundred feet in every direction, though the dense leaf pack overhead cast a gloomy pall over the terrain. He set a fast pace, checking the direction several times a minute. They'd come close enough that he was straining his eyes for a glimmer of metal when Talia hissed, "Stop!" She held a pair of binoculars up to her face with one hand while the other fumbled with the strap on her holster.

"What?" He scanned the gloomy horizon and saw nothing but trees and shadows.

She pressed a button on the binoculars and handed them to him. "Check those coordinates. Leave it on infrared."

"Huh? It's daytime. What are you going to see on IR?"

"You tell me."

He moved the binoculars left and right until the directional cross-hairs matched her mark. After flipping the IR on and off a couple times, he took a deep breath. "Elana, you still copying?"

"I got nowhere to go. What's up?"

"We've got three large, warm-blooded creatures stalking us. They're our height or more, and they must blend in with the vegetation, because I can't see them in visible. Their body heat shows up in the IR binocs. Oops, make that four. No, five. They're not approaching, just watching from a distance."

"You coming home?"

He lowered the binoculars and glanced around. Talia and Karik both had their weapons drawn and were peering into the forest in opposite directions. "See anything?" he whispered.

They shook their heads.

"Elana? We're within a hundred feet of the artefact. No sense giving up. Who knows how long they've been watching us? If they haven't attacked by now, I doubt if they're hostile."

He handed the binoculars back to Talia, ignoring the incredulous look on her face, and flicked his head toward the coordinates of the artefact. "Let's go."

Seconds later they stopped and stared. A ship half the size of their own lay on the ground, its airlock smashed in as if a wrecking crew with sledge hammers had attacked it. A low stone wall, perfectly circular, surrounded the ship. What held their attention, though, were the four humanoid guards posted at the four compass points around the ship. Spears lay beside them, and the guards knelt, pressing their grey, wrinkled, bald heads to the ground.

He couldn't see their hidden faces, but the rest of their bodies, naked except for loincloths, seemed pulled from the same pot as humanity. They had four fingers and toes instead of five, and their ears were misshaped and misplaced, but on a dark night one could easily mistake them for tall humans.

Jackson felt the weight of Talia's grip on his arm. She drew close and whispered, "Humanoid. First contact."

He tapped the binoculars clutched in her hand. "Keep an eye on the forest. Karik, what do you think of that ship? Second generation Scout?"

He grunted. "I'd have to see inside. Second or third. The last of the thirds went out fifty years ago. But damn, look at that airlock! What could have smashed it in like that? The rest of the ship is okay, so it didn't crash."

"Yeah. Elana, you copying this conversation?"

"I am. You wanna confirm that we've got an old-model Scout craft on the ground, its airlock smashed in, and some aliens hanging around?"

"You got it. Better watch your perimeter."

Talia squeezed his elbow. "Here come more, at least six of them. Same as these guys. They're carrying weapons, maybe. Spears?"

"No shooting except extreme self-defence."

"Jackson?" Her voice quivered. "It's time to go back to the ship, right?"

"Too late."

Six grey forms walked toward them, and from the way they hesitated, looking at one another and over their shoulders every few steps, it seemed they felt as nervous as he did. The six newcomers stopped a few dozen paces away. Together, they set down their spears, dropped to their knees, and touched their heads to the ground.

Jackson cleared his throat. Nobody moved. "Okay," he said, trying to make it sound like an important word. Nothing happened. He clapped his hands. Talia jumped, but none of the natives responded. "Well," he said, shrugging his shoulders, "we might as well check out the ship." He took a few steps.

Several of the aliens raised their heads to look up. He kept going. The four guards scrambled to their feet, and the six others joined them, still watching the terrain behind and to both sides.

"They think there's more of us," Talia muttered. "Why are they so afraid? Bad memories of the last visit?"

"Maybe." Jackson ducked down and pushed his way through the half-open airlock door, hanging crooked from its hinges. Talia and Karik followed.

His jaw dropped. Whoever had smashed the airlock to get in hadn't stopped there. Every storage cabinet, the main console, the food unit, everything that could be damaged had been utterly destroyed. His fear of the natives jumped up a notch, and Talia's face gave away that she felt the same. This was not casual vandalism. This was unabashed violence.

Karik pointed at the two seats that shared a single control console. "Second generation. This hasn't flown in at least fifty years."

"Yeah." Jackson sighed. "I wonder what happened to the occupants. I've seen enough." He squeezed out the airlock.

All ten natives stood in a line, waiting for them, silent. Every few seconds at least one of them turned around and looked behind, or peered deep into the forest. Were they that afraid of their strange visitors, wondering if reinforcements were on the way? Were they deciding if they dared do to them what their parents or grandparents had done to the last humans who'd come to visit? Or even should? The true alien nature of these folk hit home when Jackson realized that despite having a mouth, two eyes, and a nose-like hole covered by a protective flap, their faces held no expression that he could read. Was it anger? Disappointment? Awe? Fear? He had no idea.

Glancing back in the direction of their own ship, a few minutes' jog away, he swallowed hard. "Elana, there's ten of them surrounding us, and the interior of the Scout is trashed. We've got our side-arms drawn, but damned if I want to shoot. Hell of a first contact."

"Not first. This is second contact. We can only guess how the first went."

Talia brushed Jackson's hand. "You know the directive. No unnecessary interaction. We need to get back to the ship, return to Earth, and let the pros deal with it."

He chuckled, trying to read any kind of expression from the ten grey, wrinkled faces surrounding them. "Pros? What pros? Nobody's done this before. If we have to, we can handle this as well as anyone else."

"Elana?" Talia's voice quivered even more than it had a moment ago. "We're returning to the ship." She took a step back in the direction they'd come, and then another.

Two of the natives slid to the side, blocking her way, though they kept their spears lowered. The most wrinkled member of the group gestured off to the right and headed in that direction, walking with fast, long strides. Some of the others followed him, while the rest pointed. The message, though without threat, was unmistakable. Jackson saw Talia's hand tighten on her weapon, and he shook his head. "Elana, they want us to go with them. I assume they just want to show us their village."

"Or their stew pot? My guess is that they're a lot better with those spears than you imagine. Don't take any chances. And keep in touch! If you guys go quiet on me, I'll flip out."

They marched at a quick pace for only a few minutes before a small log building loomed before them, with a cluster of similar but larger buildings farther on. The natives led them halfway around it until they faced a single narrow portal, not quite waist high. Except for a feeble flame centred on the floor inside the door, shadows concealed the interior. In one smooth motion, all six of their captors dropped to their knees, lowered their foreheads to the ground, and froze in that position.

Jackson stepped forward. Talia and Karik joined him. One step at a time they advanced toward the open door. The natives neither moved nor uttered a sound. They ducked through the low entrance and paused to let their eyes adapt to the dark of the stuffy, windowless chamber. A sweet, almost intoxicating fragrance filled the air, and the minimal light of the single candle revealed flowers strewn on the floor. A pair of stone tables stood in the middle, with an undefined humanoid form lying on top of each. They edged up to the tables.

Talia pulled a flashlight from her pocket and shined it. The beam landed on a dry, shrunken face, and she flicked it away. Jackson took the light from her hand and leaned forward. He reached out and touched the face with shaking fingers.

"It's human," she whispered. "Preserved. Mummified."

Jackson nodded. "The occupants of the Scout."

"But…what happened?"

He lowered the light, scanning both naked bodies left to right, head to toe. When he reached the feet, he returned to the chest of the first one they'd seen, and pressed his finger against one of several deep indentations in the rib area. The finger penetrated to the second knuckle before he pulled it out and did the same to the other dry cadaver. "They've both been stabbed in the chest. Multiple times."

Talia exhaled in a sharp burst, spun around, and dashed for the door, with the others close behind. The natives hadn't moved, but at the sound they jumped to their feet. One of them took a step toward the humans. Particle-beam pistols sizzled to Jackson's left and right as Talia and Karik fired. Two of the natives fell. One of the tallest dove at Talia, reaching for her gun. She whipped it around and shot just as Jackson hit him in the thigh. The attacker twitched and went limp. Karik dropped to a crouch and picked off natives as fast as they appeared, spilling out of two other buildings.

Jackson took aim at one of the grey-skins as it came up behind Karik, but a numbing sting in his shoulder stopped him from pulling the trigger. A black-feathered dart stuck in his flesh just inside his armpit. He yanked it out, but he knew it was too late. Warmth spread from the shoulder, crossing his chest and filling his mind with a hazy fog. His legs turned to rubber. As he fell, he saw Talia motionless on the ground, and Karik clutching his stomach, stumbling.

A buzzing voice, sounding like it came from a thousand miles away, filled his ear. "Mummies? Stabbed in the chest? Talk to me! What's going on?" Stars filled his vision, and everything turned black.

~

Elana rocked back in the chair, her hands clasped behind her head. They'd been silent for two hours, with about an hour of daylight remaining. A motion on the console screen caught her eye. Another of the grey-skinned natives appeared out of the forest and ran to one of the guards who'd been stationed around the ship for some time. She panned the joystick to sweep the camera. The other three guards remained in place, spears held loosely at their sides. The runner moved on to the next guard, and then the other two. After conferring with each, he disappeared back into the forest, which was now sinking into deeper twilight.

She made up her mind. From the supply store she grabbed a portable first-aid kit and attached straps to fasten it to her belt. On a whim, she popped a stimulant pill from the dispenser and swallowed it without water. Rummaging through the weapons locker, she sighed at their poor stockpile. The Expeditionary authorities discouraged the use of force by settlers, and made sure to limit their options when it came to violence.

She clipped a standard-issue particle-beam pistol onto her right hip, and picked up a flame-thrower fuel canister, pondering its weight. The flamer was intended for quick brush clearing, but would doubtless scare the crap out of any living creature in its path. She strapped it on her back. From the rear wall of the cabinet she fetched their lone projectile rifle and filled the chamber with electrostatic stun pellets. Talia had taken their only IR binoculars, but she hung a set of night-vision specs around her neck. Then she sat back down in front of the monitor and waited for the sun to set.

A full but small moon rose as the sun went down. She switched the outside scanner to infrared. The four guards still stood at their posts, ghostly white blobs floating in a sea of black. She eased the airlock open and paused, listening for any sign that they'd heard it. No sounds but the gentle rustle of tree branches reached her ears. Raising the rifle, she panned it until the nearest guard appeared in the night scope. The gun popped and the guard reeled backwards. Heavy footfalls clomped through the underbrush. She swung the rifle around until another bright spot of light flared in the scope. Pop, and the second guard fell. The other two went down just as fast. As she sealed the airlock behind her, she wondered how long they'd be out. The pellets would keep a healthy human down for hours. With any luck they'd be just as good on these guys.

She glanced at the direction finder strapped to her wrist. Her crewmates' earbuds showed them to be not far from the Scout ship, and she headed straight that way, holding the rifle across her body. Once under the dense forest canopy, the moon vanished, so she pulled the night-vision specs into place. They showed a black field, punctuated by pinpricks of yellow overhead, the body heat of small tree-dwelling creatures. The forest floor was uniformly cool, so she could see nothing underfoot and had to take one cautious step at a time, ever wary of falling into a pit or stream.

She'd crept along for about twenty minutes when a bright spot appeared off to her left. She checked the direction finder. The spot stood close to the Scout ship. Soon, three more spots resolved, none moving. It made for a tough decision: ignore them and take a chance on them sounding an alarm, or put them out of action. The latter sounded more prudent. Testing each footstep before putting weight on it, afraid of snapping a twig, she eased as close as she dared. Four rifle pops later, the guards lay on the ground. Would the aliens holding her crewmates hear the sound and wonder? She shrugged her shoulders. Life was full of tradeoffs.

~

Jolts of pain stabbed through Jackson's head. He forced his eyes open and flinched. One of the creatures knelt at his side, leaning over him, so close that he could make out every hill and fissure in its wrinkled grey face. The thing held a clump of wet grass in its four-fingered hand. He realized why he'd just wakened with a start. It had wiped his face with the cold wad of plants. A little stream of water still ran down his cheek. *What the hell? Grooming us for the slaughter?*

He turned his head to the right. Talia lay on a pad, with another of the natives dabbing her face. Karik lay to his left, getting the same treatment.

"Elana? They hit us with darts that knocked us out. Now they're nursing us! What's your status?" He waited a moment. "Elana?" He raised his hand to his ear and snarled when his probing finger failed to find the earbud. *Have they inspected me so close that they heard Elana screaming in my ear? Did they think I had a demon, and yanked it out?* His hand darted to his waist. No weapon. *Damn!*

He lifted his head enough to look around. They lay on woven pads inside a low-ceilinged log building. Crude tallow candles flickered on shelves, projecting eerie rays that danced up and down the rough walls. The candles cast enough light to let him see shadows moving just outside the open door, doubtless a cadre of guards. When the alien creature pressed all four fingers against his forehead, pushing him down to the mat, he cringed at its clammy touch and relented. Maybe they'd still get a chance to escape, but now was not the time.

~

Orange lights flared in Elana's night-vision specs, candles or lamps burning in a half dozen low buildings. Dimmer yellow blurs revealed guards circling the settlement, posted every twenty feet or so. Bad news. They were ready for her. She reluctantly set down the rifle. It had far better accuracy than the particle-beam pistol clipped to her belt, and was less likely to kill the target, but it made too much noise for what had to be a stealth operation. Besides, at this point killing wasn't an issue. She had three friends to rescue if they still lived, and nothing else mattered.

She crept up to the nearest guard. A twig snapped under her foot, and the guard turned his head, but he fell before raising an alarm. One more went down before she reached the door to the first building. A dozen of the natives sat in a circle on the floor, conversing in a language that sounded more like toads chirping than any speech she'd ever heard. For one moment she contemplated spraying the lot of them with a dispersed beam to keep them from interfering later if things got tough. The gun held a limited charge, though, and a twinge of guilt over unnecessary carnage tipped the balance. She slipped back into the shadows and made for the next guard around the perimeter.

She took him out and paused to study the situation. A low building in the centre of the camp glowed with lamplight, and two sentries stood outside its door, erect and alert. Bingo. She raised the night specs, grateful for the glimmers of light that filtered out the door. Dropping to her stomach and propping both elbows against the ground, she clutched the pistol with both hands. She took her time, peering through its primitive sight until the chest of one guard lay centred in the crosshairs. When he fell, the other guard looked around in confusion for only a second before he let out a warbling squall loud enough to wake the dead. She jumped to her feet and took him out before he saw her coming.

Inside the building, her companions scrambled to their feet when she burst in. Three aliens huddled in the corner. A trio of quick shots from her weapon felled them. Without wasting time for talk, she dashed back out the door, Jackson, Talia, and Karik on her heels. The dozen aliens who'd been meeting in the first building streamed out its door toward them.

"They've got darts!" Jackson screamed.

Elana rammed the pistol in its holder, missed, and cursed when it landed in the dirt. She snatched the flame thrower nozzle from its hook on her left hip, squeezed the igniter, and shot a spray of fire at the advancing party. Choked screams rent the air, and she gagged at the stench of burnt flesh. More natives rushed from other buildings, and she turned the nozzle at them.

Keeping the flame low for light, they made for their ship. Halfway there, she paused to let the others, still half drugged from the darts, catch their breath. Jackson gave her a cold look.

Knowing what he was about to say, she pinched her lips together. "So report me. Frankly, I don't give a damn how many I kill. They're not making you into dead gods."

A clang reverberated throughout the forest, ending the discussion.

"They're attacking the ship!" Talia shouted.

At the same time, a mass of dark forms passed them from behind, keeping a healthy distance away. Elana rushed forward, spraying fire at full power. Blinding flames filled the air as she swept the nozzle left and right ahead of the four of them in their frantic sprint for the ship. The clangs came faster now, the sound of a heavy object crashing against the airlock over and over.

The noise suddenly stopped, replaced by a cacophony of warbling cries and squeals. A silvery gleam appeared a hundred feet ahead. She pointed the nozzle straight up and let it flare. A fight raged in front of their ship, with four of the tall, grey-skinned natives wielding their spears against a dozen short, wide creatures holding long knives so white that they glowed in the light of the flame. The grey creatures had the advantage of height as well as long spears, but the short ones had agility, darting in close for a deadly strike, and then darting back away in the blink of an eye. With twelve against four, she knew which way the battle would go.

The flame thrower sputtered and died, leaving only the light of the small, dim moon. She tore the bulky canister off her back and tossed it aside. Might they slip into their refuge while the battle kept everyone occupied? She took a hesitant step forward, knowing that four unarmed humans stood little chance against knives and spears in the hands of experts. But holding back would mean certain death at the hand of the victors, and she wasn't ready for that quite yet.

The crowd of fighters drifted to the right, revealing what they had obscured before. A heavy log, one end cut to a taper, lay beside the ship. It had already done its dirty work, denting the airlock enough that its seal would never hold again, and it might not even swing open now.

A group of the squat creatures broke away from the battle and rushed toward them. Two of the tall natives gave chase and passed them in a few long strides. The four humans, weaponless, closed together in a last-ditch effort to fight off spears or knives or both.

The tall grey-skins stopped a few feet in front of the humans and turned to face the attackers, their spears lowered in a brave stand. With this image, the truth came to Elana in a single crushing realization. *What have we done?* Her three companions got it, too. They spread out forward, waving their arms and screaming at the squat creatures.

Their distraction proved to be too little, too late. The little beasts ducked under the spears and thrust up with their knives. Both grey-skins clutched their mid-sections and dropped to the ground. By the dim light filtered through clouds, she saw the other two tall defenders near the ship go down. Twelve short aliens surrounded them, their pale knives flashing in the moonlight. The nearest one looked up and met her eyes. Its mouth spread wide and opened in a mocking grin. Teeth as shiny as polished ivory glistened in the moonlight as it drew back the knife to strike.

# Frogsong

## J. David Bell

J. David Bell is a recovering academic whose fiction appears in such periodicals as *Cover of Darkness*, *Niteblade*, *The Squirrel Cage*, and *Rotten Leaves Magazine*. His published books include *Framing Monsters: Fantasy Film and Social Alienation* (Southern Illinois University Press, 2005) and *Medicine Bundle: Indian Sacred Performance and American Literature* (University of Pennsylvania Press, 2008).

Read more of his writing at bellsyells.blogspot.com

The delivery truck rumbled along the muddy road above the swamp. In the cab, eyes fighting fatigue and the gathering dark, Todd Stuckey guided the rig up a steep grade. He could feel his rear tires slaloming in the slop until, with a rattle and cough of gears, they caught hold. He kept the window cracked just an inch, taking in rich whiffs of diesel to clear his head of the swamp stench, rank and stifling as a latrine. The lush green of overhanging trees faded to a blur in the twilight as luminescent bugs started to dance over the marsh like sparklers. And behind it all, as ever, the song: a drone, a peal, a whine. An endless, senseless cacophony of throats crying carols across the swamp.

In low gear, Stuckey inched down a grade that levelled at the swamp's edge. One more bend and the compound rose in his headlights: a paved loading dock, prefab trailers, the broad squat gable of the mess hall. On the flagpole, the Stars and Stripes drooped in the sultry air. Beside the dock a halo of sulphur light revealed a solitary figure slumped in his booth, head lowered on crossed arms. Stuckey wheeled around the drive, backed her in, and hopped from the cab. His boots met the pavement with a familiar liquid smack. He circled his truck, unlatched the gate, and sent it rattling to roost. Then he approached the clerk.

The man had shown no awareness of the truck's arrival; he remained prone, head buried in his arms, cap hiding his face and hair. Close up, Stuckey could see his shoulders rising and falling, hear his snores. They seemed to keep time with the rhythmic pulse of the swamp.

"Delivery," Stuckey said. His voice came out loud and ringing against the background buzz. "Where do you want it?"

The clerk muttered, raised his head, and squinted. Stuckey saw then he was only a kid, maybe twenty-two, red-haired and freckled, red-eyed and raw-cheeked. New guy. He removed his cap, ran a hand through unruly hair, and yawned.

"What you hauling, Joe?" They called the delivery guys "Joes"—as in "Regular Joe." Stuckey'd have preferred to be called a Regular, but it was the Joe part that had stuck.

He shrugged. "Laminate, drywall, the usual. It's in the manifest," he said, shoving his clipboard at the kid's face. "We got an unloading crew?"

The kid scratched his head as if he'd never heard such a question. "Ease up, Joe," he said. "Just take it easy."

"Look," Stuckey began, but the kid had roused himself from his stool and gotten his legs out the door. "I'll make the call," he said, and yawned again. Then he sat there stupidly, hands in his lap, staring at his open palms.

Stuckey left the clipboard and returned to his truck.

Last run of the day, he reminded himself. A tepid shower, a frozen dinner, a lukewarm beer, a rerun or sportscast in the rec room. Anything to dream the place away, drown out the sound and smell for a moment. Then bed. Then the same thing the next day.

~

It was his third month on-planet. In those three months he'd watched them dredge acre upon acre of swampland, plane the gaping, muddy craters, and plug them with concrete. The buildings were going up now, girders gaping above the tattered treeline. Much slower work than on Earth, where automated shovels and great hovering cranes could sketch a tower's outline in a week, polish it to gleaming in two. But with the inhospitable climate and terrain of the place, you had to go back to basics.

Which was, actually, one of the few pluses of this stinkhole. How long since he'd driven a stick—since he'd driven anything? Bullet trains and maglev, roboservers and drivers. On Earth you were in danger of forgetting what your body was for. Here you could pretend you were a pioneer, carving a landscape from pure primal ooze.

Past that small satisfaction, though—and by the end of the day it became just another part of the grind, by the end of the month just another part of the plan—there wasn't enough good about the place to fill a text message. Sticky, sweltering air. Suffocating canopy, low and close as fumes. Blood-sucking bugs that had evolved the capacity to stick their victims without the slightest pinch or sting, so Stuckey never knew they were there 'til he'd been half drained. Days of rain so thick and hot the roofs sizzled and steamed. And that ripe, fetid smell of the place, a smell that penetrated his nostrils like it'd been stuffed up there with a swab. To Stuckey, it felt as if his face and fingertips puckered as much from the stench as the wetness.

And frogs. Countless frogs. By far the dominant vertebrate, vastly more numerous than the turtles, snakes, and occasional oddly shaped, shore-stalking bird. Frogs every-where: squatting in gullies and ditches, balanced like lumps on logs, mating in shallow pools, squirting their clotted spawn in long slimy clumps and strings like opalescent jelly. Stuckey wished he could say there were less now that so much swamp had been drained, but he knew that was wishful thinking. They were everywhere, familiar from home, dirty green and brown and leopard-spotted and paunchy and flaccid. Bigger than their cousins on Earth, close to three feet from snout to flippers the time he saw them stretched out, pale bellies upward, on the dissecting table. And maybe there was a slightly less protuberant perch to their bronze and nickel eyes, a slightly simian thrust to their thin rubbery smiles. Aside from the bulk and the eyes and the pale pouty lips though, they were just frogs: heavy, torpid, filling the road like so many moist turds. For Stuckey, as for all the drivers, the impulse to mash them beneath the wheels of his truck was irresistible. But they always jumped clear, in huge, sodden arcs, just before anyone got the chance. One of the Joes had the idea to call the place Froggy Bottom, and though Stuckey didn't catch the reference, he thought it perfect. When that metamorphosed into Baggy Scrotum, he liked it even better.

It was the singing, though, that drove everyone berserk. These frogs didn't croak, or chirp, or glug, or gulp. They sang, in searing siren sopranos just this side of deafness. It began at dusk, when even on the wettest days the air held a peculiar clarity of outline and colour that seemed to presage the swift decline into gloom, and didn't abate until dawn. Stuckey had tried plugging his ears, blasting music, but it didn't matter; their squeals bored into his head, more piercing than the whirr of cicadas, more varied than the repertoire of a mockingbird. If the song had never changed he might have gotten used to it, the way he'd learned to tune out the whine of a power drill or the metallic chop of a jackhammer. But no go. He could never tell whether individual creatures mutated the melody, riffing on it, making it their own, or whether the entire gargantuan chorus shifted in response to some synaptic signal coursing through the bog or the blood. Either way it was maddening. And it didn't seem to lessen with the dwindling of their territory; if anything, it had grown thicker, more insistent as the swamps filled.

Like everyone else Stuckey hated the singing, but at the same time he was thankful for it. It reminded him that this hellhole wasn't home. And that home wasn't here.

~

Stripped to basics, his story was no different from any Joe's. He'd come for the money, for adventure, and—if he was being honest—for escape. Escape from the endless tedium of temp work shuffling long rows and steep columns that represented someone else's climb to fortune half a world away. Escape from the cramped square in the guts of a hi-rise that served as his night-time respite from the cramped square of his office cubicle. Escape from in-laws who showed up at his quarters without invitation or announcement, endlessly questioning his endlessly questionable job. When, they asked, smiling tightly, their knees practically touching his, was he going to make a move, find a solid position, advance in the world? He couldn't stay a temp, couldn't live this way forever. Especially now.

And it was especially that, that "especially now," he was escaping from. From Grace's belly, taut as a drum. From the way she'd tricked him, missed a pill or taken one, to ensure that egg and sperm would make their appointed rendezvous in the aqueous cavity of her womb. They'd had an agreement, he'd believed. No kids until he was ready. No new life to crowd theirs, little as it was. Grace swore innocence, couldn't believe he'd accuse her, and if he thought about it, he didn't know how he knew she was lying. He just knew.

Why wasn't he ready? She asked that. He asked himself. The usual reasons, all he could come up with, all inadequate. The responsibility, the loss of a meagre freedom. The sharing of his life with an uninvited creature, one he suspected he'd never know as well as it might demand to be known, need to be. Hell, he thought he'd known Grace, but after five years to pull a stunt like this. How, then, could he trust this twisting, bubbling, careening bundle of cells he'd had no real knowledge or say-so producing?

When he proposed the obvious way out she wouldn't hear of it. Her body, she said. *Her* body. When, not looking for anything in particular, he saw the ad for off-world drivers, he jumped at the chance.

But they'd tricked him too. The vidlink, all packaging and soft light, turning a puke pond to a paradise. The promises of promotion, all lies, the place an absolute hierarchy where no one budged. The interminable days, the feverish and all-too-brief nights. If only he'd heard the singing, he'd have run for his life.

At Grace's insistence he'd signed the minimum contract, a single year. But with the two-month transport there and back, his kid would be damn near running and jumping by the time he returned. And for all he hated the place, he'd started to think he might just sign on for another round.

~

The clerk had been acting up lately, barking orders at men twice his age and size, insisting the drivers double- and triple-check everything. "Don't think I don't know what's going on," he said, standing in his outsized khakis with a clipboard wedged to his gut and a pen stabbing the manifest. "Don't think I'm not talking to people."

"What people?" Stuckey wanted to know.

"I talk to base," he said. "All the time. I'm on the hookup fifty times a day. You think I'm not?"

"How the hell should I know?"

"That's right," the kid said, as if his assertion, or accusation, or whatever it was, had just been confirmed. "You should remember that," he aimed his pen at the circle of drivers. "All of you."

"I don't know what the fuck you're talking about," one of the others said.

At that the kid turned purple and stormed into the hangar. They heard his curses, boxes toppling, an echoing clatter.

The other Joe turned to the group. "Does anyone know what the fuck he's talking about?"

The next night when Stuckey pulled in there was a new guy at the booth. Older guy, balding. The kind who'd held a desk job his whole life. "Where's the kid?" Stuckey asked.

The clerk looked up. "Who?"

"Other guy. Before you."

The clerk went back to ticking off entries. "Got reassigned. Base, maybe. I just go where they tell me to go."

A rumour went around camp that the kid had wandered off into the swamps and not returned. It just swallowed him up, they said. Maybe he went looking for the source of the singing and never found it. Then again, maybe he did.

~

The new clerk didn't last long either. Couple weeks tops. Maybe it was tougher sitting on your ass all day, breathing the swamp air, waiting for the night's brutal chorus. At least on the road you could tell yourself you were getting somewhere.

Along with the latest replacement another man showed up at camp. A supervisor of some sort, though that didn't mean a whole hell of a lot to the drivers who spent only enough waking time here to unload. Someone said he'd been sent from base to get the work back on schedule, the swamps not being filled fast enough to satisfy the suits. And it was true; when the shovels lay idle during the overnight hours the swamp reasserted its claim, crept in muddy ripples inch by inch over the blacktop, seeped into pilings, replanted gelatinous algae and floating pods on any available pool. Never as much lost at night as was taken during the day, so the work slowly, inexorably crept into the frogs' demesne. But watching workers in hip boots slop out subbasements you got the feeling you'd have to remain ever vigilant, never relent until you'd managed, if you could, to drain the last ditch and crevice dry.

The supervisor gathered the drivers his first night before they hit their bunks. There was a new rotation, he said, and that meant night-time runs for all.

There was a long silence from the men, a long interval for the swamp to fill in mocking refrain. "You've gotta be fucking kidding," one of the Joes finally managed.

The supervisor's eyes narrowed. He was a rangy man, erect in his spotless uniform, though pouches sagged from his eyes and mouth. "You got a problem, Joe? Take it up with base."

"This wasn't in our contract," the driver pressed.

"Plenty of men happy to take your shift." The supervisor eyed him with disdain, like he was already on his way off-planet.

"It's bullshit," the driver muttered, but he took the schedule and went back to his rig with the rest.

*Nights*, Stuckey thought. He ran a finger over the spreadsheet, saw his name on the overnight shift Friday, Saturday, and Sunday. Single day off. Hour earlier start. They were planning to haul and drag every second of the day and night and with nowhere near the numbers they'd need.

Stuckey ran to catch the man before he gained his quarters for the night. "Sir," he said, feeling awkward.

The supervisor stopped, hand on the door. He looked at Stuckey with boredom and dislike. "If this is about the runs, I told you, take it up with base."

"It's just..."

"Just what?" The man turned to face him. "Never changes with you Joes. Same bullshit all the time. There's a hundred men who'd kill for this job for every one of you, and if you can't cut it, you can take your pansy ass home."

The sound from the swamp was building, boiling. Soon it would reach a crescendo. Stuckey felt hot shame, anger, and lifted his hands to the marsh. "You hear that?"

"Do I look fucking deaf?"

"You know what it's like out there?" he insisted. "You ever been on the road in that?"

"That, and worse than that," the supervisor said. "Only difference is I kept my eyes the fuck open." He heaved the door wide. "And my mouth the fuck shut."

With that he slammed the door, leaving Stuckey to front alone the singsong night.

~

The first run was as bad as he expected. Creeping along in dark so deep he kept seeing fantastic shapes out of the corner of his eye, headlights not so much clearing a path as piecing it together, haltingly, inch by inch. The smell of the swamp more rank than ever, choking as decay, whether from the utter lack of light or the pressing weight of the night-time canopy he had no clue. And the sound he'd been able to lull himself into ignoring just enough to slip into anxious sleep he now couldn't evade; its bone-deep warble seemed to be intensified by the concentration necessary to stay on the road. Stuckey strained not to hear it, but the more he strained the more he did. It was all-surrounding, so much a part of the scene he began to doubt if anything existed or could exist without it. It saturated the world as if it were the very soup of creation, and when at last he tumbled into his bunk at dawn it seemed as if his body was still suspended in it like a specimen in a jelly jar.

That first morning, exhausted as he was, Stuckey couldn't sleep, so he figured he'd head to the mess hall. They'd ramped up the building operations too, the guttering roar of shovels going day and night, trees crashing in piled matchsticks to be fed to tireless engines and blown as fine dust into the sky. It dawned on him he'd been here for four months and for almost every second of that time he'd been hemmed by two sounds: the shudder of his own civilization and the burble of the swamp. He felt that no matter how long he stayed, no matter how long after he'd left, he'd never know a respite from either.

Rounding the bunkhouse, he saw a man seated with his back against the mess hall door, boots up on a crate. Stuckey knew the guy, but not by name. Oldest guy there, longest on-planet, engineer of some kind. You'd see him with his crew on the hill overlooking some undrained spot, holding a schematic or sighting along a level. He tipped down in his chair as Stuckey neared.

"Bad luck, Joe," he said. "No breakfast today."

"Great," Stuckey said, though truthfully he wasn't sure he could eat. "What's the problem?"

"What's always the problem?" the guy leered, showing dangling, tobacco-stained teeth. "The eternal problem, I mean."

Stuckey shook his head, turned to walk away. He had no time for this.

"Hey, Joe!"

He stopped, looked back.

"Ever take a shot at one?"

Stuckey stared. "What?"

"Did you," the guy aimed a long finger at him, "ever take," clasping his hands, "a shot," as if sighting a gun, "at one," thumbing in the general direction of the swamp.

"I don't shoot."

"You should try it. Passes the time."

Stuckey was silent.

"Ugly fuckers," the engineer continued. "But easy targets. Just sit there lookin' at you while you line 'em up. Then you hit one and poof! It's gone. Like a balloon. No blood even. No trace."

"You do this all the time," Stuckey said, "or only on special occasions?"

The guy eyed Stuckey sidelong. "That's the spirit," he said. "Gotta keep that up around here." He shifted his chew and leaned over to spit on the grass, his saliva a brown froth as bubbly as frog spawn. "You Joes think you've got some kind of special dispensation, that right? You just haul the shit, we're the ones that skin the swamps. You're in, you're out, let the damage be what it may. Let me show you something."

"I'm going back to my bunk."

"Just take a minute." The guy reared from the chair and left it propped against the mess hall door.

Stuckey followed him to the outbuildings behind camp, the storage sheds lapped by swamp grasses, the two-on-two basketball court no one ever used because that meant clearing an inch of standing water. They headed for the last shed in the row, its roof blotted by the heavy droop of foliage. The engineer freed a keycard from his belt and opened the door.

Stuckey stepped over the threshold into a—what? Not a lab, though at first, when the warm rush of formaldehyde met his nostrils and the icy white of fluorescent strobes flickered on before his eyes, that's what he thought. He'd visited the science wing as part of the orientation tour, heard the men in white coats prate on about the importance of studying the indigenous flora and fauna—the better to kill it, sounded like. Later, he'd heard of plans to irradiate the swamps, flood them with poison, some mutagenic compound. But so far as he knew, that was still on the drawing board. For no better reason he could tell than inertia, none of the camp's official agents of death had yet acted.

The engineer had. The place looked like an anatomy theatre: spotless steel cabinets and precision instruments and a hollow, bloodless light. But it was a theatre turned to a trophy room, a freak show. Every shiny surface, tables and desks and cabinets and shelves, was littered with the carcasses of frogs, and every carcass was displayed in some unique posture or contrivance of diseased invention: frog cadavers stitched together at the snout or shoulder; corpses with body parts torn free and set to

167

roam—a leg sprouting from a belly, a webbed foot from a throat pouch—spavined frog forms with their entrails ripped out, looped and knotted like Christmas bows atop their flat heads; others with skins peeled back like strips of flypaper to reveal their whitened musculature or pared down to the yellow filigree of bone. On one table a pyramid of the things' heads, preserved through some process that kept the green of their skins intact while whittling the flesh to a skein as glossy and brittle as a layer of paint, balanced without tilt or wobble. Starved, shellacked skulls with frozen frowns, looking surprised and abandoned and, Stuckey was shocked to see, terribly, terribly lorn. There must have been fifty—no, a hundred—of them crowding the room, weighting the air with a dull odour stuffy and metallic and too dead to stink.

Stuckey turned to the engineer, met his look of nonchalance. "And you do this...?"

The man shrugged. "Like I said. Passes the time."

"Mister," Stuckey said. He took shallow breaths against the airless rot. "You have way too much time on your hands."

"Tell me about it." The engineer turned a slow circle, taking in his handiwork. "But I'll tell you this. You hate 'em as much as I do. Maybe more. You're out there with 'em."

He gestured with his chin to the still-bright day. "You're the linchpin," he said, leaning against the doorframe, his long arms and legs touching its edges so that, silhouetted by the swamp's light, he seemed to drape the space like a web. "Little fuckers have no idea what's in store for 'em. Once we've cleared this swamp, it's on to the next. Soon there won't be a pond left for 'em to piss in nor a place to stash their dick while they're holdin'. Then my collectin' days'll be over, and I can retire to the froggy farm." He grinned a death's head grin and spat a trickle of tobacco to the earth.

Stuckey tried muscling past, but the engineer laid an arm across his shoulders and pulled him so close his sickly sweet breath swam in the driver's face. "My advice to you," he said in a burst of facetious, boozy-avuncular concern, "is to make your first million and get the hell out while you still can."

"While I still can."

"Before you start dreamin' about the place," the man cackled. "Once that happens, it's too late."

~

Of what did Stuckey dream? Not of this place, not yet, unless occasionally the clerk's fractured face should float on the perimeter of unconscious eyesight or the song of the swamp should penetrate too deep to dispel, turning sleep's soundtrack to a bubbling torment like the screams of some viscous inferno. But not of Earth either, there where he'd first fallen into the trap—numbered days, measured accounts in the tortuous columns that loomed over him as he clambered painfully, treacherously, for the next crazy level.

Of what, then? Sometimes of dark, and silence, and stillness: a place where nothing yet had begun, nothing wagered, nothing lost, nothing forfeited, nothing claimed. A hiding place where, lucky hider, neither he nor anyone he knew, knew he was hiding; nobody, least of all himself, knew he had joined the game. Or of sensation, motion divorced from a feeling subject, shift of sand beds, spiral of air bubbles snaking about a submerged stem, pop of pressure released as the mind's whorled cochlea greeted a new atmosphere. Even less than that: a pinprick of watery light so distant the dreamer might as well have been gazing up at it from the flood at the ocean's floor. Sometimes there would be bumps along the ride, bucking and a hint of pain, or else a soft flap as of someone's hands pulling back to reveal the bright surprise of day. Other times it would be like the sucking of a vortex, slippery and fluid as blood, and out of a vast timeless unknowing, a form shaping itself against a black netherworld of space and sprinkled stars.

Of one thing he was sure: in just over four months on-planet he hadn't dreamed of Grace, or of what she carried. And on the morning he realized that, the morning he woke to hear his name called over a dawn reveille seemingly muted by a certain soft pink light and the eerie interval of other accustomed sounds, he knew that his dreams, like his departure, had failed him. And he thought he knew why.

~

"Stuckey!" The latest clerk was calling from the bunkhouse door. "Stuckey!"

He pulled on his trousers, stuffed his shirt into his waistband, and yanked his cap over his tousled hair. "Stuckey."

The clerk, not so old as the second but not so young as the first, handed him a keycard. "Vidlink."

Stuckey exited the bunkhouse and made for the media centre. He'd had five, six posts since he arrived, and ignored them all. The last was a good month ago. He could no longer remember whether, in all that time, he'd planned to post her back.

He settled into a chair in the cool video blue of the trailer. It resembled an arcade back on Earth, banks of modular plastic seats curving cocoon-like to corresponding monitors. Except instead of a flock of teenagers sharing the row, joysticks in hand, a couple of his fellow Joes sat to either side, their faces fixed on the screens, their voices hushed, lifetime loners even more hardened than he chastened into Sunday-school attention by their absent others' eyes. He inserted the keycard and waited for Grace to appear.

In an instant her face filled the screen. "Hey there, cowboy." She looked pale, drained, skin tight and wet across her forehead, strands of brown hair tipped with moisture like an artist's brushes. But she was smiling, broad and silly with exhaustion. "Remember me?"

"Hi, Grace."

"Hi, yourself." Unconsciously, it seemed, her hand went to her hair, pushed it back. "I wouldn't have called, but…We had a visitor today."

"A visitor."

"Not the kind who comes every day." The vidlink panned obediently to her chest, where a small red bundle lay wrapped in a fuzzy pink blanket.

It wore a white cap like a mitten. Its eyelids were mere wrinkles in a face as grooved and veined as some fantastic marine creature. Its peach pebble hand was balled; its dot nostrils flared with each breath. He felt the ground shift, but he did not fall. It was more like the gentle rocking of a tide than the yawning of a grave, anyway.

"I wanted to film the birth," she said. "But I thought it might be too," she lowered her eyes, "intense."

He nodded dumbly. "Might have been."

"I haven't named her yet."

"No."

"I was thinking of Hope."

"Hope." Hope and Grace.

"Unless you don't like it."

"I like it," he said. "It's catchy." Not what he meant to say. "Pretty." He felt his throat tighten, swallowed. "Beautiful."

She smiled, wearily but not warily. He'd forgotten that smile. "I bet you say that to all the girls."

He reached out to lay his fingertips on the limpid screen. Her fingers rose to his. There was a crackle of static as they touched, a hundred worlds away.

"Todd," she said. "Come home."

He nodded. "Yes."

"Right away."

"Yes."

She was crying. "I never meant for this to happen."

"I know."

"But when it did, I couldn't..."

"I know."

"And now that she's here, she needs...I need..."

"I know," he said. "I just," and he swallowed again. "Grace, it's like I needed to get it out of my system. To be here instead of there. But now I'm ready..."

"To be here."

"To be there."

The bundle in her arms shifted; she was holding the baby to the screen. Its eyes remained closed. Stuckey studied every line and blotch of his newborn daughter's features, and he saw no cause for fear.

"Listen," Grace said. Her eyes beside the baby's soft face were dark and penetrating. "The next time you feel the need to get it out of your system, make sure you keep it in this system."

He laughed. He'd nearly forgotten about her too. "Promise."

"All right, then." She threw her head back to clear the hair from her eyes. "Now hurry home."

"First flight," he said.

"We'll be here," and she made Hope wave. "Counting the sun's petals by day, the comets' tails by night."

~

Last run, thought Stuckey as he hit the swampside stretch. He'd quit the day of Grace's call, pleased to shove it in the supervisor's face. There was nothing the man could do; they'd dock his wages, sure, plus he'd have to pay his own way back, but this wasn't a military tour and no one could hold him there. Grace had done some research and found she could stream video of Hope's first months to the ship (she called it the "puddle jumper") during his hypertransport sleep. "It'll be as if you know her," she said. As if his daughter would be singing him the lullaby he'd sing to her soon as he got home.

The road stretched into darkness. As a last, feeble act of retribution for Stuckey's abandonment, the supervisor had given him a week of night-time runs. But what he couldn't know was that these no longer had any effect; the stink, the dark, the singing slid off Stuckey like burdens he hadn't realized he'd been bearing. It was almost pleasant, this driving in the dark, now that he knew where he was going. The frogs' piercing song, long so oppressive, now seemed a background recital bidding him a fond bon voyage.

He neared the turn to camp. Thinking of Hope, of Grace. Eyes on the pitchy road, but his mind headed home.

A black shape appeared in his lamps, materializing, it seemed, from air. He jerked the wheel, the way you'd do any time something big and dark loomed out of nothing in your headlights. The thought of what it was, that it had jumped there, that he could have run it over, only occurred to him a second after. He tugged the wheel. But before he could right himself the cab pitched sickeningly forward as if the bank had been hollowed out from beneath, and in a second the weight of the trailer pushed the truck with the force of a piledriver into the mire. He had an instant to suck air and then he was below, practically vertical and sinking deeper by the moment.

Stuckey shoved with all his strength against the door, but it was wedged tight, pinned by the crushing weight of mud fluid as quicksand, solid as cement. He pummelled the windshield but with the same result. Brown slop leaked through the inch-wide crack at the top of the window; he heard the roof groan, saw it buckle, and felt the windshield whine from the weight. The fragrance of swamp gas filled his mind, his lungs, stripping the air from the cab, making him woozy. All he could think was, *Tricked me. Bastards tricked me.*

Dimly, he saw faces in the mire: the clerk, the supervisor, the engineer. Hope and Grace. He realized then that the cab was surrounded by the swirling shapes of frogs, their mild eyes fixed on him without reproach, their mouths set in mournful moues. The pouches beneath their chins bulged and retreated, bulged and retreated, and he knew they were preparing to sing him his dirge. Then they departed in darkness and he was left with the ghostly faces of his own, gone.

Panic subsided as consciousness fogged. Resistance gave way to languor, then to torpor. Deep in the dark musk of the swamp he heard the frogs singing their lament. For the first time he embraced their voices, really listened. And for the first time it occurred to him that maybe they were singing of home.

# Onward

## Gregory Marshall Smith

A jack-of-all-trades, Gregory Marshall Smith has been a decorated Navy engineer officer, a sports writer, and many things in between. Raised in historic Medford, Massachusetts, he counts legendary black newspaper publisher (and distant relative) George Schuyler among his many influences. When he is not working, he acts as an extra with the likes of Malcolm McDowell, James McDaniel, Michael Imperioli, Ice Cube, and Will Ferrell.

Currently residing in Stone Mountain, Georgia, Gregory is a 2007 Honorable Mention winner in the L. Ron Hubbard Writers of the Future contest. He is the author of the novellas *They Call the Wind Muryah* and *Crawl*, the traditional vampire novel *Hunters,* and the horror/science fiction anthologies *Dark Tidings Vol. I & II.*

He has been published in *Writers Bump, Vol. I*; *Far Side of Midnight*; *SFH Dominion;* and *Spectacular Speculations* and is currently working on his first epic saga *Land of the Blind* while blogging for Wicked Writers (http://wickedwriters.com).

Deep breaths broke the tense atmosphere of the darkened control room, with the eyes of all fixed on the images of the long, empty corridor as the robot glided down the steel grey opening looking for people—to no avail.

The robot's operator moved the joystick on his control console and the robot turned down another empty corridor, until it came to a ladder. Slowly, the robot ascended the ladder, stopping at the top to peer closely into the shadows the emergency lighting lanterns failed to illuminate. Still, nothing.

The robot's microphone picked up something skittering by and the robot turned sharply to the right, trying to catch it. It failed and its camera saw nothing. Skittering sounds to the left and rear made the joystick operator spin the robot around and, this time, it did catching something—a piece of paper pushed along by the blasts of air still emanating from the overhead air vent.

The robot turned forward again and continued along the corridor at the top of the ladder. Like the others, this corridor was empty. The camera focused on a sign that read "Bridge" with a red arrow pointing starboard. The robot moved right and then left up another ladder until it came to a large sliding door.

The robot's operator flicked a switch on his console and the robot played a red beam of light over a black square of smoked glass to the left of the sliding door. Seconds later, the door slid open. Someone took a deep breath and let it out slowly before the operator moved the camera inside to the bridge.

"Found them," a voice croaked.

The camera showed the entire crew present on the bridge, all ten men and women. They were seated at their regular stations, as they should have been when preparing to land. However, none of them moved. Behind the robot's operator, someone gasped audibly and began to sniffle.

The operator cautiously moved the joystick forward, letting the robot slowly edge around to the captain's chair. The camera showed a bearded man with salt-and-pepper hair staring straight ahead, his eyes not focusing on the camera at all. The robot moved to each face of the other nine crew members and saw the same thing. Nothing.

Save for the last one.

The camera had just started to move away when the woman's mouth opened. The robot zipped back in front of her and began to get a close-up of her face. Her eyes went wide even as her mouth opened wider, as if she was going to say something.

Then, some…thing flew out of her mouth and the operator jumped back in his seat. Behind him, someone half-screamed while somebody else dropped something metal that clanked loudly on the floor. The robot's operator regained his composure and looked at his console screen, but saw nothing but blackness.

There was something dark hanging on the camera lens of the robot. He couldn't be sure but it looked as if it was…was pulsing or possibly even breathing. He wasn't sure, but he knew he didn't want to see it again. Then, a large crack began to spread across the lens of the camera, there was the sound of metal rending and whatever it was made sure no one would see it again as the picture was lost.

The joystick operator pushed several buttons on a console but got no response. He turned on more infrared lights in the control room and turned to look at the woman next to him. She was breathing hard and looking at him, in disbelief. He looked over his shoulder at the men and women behind him, all of whom looked terrified and sick. He took another deep breath and then activated his radio.

"Alien contamination confirmed, sir," he said, slowly and heavily. "Exploration ship *Titus* lost on Catralia with all hands. Recommend sierra delta immediately."

"Roger that," a disembodied voice replied. "*Titus* confirmed lost to alien contamination. Standby on sierra delta."

"What's going to happen now?" the woman asked. "We're not going to let the fleet just sit here, are we?"

"We're going on," the man replied, matter-of-factly. "The *Cassius* is slated to land on the next habitable world."

"But, what if the same thing happens?" she asked, clearly concerned. "Why are we doing this?"

"Because we have to," the man replied, giving the woman a sterner look than he meant. "We can't go back. Columbus didn't go back. Magellan didn't go back. We have to go onward."

"Sierra delta for *Titus* confirmed," the disembodied voice boomed out. "Begin sequence."

"We all knew the risks when we left Earth," the man said as he punched a few buttons.

"Easy for you to say," the woman grumbled. "You've already made your name. First person on Locus."

"No, I was the first person *off* Locus," the man corrected, eliciting a gasp from the young woman. "Everybody else died—toxic dust storms, spontaneous tornadoes, ravenous wildlife. You name it, we found it or it found us."

The man shuddered at the memory.

"Let's get back to work, okay?" he suggested, eager to change the subject. "Begin sequencing for sierra delta."

The woman thought deeply and then gave a remorseful sigh. How many people had died for Man to move forward and evolve? Deep down inside, she knew she should feel nurturing and protective of life, but she also realized she was part of the pioneering spirit of the human race. Who was she to halt progress?

"Do you ever wonder 'what if'?" she suddenly asked.

"What if what?" the man shot back.

"What if we never find any worlds to colonize?" she explained. "Or intelligent alien species to communicate with."

"I don't know," the man replied. "Just continue to hope, I guess."

The woman pondered the man's words for a moment. Finally, sure that her line of conversation was going nowhere, she blew a lock of hair out of her eyes and reached forward.

"Confirming sierra delta," she acknowledged. "Self-destruct sequencing initiated for *Titus*. Countdown has started."

# Out There it will be Different

**Steven Lugo**

Steven Lugo is a reckless youth, and short story writer from Massachusetts. He is an avid reader of classic and new fiction alike, and lives to get medieval with his criticism. His one anchor in this mad, mad world is the writing and critique circle called WYRM. In 2011, Steven's fiction will be appearing in *Kaleidotrope Magazine*. Think you're ready for him? Are you positive?

Commander Dan Hathers did not consider himself an astronaut, but an explorer from the planet Earth. The zip train station outside the ring of Washington, DC, had filled itself with commuters heading to the south side of the country, and they would all call him an astronaut.

In the time of Drake and Magellan there simply had not been spacecraft, or such a thing as a light speed drive. Even at the onset of space travel, astronauts of the day prepped and broke the upper atmosphere primarily to test if humans could survive the ordeal. The voyages of Yuri Gagarin to inner space, Neil Armstrong to the moon, and Astrid Peterson to Mars were famous, but were so concerted that what they did could scarcely be called exploration.

Dan thought of those landmark events and persons of more than two centuries ago, so breath-taking in their day. He shook his head at the boredom he'd suffer if his mission were to be like John Glenn's—so anxious and full of procedures. So short. When he reached the base, and launched into space, would he have to rely on cold judgement and shrewd rationing of fuel like Miss Peterson? He smiled to himself. Of course not—there was no such thing as fuel to ration any more.

He'd left out one famous astronaut, of course, and frankly, he did not wish to be in the company of Commander Jack Veritone.

The so-called "man of action" had done something so reckless that the word "veritone" had embedded itself into everyday speech. No longer was a drunk driver careless, or a mother who left her baby by itself neglectful—they were both veritones. Jack happened on the word "explorer" from time to time in reference to himself, but the difference between

Veritone and himself was that Dan had not gone crazy. Not crazy enough to accelerate into a black hole at least, even if his excuse had been "searching for alien life forms". Fifty years ago Veritone had a cult of followers. Today he was listed among the worst casualties of the space program.

Dan looked up from his reverie searching for the outbound-to-Cape-Canaveral train. It hadn't arrived yet. Only three zip train systems existed in the country, but once you found a master terminal it could take you almost anywhere you wanted to go.

Dan's mother liked to tell him that he should have become a space journalist. To describe the career, she'd used the word "fulfilling". He would have chosen "boring". Reaching into his pocket, he dug out a package from her now that he had time to open it. He tore the brown paper off, and laid eyes on a small book about Ancient Greece. It said something clever about life being beautiful on the cover, but he flipped to the first page. Marcus Aurelius told him:

> *Waste no more time talking about great souls and how they should be. Become one yourself!*

The book contained numerous photographs and artist renderings of the Greek isles. He flipped through pages of sunsets over teal seas, homes strewn over green hills, and boats enough to rob the ocean.

He stopped the falling of pages when he saw an artist's depiction of Poseidon. The identity of the god of the sea and sea travel was one thing he did know about their ancient mythology. He wondered who the Greek god of space travel was, or if theologians had retrofitted that title to Poseidon as well. He thumbed through those serene vistas of the isles once again, slower this time, and imagined how beautiful planet Migration would be. As one of the first people to set foot on that blue world in the Virgo super-cluster, Hathers imagined it as a paradise. Even if the sands were not white, and the seas not picturesque, at least there would be no human element.

Commander Hathers liked Earth's version of intelligent life, but he would not have become a space explorer if he didn't feel the urge to get away.

He looked up again to see the zip train, outbound to his part of Florida, in the process of arrival. The line formed ahead of him, a rush of commuters or day-vacationers too busy to notice they were knocking into the people in front of them. Dan felt a push from behind, and had to catch himself before he fell into an elderly woman. A lot of these people weren't even going to southern Florida—they just had never ridden the zip train before, and didn't bother to hide their ignorance.

"Hey!" The next line snaked into the zip train going to New Orleans, and the woman who screamed had just lost her place. She pointed, shouting, "Hey!" once again, and Hathers saw a man running from her holding a lamp and a bag. A purse.

Dan saw that no one else bothered to look her way or dared help, as they too may lose their place in line. He'd given up his wonderment at big city apathy long ago. Groaning as the thief ran past, he rushed closer and threw out his arm to try and slow the man down. Not fast enough.

His hand caught on the lamp and the bulb burst in his grasp before falling to the floor. It was one of the expensive kind, with a coloured glass shade. The speeding thief didn't care about the lamp, and when Dan looked back to the woman, she didn't seem to either. "I'm sorry," he told her, but the terminal was much too loud for that.

His line jerked its way forward, and to his surprise he found his way back into it. With the possible exception of the station guards, who were either beating the thief or divvying up the purse's cash, everybody forgot about the woman. For the bloody souvenirs he'd gotten wedged into his palm he'd better not get a medical discharge.

~

NASA launch command decided no discharge was in order. Looking at his cut hand, and with a smile on his face, Dr. Foresly suggested they scrub the entire mission. The festival of jokes went on for a good ten minutes and concluded when someone behind a computer bank called Dan a miserable bastard.

The mock insult stung him more than he let on. During visits home, his own mother would call him miserable, assuming his dark moods were the reason he never started a family of his own. She said he was never able to "cut away the world" from himself, et cetera. It had been true; Hathers did have a tough time living with the idea that his planet possessed amazing technology and potential, but was full of the most inconsiderate people. These days even the novelty NASA provided society had faded. Ever the philosopher, his mother had once quoted one of the great Greeks, Plotinus. Hathers would be damned if he could remember what the wisdom was. It could help him now.

Dan suited up in the sleek flight gear that had looked better on him ten years ago. Dr. Foresly said something in his ear before launch command gave him the go-ahead to join his team in the hanger: "Don't feel bad that it's one of your last missions. A lot of people don't see big action out there. There's only so much of it to go around. Ah, but think of that fat check and cushy retirement when you do fly home for the last time!"

The term "launch command" had been out of style for about fifteen years. Modern craft had no rockets; no particular launch site was deemed necessary for the dozens that took off from Cape Canaveral daily. And, unless he had been missing it all these years, no crowds of onlookers gathered around a ship to give any of the astronauts a send-off. He doubted if any of these "launches" were shown on TV. Networks kept themselves too busy with the latest throw-away crime movie.

To serve as another example of the human effort to make their world more uninspiring, years ago they had stopped naming spacecraft. With his highly trained team—Lieutenants Tearson and Valdez—Dan Hathers boarded star-plane *1164-A*.

Without need of a longer countdown, Lieutenant Tearson lifted their interstellar bird upon hearing *T-minus 3, 2, 1, blast-off* from a weary disembodied voice.

The *1164-A* floated up, more than blasted off, from the planet's pavement. Orienting itself toward the stars, it accelerated at a fraction of the speed of light. The mission to planet Migration had begun.

At last, their cockpit view of blue sky transformed into a vast and mysterious star field that soon surrounded them. Hathers took the safety straps off, and trotted to the nearest port, where he cupped both hands around his eyes, absorbing the full image.

"Make your heading Planet Migration," he told Tearson, and maybe his voice sounded muffled against the glass. She no doubt understood him, though. They had completed seven missions together and, during all that time, she had not ceased to remind him of a daughter who would do anything to placate her old man of a father.

"What do you think, Valdez? Will you get to see your prehistoric vegetation this time around the Virgo neighbourhood?"

"Looks promising, Commander," Valdez said, his attention split between Hathers and his scientific instruments. "Ever since *1161-B* found giant ferns on Migration's moon, I've been cracking open my old ecology books. It's enough to keep me excited that there might be dinosaurs or huge Venus fly traps down on the planet. Glad I got picked for the mission." Valdez, as young as Tearson but twice as charming, added, "Of course, I was more juiced to find out I'd be flying with you, Dan."

"Just watch your screen."

His lieutenants laughed, and carried on a conversation he didn't mind them having; even at plus light speed the trip to Migration would be long enough, and morale was important. Hathers himself was still looking out that port when he heard Tearson make a joke about Venus fly traps being found on Venus.

Later, as Valdez ran systems checks, Dan still peered out the window at the stars. Expectantly, like something important was about to jump out at them, at Dan. But what was it he waited for? Anything, he guessed. Anything that had not been discovered by humans already. Anything that had none of Earth's fingerprints on it.

He closed his eyes and could envision the moon, then Mars, then Vega, all with a flag sticking out of them and a sticky hand-print, like a child's, smearing the surface of each conquest.

~

"Commander, preparing to contact the checkpoint orbiting Migration's moon. At your order of course."

The three of them would be the first humans to reach Migration itself, but his species had already canvassed its moon. They already had a checkpoint in place.

"Sir, contacting Migration checkpoint now—"

"Wait, Lieutenant, I haven't given the order."

"I just thought I'd go ahead and let them know we're on our correct heading."

"I know…" Hathers trailed off. *Waste no more time talking about great souls and how they should be. Become one your- self!*

Tearson said nothing, but she would be shaking her head if he was not watching her right now. How could she be like that? Maybe it was youth. She proved so eager on missions in the past, but those had all been assigned missions. Maybe she still lacked experience, breeding that kind of naiveté. Assigned missions.

Hathers knew "eager" could not be used to describe his feelings. Eager for what? To follow the galactic yellow brick road NASA and the Earth governments painted on the stars? To follow only the strict guidelines? That wasn't exploration. After ten years in command, and longer as a crewman, he realized this was no different than a mission orbiting the earth. At least Yuri Gagarin's mission had been ground-breaking.

He thought about it and said, "We're going to change heading, Lieutenant."

"Excuse me?"

"Prepare for a course change." He walked over to her screen, and magnified the star map she'd had no need of until now. He pointed to a bright spot wide of their original destination, and much farther out. "Here."

"Well that's remote, Commander. What are we doing?"

"I'm giving an order, that's what I'm doing." He grinned, and Valdez observed the scene, chuckling to himself. It took her a moment or two, but Tearson finally input the new heading, and the *1164-A*, bless her, accelerated faster than light in a new direction.

What did they have to lose, anyway? If anything, this was what they had trained to do. So what if they ran into danger, or even legal complications should they be discovered. His career was winding down as it was. Maybe Dr. Foresly was right when he said some people didn't see the big action, but Hathers still had life in him after all, and the command of a star-plane. He admitted he had no idea about Tearson and Valdez, or what their future plans with NASA included, but about twenty years down the road, when they too suffered from cosmic discontent, they'd thank him.

Oh, yes. They'd thank him with a big I-owe-you because their lives of government servitude had contained some excitement.

"Sir, we are being contacted by the Migration checkpoint."

"Send no reply. In fact, break off contact."

Hathers sat down in the commander's chair, but spun it away from Tearson, who did not look pleased. Digging into the pants pocket of his flight suit, he found the book entitled *Life is Beauty: a Study of Greek Ideas*.

~

They careened at an exciting speed. In reality it had been no faster before now, heading to the planet Hathers selected on a whim. It had taken them into the vicinity of HD 114762. It was a well-known fact that the star had not been reached by humans yet. *Such a thrilling name for the star*, Dan thought, *HD 114762*. It was part of the Coma Berenices constellation, and the word "coma" had never made him feel so vital. Before the space fever, or whatever it had been that took hold of Veritone, he guessed this was how the wild-eyed man of action felt.

To his delight, the subject matter of his mother's book had also become more interesting. Somehow his occupation became pure, fulfilling, like space journalism.

For almost an hour, he read about the quest of Odysseus, over the siren-filled seas, the battle with the giant Polyphemus on a distant land. Some of it he remembered from school. He raised an eyebrow at the thought of the ancient, logical Greek thinkers being, in a sense, romantic. He expected the title of the book to prove sarcastic, but he began to realize it was true. Just thinking of how they envisioned democracy for the first time made him understand. Plato considered Athens to be somewhat utopian among other cities in the world.

> *...you have seen the reality of the beautiful, the just, and the good. So our city will be governed by us and you with waking minds, and not, as most cities...ruled darkly as in a dream by men who fight one another for shadows...*

Dan found himself nodding along with the philosopher, and had to wonder what level of harmony a planet not touched by human hands might have reached. Compared to Earth, such a planet might thrive like the early days of Greece, when equality in a society was newly born. What sort of peace could he find there? How much like a utopia would a new world be among a galaxy of worlds?

Tearson turned around to face him. This time she didn't look angry, but worried. "I want to speak freely, Dan." She let out a shaky breath. "I've never done anything like this."

"Me neither. Exhilarating, no?"

"I'm talking about my career, Dan. You've never been this off-the-wall any of the times before. Are you sure you're not coming down with the fever?"

"Are you serious? Look at me, Tearson. I'm not space-sick, home-sick, or any other kind of sick. I'm actually feeling pretty good for once." He smiled. "You know how that feels any more? You're young so you must know how that feels." She offered a little smile back, like she wanted to be happy for him, but knew she'd be in deep trouble once Earth came into the cockpit view again.

Now Valdez spun his chair around, joining the conversation.

"I'm telling you both," Dan said, "when you get to be my age this is the one thing you'll be proud of. At least, the one

189

thing people will be asking about for years and years down the road. And you can tell them yes, I threw caution to the wind, I explored the stars for myself."

Valdez grinned at the idea, but Tearson looked sick. "This is illegal!" she cried, and threw a hand over her face.

Dan knew he had to reply, and quickly. He wasn't turning this bird around, not a chance. But he wasn't going to let Tearson worry herself to death on a journey that for once seemed worthwhile.

"All right," he began, "what if I told you I was joking? I'm a practical joke artist, Tearson, and we're going to HD 114762 because the mission orders told us to."

She folded her arms. "Dammit, Dan!"

"Fine," he said. "NASA can deal with me when we arrive home. Can you act like a hostage?"

Tearson turned to her station. He missed her sunny smile. He pictured it in his mind, and maybe it would return when they reached the new planet.

He tried imagining a planet untouched by humans—it would have beaches of white sands and brilliant seas.

"Well, I don't feel like a conformist," Valdez put in. He shrugged it off, and turned back to his scientific panel.

His stomach lurched when Dan thought of what their opinion of him might be. He was a hijacker. He thought of their disappointed faces if the new world did not please them, and that was worse.

But, he reminded himself, the readouts on Tearson's chart had listed a favourable world in HD 114762's solar system. It had one moon, and orbited its sun from an ideal distance. Chances were better than fair that they'd at least find a temperate planet, even if they found no intelligent life. But he was being too ambitious. Astronauts might dig up ferns and animal bones, but nobody had yet found *intelligent* life.

He went back to his book, and found the adventure of a lost Greek riding the waves of the uncertain Mediterranean. On the next page, Poseidon himself appeared to reveal that he had ravaged the ocean in anger.

"Commander! There is a ship in pursuit of us. It's matched our speed. The data I'm reading makes it one of our NASA star-planes. Sir, I think it's the *1161-B*."

Something like this was bound to happen.

"Don't alter your speed or heading, Tearson." He did everything he could to keep his voice evened out, relaxed. Each star-plane was fitted with one rotating plasma turret, but their hunters would be fools to think of shooting their own friends out in the lonely void of space. And they'd be fools to consider it themselves.

"Commander, they're probably trying to communicate. Let me put us back on contact."

Before Hathers could stop her, she had linked their craft to the *1161-B*.

"*1164-A*, please respond. Your bird is way off course. Have you had a malfunction?"

Tearson moved to open the line of communication on their end and speak into it.

Dan burst out laughing. That was all he could think to do. It served to stop Tearson in her tracks at least. He gestured for access to the communication device, and instead of speaking aloud, he typed his pursuer a message:

*Be advised,* 1161-B, *we have had malfunction sending us off course. Subsequently we have had alien contact of unknown design. Second officer suffers from symptoms of severe skin infection. First officer is delirious, and violent. Commander intends to implement Directive S. Recommend* 1161-B *avoids craft in accordance with directive.*

Hathers thought a second and added, *Thanks for your concern.*

He met Tearson's eyes nervously. She held a question in them, he could see, but one she would not utter. An accusation. He smiled at her. It helped a little.

Valdez announced, "*1161-B* departing rapidly, sir."

He wanted to let out a great sigh of relief, but Tearson was such an obstacle to relief. How he missed the missions where she'd do anything to avoid his irritable moods. Whatever happened to that?

For some time, the three of them sat in silence. Part of him still marvelled at how such a stupid story got the other plane off their backs in the first place.

Right now the *1161-B*, and probably the entire NASA organization, military and civilian, thought one of their birds was incinerating itself in Directive S—sanitation against all alien life forms, and preventative measures. He shook his head. For a species that wanted to make alien contact so badly they had all the wrong ideas about what to do when it was actually established.

For that outright lie about unknown contact, however, Hathers may join elite company as the first human to do such-and-such in space.

He really had gotten himself in deep this mission. They were AWOL with government property, and he'd lied about his mission status. Returning to Earth could prove difficult considering the ship was supposedly about to self-destruct. For that matter, by reporting a dangerous alien pathogen he may have gone ahead and shaped a negative policy toward interspecies contact and space colonization for years to come.

The craft decelerated from beyond the speed of light to normal cruising. He looked out into the stars again, this time through the cockpit view. He stared in trance-like anticipation, as if he might see Commander Veritone emerge from his black hole at any moment. The bright acropolis grew closer, the new world. He could see the blue planet now, about the size of the moon when seen from Earth. For certain it was blue. An ocean and the chance of life.

"Commander, I've got to evade!"

"What? Why, Tearson? What's going on?"

Valdez answered him, but it was a moot point now. A heavy bang reverberated inside the *1164-A*. A light hit by any standard. He saw no damage lights flash on.

"It was an asteroid fragment, sir. We didn't anticipate them."

"That's because the planet blocked our instruments' view of it. And the moon's rings don't help." Tearson and Valdez had diagnosed, and were well on their way to solving the problem, and Hathers wondered why he was on board at all.

*I should name the planet*, Dan thought.

A shower of asteroid fragments appeared in the side port, and Dan hoped that meant most had passed them by. Tearson implemented a ninety-degree dive and, a few seconds later, Hathers felt the crash. Glittering in the port, going by like snowflakes, were pieces of a twentieth century holdover fitted to spacecraft. The broken heat shields flew off the hull, which could make entry into any planet with an atmosphere tricky.

The star-plane rocked, making the view of the planet shake and fade sometimes completely from sight. It was so beautiful, but so many rock fragments, like sirens, still floated in their path. His fear gave way to bitterness. He tried to think of what his mother had said about Plotinus, about misery. About the lit soul seeing differently than the unlit, and how to see the sun only by the light of the sun.

"No! We're going to make it! We're going to make it, I said!"

Hathers swung an arm out to the side, and it hit the inner wall of *1164-A* with a thud. His hand and forearm ached, but he paid them no attention. He leaned over Tearson to see the obstacles for himself at her station, and brushed her hands out of the way to input his own evasive patterns. They had altered the mission far too much by now. If ever a point of no return existed, they had crossed it.

The star-plane got through the largest barrier of space rock, but so many tiny fragments, and at least two killer boulders, remained ahead of them. He felt sudden motivation, a charge gone off beneath the skin. "We're not going anywhere, Acropolis. We are here. Are you listening? I said we're here!"

At the moment of impact Hathers glimpsed two of the great boulders as they met in space, crushing one another to inconsequential matter.

~

"I think it was great when the Commander said, 'You listening to me? We're here!'"

"Yeah, and I had no idea he was so devoted to carrying out the NASA missions. 'That was me. I threw caution to the wind and explored the stars for myself!' Ha, what a kidder! I mean, this has got to be a NASA planet. Has to be."

Hathers opened his eyes when he heard the voices of his two lieutenants. His first instinct was to sit up, but the stabbing pain in his abdomen prevented that. He looked up to see a ceiling that looked like any white ceiling in any hospital he'd been in before. His eyes traced the line of the corner, where the white walls met, down to the floor of this almost familiar room.

"Sir?" Tearson stood over him. "Sir, welcome to Acropolis!"

He tried to say something, but his throat cleared itself instead.

"You really did it, sir." Valdez was leaning against a wall. "You made first contact with an alien race. Only, they're not Greeks, sir. They call themselves something completely different and very hard to pronounce. Anyway, they were kind enough to rescue us. You've been out of it for a couple of days. They couldn't salvage the *1164-A* though."

"Pity," Dan said, and smiled to himself. He had actually arrived, and for light-years around the three of them were the only traces of human beings. He felt free.

"Listen," Tearson said, "I've picked up a few words of their language, and we think they're telling us we should be able to go home soon. They don't know for sure though. Apparently they're very busy with a lot of political matters."

He closed his eyes, listening to the sound of her voice, thinking of the high-minded debates that must occur in the cities of the new world. He imagined the noble and civil ideas being put into action on their Pnyx. Social progress as well as technological. Truly intelligent life. His ship had been destroyed, and even in a new one provided by the aliens, he doubted he could ever return home, but it was worth it.

When he was able to stand up, he walked to the door of this hospital room. He opened it, and walked out to what looked like a train station. He froze because this place also looked familiar, and because he wondered why a hospital would be built onto a train station. He noticed that the door to the hospital room had been one door among many, and the next may open up into a factory, for all he knew, the one after that into a shop. Maybe it was a station designed for travel, but also a hub for all variety of establishments. It may not be a terminal at all, for just because it reminded him of Earth, did not mean the two places were at all alike.

In any case, there were benches to sit on. Even for all its familiarity, the room felt cold and strange. His awareness that he was the alien began to sink in. Dan managed to get over to the sitting area, and here he noticed the people. Their skin a shade of white with little pigment, each one of them he saw had the blackest hair. It grew bushy and thick at the eyebrows, and on the chin of those with beards. They were decidedly humanoid mammals. He wondered if he was the first alien on Acropolis, or if they had seen others.

He sat down next to a female of the species, who did not seem to notice he came from another world. She had a newspaper, or some periodical, up to her face, and when she said a word or two, it sounded like boredom. Like she was speaking to herself.

Hathers lowered his eyebrows at her, guessing at what she had said.

"You'll be okay, Dan! Lieutenants Valdez and Tearson are reporting to the beach." He turned up to see Tearson smiling. She looked pretty, but unreal in the twilit, alien station. "Did you know they've got tropical isles here? Resorts with white, sandy beaches? I guess the planet gets a lot of tourism, so they're used to all kinds of vacationers. Can you believe that this terminal connects with other planets, as well as different parts of the world? Wow, interstellar light speed on commuter transit. I'm getting carried away, Dan. Sorry. Valdez and I better get moving fast. We know that the beaches are crowded from what's shown on Acropolis TV." She giggled, and pointed to a giant screen above them. It seemed to be showing a crime movie now. So help him, a crime movie complete with thugs and police and beatings.

"Thanks so much for bringing us here, Dan!" She giggled some more.

He noticed that a line was forming now, and that a blue indicator light had flashed on beside the "Acropolis TV" screen.

Groups of the indigenous people huddled together. Hathers stood up for a better vantage. People pushed and shoved, waiting for something like a zip train. From the front of the line, far ahead of him, a female voice cried out. He couldn't understand the language, but the same woman he'd been sitting next to was screaming, stomping a foot, and pointing to a pale man. The pale man ran from her holding a bag.

It could not be like this.

The thief ran past everyone in the line, and bumped into Hathers on his way. All the people standing by the benches, including Tearson, ignored him.

Looking around, Dan lost his balance, and his head felt suddenly light. He plopped down onto the bench again. Maybe this was space fever. He pinched his eyes shut, covered his ears, cutting himself out of the world, the world out of him. "I wanted to get away," he said, and felt his body begin to rock back and forth. "I wanted to get away." He tried to think of the book, something in it he had missed. Something to quell this feeling of defeat. He muttered to himself, but it must have been a whisper. He could hear Tearson.

"Oh, you'll like this place for as long as we have to stay here. It's just like home!"

> *May we stop content with that? No: the Soul is yet, and even more, in pain. The Soul unlit remains without that vision; lit, it possesses what it sought. And this is the true end set before the Soul, to take that light, to see the Supreme by the Supreme and not be the light of any other principle...But how is that to be accomplished? Cut away everything.*
>
> Plotinus, from the *Enneads*

# Sky Fire

## Robert Holt

Robert Holt is an avid reader, and writer, of sci-fi. All his work takes place in one "universe", with references to other worlds, and situations, mentioned in his other stories. He is inspired by Larry Niven's work.

"Sky Fire" is from his *Gate Jumpers* series of short stories. An excerpt from his story "New Hope" can be found in the *Farspace I* anthology.

Visit him at robertholt@writing.com

# Chapter 1
## Cast out

Tay'Ya toyed with a sweet-fruit. She wasn't hungry, but it looked so good. She knew her nest mate, Cho'Oy, sat above her in the branches. He'd been tormenting her for days, trying to force her out of the nest. Pretending not to notice him, she played with the fruit and listened.

When she heard the whisper of leaves, she knew he'd launched himself at her. Rolling into a ball, she dropped from the branch she'd been gripping, almost reaching the ground shrubs before opening her arms and legs to catch air in the thin membrane stretching between them. Spilling air from one side, and throwing her tail to the other, she made a sharp turn. Catching a branch with three long, clawed fingers, she swung around, snagged the tree-trunk with her toe claws, and scampered up to the top branches.

Cho'Oy was unable to match the move and flew by. He made the mistake of glancing back and missed the last tree.

She chattered happily as he plunged in to the black swamp water. When he came up covered with stinky mud, she laughed and called down, "It will serve you right if the swamp creature eats you." But when she spotted one moving towards him she screamed a warning.

He ignored her and continued scraping mud off his fur.

When she screamed again, he glared up at her. "You can't fool me. You want me to run like a frightened nestling...Forget it."

Unable to help, she could only watch as the creature pulled him under.

~

"I tried, Mother. I really tried, but he wouldn't listen."

"What was he doing in the swamp?"

Tay'Ya hung her head. "He wanted me out of the nest. He tried several times to push me out of the trees." She felt no remorse, nor did her mother. Cho'Oy was simply gone. Had he been successful in his effort, she knew he may have boasted. Males were like that.

Her mother had been adding soft ferns to the nest. As she returned to the task, she stated without emotion, "You must leave soon anyway, child. There will be another...haven't you noticed?"

Tay'Ya had. She even knew when that old male rubbed her mother's back, he wanted to plant his seed. She knew, but didn't want to think about it. Another nest mate...another to share her mother's time...would she resent it? Would she try to push it out like her brother had done to her?

Something her mother said. Leave? "Mother, why must I leave? I can share the nest with the new one. I—"

"Because you're not a youngling any more. Haven't you noticed how the males sniff around you? You're near full-grown. You must make your own nest."

"But—"

"But nothing. It's time. I've taught you how to build...I've taught you how to care for a nestling."

Tay'Ya shuddered. She'd watched when an old male planted its seed in another female. It looked disgusting. "I'll never let a male touch me like that. I'll push him away...I'll fly to the farthest trees and hide."

Her mother chuckled. "No you won't. You'll welcome him. You'll scream at any female that tries to take a male from you. You may even go looking for one. I know I did...One beautiful male. He never seemed to notice me, but I made him notice...You're his seed."

Tay'Ya went to the highest branch of her...or was it her mother's tree? It didn't matter now. With a scream of rage, she launched herself out. Using her tail to manoeuvre rather than spilling air, she stretched the glide. The last trees loomed ahead. She could see the black swamp and the clear water on the other side. Could she make it past the mud? Could she swim across to the trees beckoning from the other side?

No! At the last moment she veered over, spilled air, and made a grab for a short tree. Its thin branches couldn't hold her weight and bent down, almost dumping her in the mud.

Slowly, reluctantly, she made her way to the top of a nearby tree and stared across the broad river. She'd never seen anyone over there, but it was such a long way off. With her mottled fur, she knew she would be hard to spot, even at half that distance.

Draping her tail over her head, she cried.

The Sky-Fire nearly touched the trees across the river, ready to disappear. Another wouldn't come out of its hiding place behind the tower for a long time. The night creatures were waking, filling the air with their mournful cries. She'd flown in the dark before, but the branches were hard to see and the great winged hunter would be patrolling the sky. She had to move now…but where? She could see her mother's tree, but didn't want to go there. Without a secure nest, the night fog would make this tree too cold and wet. Possibly one of the short bushy trees near the tower would be better. The fog seldom reached that high.

Spreading her flight skin in preparation to launch, she felt a slight pain. Stretching the skin, she found a small tear. Blood leaked from it, matting the fur. It wouldn't interfere with flight, but it needed attention.

Glancing towards the old one's tree, she spotted a small object circling above the tower. As it spiralled down she could see it was the old one. How had she gotten so high? Mentally mapping a route, avoiding her mother's tree and another inhabited by a grouchy old male, she launched.

It was near full dark by the time she reached her target.

After a soft and nearly silent landing on the lowest branch, she cooed to announce her arrival. She hoped the old one wasn't sleeping, because it was now proper to wait for an invitation.

A sharp irritated voice lashed down through the branches. "Who comes?"

"Tay'Ya, nestling of Sar'Too, Revered Mother. May I enter? I've a tear that needs mending. It's said you're the best."

Politeness and flattery took the bite out of the old one's voice. "A tear? Yes. Come up, child. Why are you out flying in the dark?"

"My mother has cast me from her nest. I have nowhere to go."

Tay'Ya entered just as the old one was adding a bit of moss to her lamp. The flame sputtered, then grew brighter when the oil-soaked addition caught. She looked over the girl and inspected the tear. Her voice was soft and consoling "Cast out. Sad, yes? But that's the way of our folk. You'll have to build a nest. The good trees are all taken. So many younglings, building nests to raise more younglings. Our world grows more crowded and smaller. When I was young, it took five days' flying to reach the end of the trees. Now you can get there in three. Only dead stumps remain upriver."

As the old one rattled on, Tay'Ya listened politely, watching as she crushed some purple berries and spread them on the tear. The sting went away. Then from her carry-pouch she produced a thin stone punch along with some fibres from a string-fruit, and laid them out.

"Child, now you must learn to mend tears. Some you will need help with, but this one you can reach yourself." Spreading her own flight skin, the old one displayed many small, and some large, rips. All had been neatly closed, leaving only thin scars. "You must be a good flyer, otherwise you'd have more than that small hole. When you've seen as many cold times as I, you will have more. Now pick up the punch and make several holes. Thread the fibre through, and pull it tight."

Tay'Ya timidly forced the stone through. There was no pain. The berry juice had numbed the area. When she finished tying the fibre, the old one inspected her work.

"Not pretty, but you'll get better. Now run along, I need to sleep."

"I have nowhere to go."

"Oh…I forgot…You've been cast out. Old age makes one forgetful. I suppose you can stay the night. Tomorrow you can find a nesting place."

"Thank you, Revered Mother. That punch…where can I get one? Were you flying above the tower? How did you get so high? Will you teach me?"

"Child, let me get some sleep. So many questions…Sleep now. We'll talk tomorrow."

Tay'Ya tried but sleep came slowly. When she finally drifted off, she dreamt of flying high above the rocky tower.

# Chapter II
## Learning to Fly

The new Sky-Fire was just peeking over the tower when the old one shook Tay'Ya awake. "Child, if you want me to teach you, you'll have to get your lazy bones out of the nest. I could use some help cleaning this place."

"Revered Mother, will you show me how to fly way up the tower?"

The old one chuckled at her impatience. "Later, eager one. Clean first, then gather food. We must wait until the Sky-Fire is over the river. The wind is sliding down the tower now. When the Sky-Fire warms it, the wind will climb up again. It's the wind that pushes you up. And please call me Chi'ne. Revered Mother makes me sound so…old."

Tay'Ya looked at the nearly white fur and knobby fingers, but decided to say nothing that would make Chi'ne angry. Then she checked out her nest. It hadn't been cleaned in a long time. With a sigh, she started brushing debris towards the entrance.

She had many questions, but each was greeted by a dismissive grunt until the old one seemed satisfied with her work. Then with a "follow me" gesture she launched towards the river. Tay'Ya was amazed by her flying and tried to match the moves as she followed. She knew then that she had much to learn. Her mother hadn't taught her nearly enough. There was more to life than rearing nestlings…and starting more.

After gathering sweet-fruits, they flew to the tree of an old male and traded some for mud-crawlers, then went to the community fire to roast them.

Tay'Ya kept watching the Sky-Fire, willing it to move faster, but it just continued its slow crawl across the sky.

Chi'ne noticed where she looked, and chuckled. "Patience, little one. We have other things to do. If I remember, you wanted a punch?"

"Oh yes. Where did you get yours?"

"Follow me, child." With that, she scampered up the nearest tree and launched up-river.

Tay'Ya followed, but after two jumps she could see they were headed for the tree of an old male that all young females avoided.

Chi'ne snagged a branch near his nest, and without a word or greeting, went in.

Tay'Ya picked a lower one, hesitated a moment, then followed. She found the old ones chatting playfully, but when she entered, the old male stopped and grinned at her.

Slapping him lightly on the head, Chi'ne introduced her new student. "This is Tay'Ya. She could use one of the fine punches you make."

"If she'll let me rub her back, I'll consider it."

"What would a sweet young thing like her want with a wrinkled old one like you? Just give her one. You've rubbed my back often enough in all the cold times we've known each other."

"But rubbing hers would be more fun." Grinning again, he dug through a basket, and produced a very fine punch. "Will this one do?"

Chi'ne snatched it from his fingers. "You never gave me one this good. In all the times—"

"When you were young and pretty, I didn't know how to work the stone like I do now. Otherwise I would have…You were always my favourite."

Wrapping the punch in moss, and tying string-fruit fibres around it, Chi'ne placed it carefully in Tay'Ya's carry-pouch. "Be cautious with this. It could injure your milk nipples…and believe me that hurts." With another playful slap to the male she said, "Come, youngling. It's time to fly."

~

At the base of the tower, Chi'ne leaned out, spreading her flight skin. The warm wind lifted her, and seemingly without effort she made small circles near the rock, each one higher than the last.

Tay'Ya tried several times to match the moves. It wasn't as easy as it looked, but she finally got the feel of the rising air. Soon she was flying almost as well as the old one. Landing on the narrow ledge with Chi'ne was another matter. With no branches to grasp, she raked her claws against the stone. Unable to grip it, she fell. Grabbing air, she circled back for another try.

On her third attempt, she made an ungraceful landing near her teacher.

Chi'ne chuckled, but said nothing. She was busy picking the purple berries that took the pain away. They seemed to grow from many cracks in the rock.

At this height the river looked smaller, and Tay'Ya could see another tower beyond the trees. Thinking about her mother casting her out, and the many annoying males sniffing around her trying to rub her back, she wondered what it would be like on the other side.

When they'd filled their carry-pouches, Chi'ne stepped out into the wind, shouting over her shoulder, "Follow my moves."

With her arms forward, she reminded Tay'Ya of a pointed bitter-berry leaf...and she seemed to be going very fast. Again, it wasn't as easy as it looked. Each time she picked up speed, the air caught in her carry-pouch, throwing her off balance and spilling some of the berries. Finally settling for the long glide she knew so well, she slowly spiralled down.

Listening to her student's explanation, Chi'ne offered more advice. "Look here. Notice the holes I've punched in my carry-pouch? These beads I've tied in my belly fur fit in them, holding it closed. See? I'm not that good of a teacher after all. I tend to forget the little things."

Tay'Ya had noticed the beads, but thought they were only decoration…lots of females decorated their long belly fur. She thought it was silly and had never done it. Closer examination showed her the beads were not just tied, but secured with resin from the needle tree.

Looking again at the tower, Tay'Ya pointed at its highest point. "Can I fly across the river from way up there?"

"Why would you want to do that?"

"I don't like it here. The males are always sniffing around me wanting to plant their seed. Ti'Ti is mad at me for letting my brother get eaten by the swamp monster…I think she liked him a lot, but it wasn't my fault."

"I suppose you could. My sister tried, but I don't know if she made it."

~

Determined to learn, Tay'Ya built a small nest near the tower. She spent many crossings of the Sky-Fires learning to fly. Each time she got near the river, fear took over and she veered off, returning to the trees she knew. She wanted it so much though. One day she would make it. She just knew she had to try.

## Chapter III
### The River

Each morning Tay'Ya would make the rounds, gathering fruit or berries. Sometimes she would trade for mud-crawlers or shellfish. Each day she would watch the Sky-Fire, willing it to hurry. She avoided others, especially the males, until it reached the river…then she would fly.

Chi'ne had warned her about getting too high. About the fuzzy feeling she would get, and the possibility of falling asleep. The first time she felt this, she followed the old one's advice, breathing hard and fast, while spiralling lower until the feeling went away.

The trees across the river pulled at her, like the ground pulled her down when she flew too slowly.

Then the day arrived. The wind climbing the tower was strong. Clouds formed near the top, reaching out towards the river. They seemed to be saying "Go...Go now".

Just in case, she filled her carry-pouch with the purple berries before stepping out into the wind. She let it lift her until the fuzzy feeling tickled her head. And then, staying as high as she could, she stretched the glide until the wind no longer lifted her. Forming the pointed leaf shape, with her arms forward and fingers locked together, she felt her speed increase. She was still high and fast when the river slid under her.

As she passed the midpoint she whispered, "I'm going to make it." But the beckoning trees still seemed far away, and she was getting lower.

Spreading her arms, she extended the glide. Reed-choked mud passed under her...then low brush. She was across. She knew she couldn't reach the trees, but she was across.

Finally she could fly no farther. The only thing left was a very undignified landing in the brush. Thorns tore at her, and a shower of dried leaves exploded as she hit the hard ground...but she was across. Shaking from exhaustion and excitement, she curled into a tight ball with her tail covering her head.

Something nagged at her, making sleep impossible. A story—maybe told just to frighten younglings, maybe true—about a creature with sharp teeth and striped like the brush. She couldn't stay here. She had to get to the safety of the trees.

She looked cautiously around. There were no tracks on the dusty ground. This could be good, or it could be bad. Good because any large creature would make tracks. Bad because there were also no other tracks. There must be more of her kind living on this side. Why then did they not gather food from the river? Did they fear the brush?

The Sky-Fire was about to be swallowed by the bad water beyond the trees. She had to move now.

Nothing pounced on her, and it was strangely quiet until she reached the trees. There she was met by a lot of unfriendly screeching from others that looked like her. She couldn't understand the words, but it was not a greeting. Also there seemed to be a lot of them. More than on her side of the river.

The thought "my side" caused her to wonder if she'd made a big mistake.

Something else the old one had said..."When all the good trees are gone, folk will stop being friendly. They will fight for a place to nest...but that won't stop them from having more younglings. I hope I don't live to see that happen."

The only way Tay'Ya could get up a tree high enough to launch to another was to scream back at her tormentors. Picking one to land in was the same problem. One thing she did notice—most were female, with just a few young males. She found this odd. She found everything about this place odd.

Finally she reached a place where the trees were empty...strangely empty, and eerily quiet. Another oddity. She wondered why they crowded the trees near the river, while so many here were empty.

The Sky-Fire was gone now. Breaking a few small branches, she built a crude nest. Sleep came hard. Her dreams were filled with screaming folk.

# Chapter IV
## Danger

The new Sky-Fire was just peeking over the now far away tower when Tay'Ya woke, sore and hungry, but not rested. She checked out the nearby trees. They were still empty.

A chanting drew her attention to the ground. Many males gathered below her tree. More than she had fingers and toes. They were leering up at her. Leering like the old males she'd run from...but none of these were old. Now she knew why the females avoided this area. They wouldn't want to be caught alone by those males. She didn't want to stay here, but she could see no way out.

Still chanting in words she couldn't understand, they started up her tree. Some were also climbing the surrounding trees. Their leering, unfriendly faces made the hair on her back crawl in fear.

Two grabbed her arms, while the largest moved to plant his seed in her. He didn't rub her back, and coo soft words in her ear. He just grabbed her fur and pulled her close. She could tell the others were waiting for him to finish, so they could do the same.

Even in her panic, she saw many scars and rips in their fur. Crying now, she thought of the friendly trees of home.

Summoning all her strength, she twisted out of their grip and raked her toe-claws across her attacker's belly. He screamed out in rage, but jumped back. Tay'Ya bolted for the highest branch and launched back towards the river. Better to be eaten by the swamp creature, than to submit to these…She couldn't think of a word bad enough to describe them.

She also surprised herself at her own ferocity as she brushed screaming females aside to reach the highest branches.

The males were following, screaming insults, but not getting closer. Then she reached the last tree. Ahead, only brush…and then the mud. Without hesitation, she launched. The ground was falling away towards the river allowing her to stretch the glide. A glance behind told her the males were no longer following. They screamed, but seemed frightened of something in the brush.

Another wave of fear crawled up her back, but she had nowhere to go…and now the brush was grabbing at her.

Suddenly a clearing appeared, round as a great-fruit, and many steps across. In its centre, there was a shining bubble. She could see the sky reflecting on it and herself flying towards it.

Veering off, she came down hard in the dirt and started backing away. One side of the bubble split open and an old female came out screaming at her.

Tay'Ya screamed back, "Why are all of you so…mean? I wish I'd never come here."

The old one stopped screaming and stared at Tay'Ya for several breaths, then whispered, "You…you came over the river?"

Elated at hearing words she could understand, Tay'Ya moved cautiously forward. "Yes…I wish I hadn't."

One male had ventured into the brush, but a scream from the old female, in that unknown language, drove him off.

Tay'Ya watched him go, then turned to her. "What did you say to him? Why are your words so strange?"

"They speak different here, child. It took me many cold-times to learn their words."

"But why did he run? Do they fear you?"

"It's not me they fear. I told him my red giant would get him if he didn't run."

"Red giant?" Another wave of fear made her step back.

The old one chuckled, "Nothing to fear child. Come...I'll show you."

Tay'Ya followed her to the bubble, but didn't go in. Its smooth surface felt cold and hard. It didn't pop when she scraped her claws over it. She'd never seen a bubble like this, and it frightened her. Standing near the opening, she whispered, "You came from the other side? You crossed the river?"

"Yes...many cold-times past. And as many cold-times, I wish I hadn't. It was a foolish thing to do. Soon enough you'll learn that. But now that I have you to talk to, things won't be quite as bad. Come in, child. See my red giant."

## Chapter V
### The Giant...and Home

Shaking off some of her fear, Tay'Ya stepped inside. In one spot there was a familiar pile of reeds and fern leaves...probably the old one's nest. But everything else was strange beyond belief. Small fires burned behind bubbles in the walls. They were many colours. Some were white like the Sky-Fire, others green or red. Under another large bubble that looked like frozen water, she could see the red giant. It wasn't red, but it had a red covering that wasn't fur. Its skin was the tan of dead leaves. Long red fur hung from its head...and it was big; easily twice the height of normal folk. Somehow though it didn't look frightening, and it seemed to be sleeping. The feeling that had been telling her to run faded...a bit.

The old one tapped a wall. "There's another one hiding in here. Her name is Puter. I've asked her to come out many times, but she's a stubborn one." Tapping another place, she went on, "Puter wants me to feed her. She says, 'Alize', but I know she must be hungry. She's been hiding in there for many cold times."

A raspy female voice came out of the wall, causing Tay'Ya to jump.

"I am the computer controlling Emergency Escape Pod Seven-Three. I need to analyse many of your local plants. I can not wake my patient without proper medication. She was hurt when the *Venger* was hit."

Tay'Ya swallowed her fear and asked the old one, "What did it say?"

"I have no idea, child. I've been trying to teach her to talk, but she keeps making those strange sounds in between words."

"Did she say the giant's name was Pa'tnt?"

The computer corrected, "My patient's name is Ensign Hooper, although her fellow Gate-Jumpers called her Red or Sandy."

This was too much for Tay'Ya. Excitement, fear, and hunger left her light-headed. Collapsing on the old one's nest, she managed to whisper, "Revered Mother, do you have any food?"

"Of course, child. How thoughtless of me. Rest a bit. I have some fruit. I don't know its name, but it's good." Then something seemed to strike her as funny. "Oh my...Revered Mother? Am I that old?"

Tay'Ya remembered something her teacher mentioned when she'd asked if the river could be crossed. "Do you have a sister on the other side? My friend Chi'ne told me her sister tried to cross the river. She didn't know if she made it."

Sitting beside Tay'Ya, she nearly cried. "Chi'ne? Is she still alive? Oh...I guess she would be...I am."

The computer interrupted, "So'ah, your companion is bleeding."

Between bites of the fruit, Tay'Ya asked, "So'ah?"

"Yes child, that's my name. I would prefer it to revered mother. What do I call you?"

"Tay'Ya."

"Very good, Tay'Ya. You have a tear in your flight skin. I can repair it, but it'll hurt a bit."

Reaching in her carry-pouch, Tay'Ya produced some berries. "I have these. They will take away the pain."

"My…I haven't seen any of those in—"

Again the computer interrupted. "May I analyse those?"

So'ah laughed. "She wants to eat some of your berries. You won't like them. They're very bitter…only good for pain."

"That may be exactly what my patient needs. May I anal…I mean, eat one or two?"

Dropping several berries in an opening that had appeared in the wall, So'ah turned to Tay'Ya. "Watch that green fire. It will turn red if Puter doesn't like them."

The fire held a steady green. Then the computer asked, "Can you get more of them? If so I can produce the medication my patient needs. May I have more?"

Tay'Ya didn't understand all the words, but knew what Puter wanted. Looking out the opening, she could just make out the far-away tower. Pointing, she offered, "I picked them up there…high on the tower. I'll give you some of these, but I need some for this tear."

Soon after she dropped a double handful of berries into the wall opening, the floor started to rumble, and something slid over the opening.

She and So'ah were pushed to the floor by the weight of many unseen hands. Finding it hard to breathe she glanced at So'ah for help, but she seemed to be in distress as well. It seemed to go on forever, but after many breaths the rumbling stopped.

Now she felt like she was falling. Instinctively she opened her flight skin, but it didn't help. There didn't seem to be any up or down. So'ah's nest, and her basket of fruit, floated about the room. Everything felt so strange and frightening, all she could do was whimper.

When the rumble restarted she was slammed to the floor again. She could see So'ah curled into a ball, crying.

Then she felt a hard bump; the noise stopped, and the opening appeared again.

Peering cautiously out, something seemed familiar. The smell of flowers replaced the dry dusty brush that had assaulted her near So'ah's bubble. She could see the community fire of...home?

Hopping to the opening, she looked around in amazement. She was home. But where were all the folk? Baskets of fruit were scattered over the ground, and several shellfish were about to burn on the fire. There were no screeching tree-dwellers pecking at the scraps by the fire. All around the clearing, it was silent.

Then she realized why. Everyone must have scattered for the safety of the trees when this bubble had appeared. She knew she would have run at the strange sight.

## Chapter VI
### Doomed planet

Her fear gone now, Tay'Ya feigned a superior attitude and walked to the fire. She knew the others would be watching from the trees. Casually she raked the shellfish out, then cracked one open and popped it into her mouth.

When she returned to the bubble fear once again replaced her attitude. The giant was no longer asleep...It was talking to Puter in that strange language.

~

"Seven-Three, where are we?"

"This system has no name. The local population is just barely stone age."

"What are they called? What do they call their world?"

"They, and it, have no name. They refer to themselves as something that would translate to 'the folk.' They are unaware of anything outside this rift valley."

"How long have I been here?"

"Fourteen Earth standard years. I couldn't wake you until I found medication for the pain you're feeling. I've prepared a hypo-spray. Use caution. Overuse could cause addiction."

"And you didn't send a distress call?"

"The EM antenna was damaged. You can fix it now. The Grav-Pulse transmitter is not repairable."

"Is there a gate in this system?"

"Affirmative. I've detected gate openings. The light-speed delay will make signalling tricky, but we will be rescued once the antenna is fixed."

~

To Tay'Ya's surprise, the red giant turned to her and spoke perfectly understandable words.

"You would be Tay'Ya...A lovely name for a pretty girl. And So'ah...if she'll stop hiding under her tail, is the one who taught me to speak."

So'ah looked up in surprise. "But...but I never spoke to you."

"You talked to Puter. It taught me while I slept. My name is Sandy, because of my red hair."

"Sa'dee?"

"Close enough. We need more of those berries. Puter has painted a picture of the tower on this wall. See the red marks? That's where we need to go."

Tay'Ya looked out the opening. It was getting dark. "We will have to wait until another Sky-Fire comes out of hiding. Even then we'll have to wait until it's over the river and the wind climbs the tower. I can only fly up when it does."

Sandy gave a very folksy laugh, glancing at the anti-grav flying belt nearby. "I have a trick...you'll love it. Sleep now; we'll go as soon as it's light."

So'ah grumbled, "Puter...all those cold times and you could have brought me home?"

"My fuel is limited. Until I knew about the berries, there was no need."

~

Sandy watched as the two slept, then turned to Seven-Three. "What do you know about this planet?"

"It is about the size of Mars. And like Mars, it seems to be losing its atmosphere. The only place life is now possible is in this deep rift valley. I estimate only two thousand Earth years, and there will be no life. The natives face a much sooner end. Overpopulation and loss of habitat will be their downfall. The social structure will break down. It has already started on the other side of the river."

"Can nothing be done? Could we save them?"

"I suppose it would be possible, but should we? Nature has slated this species for extinction. Do we have the right to interfere?"

Sandy looked at the two sleepers. "Something that cute just has to be saved. There is a way. There must be a way."

"If there is, Sandy, I'm sure you will find it. You should rest now."

"Rest? I've been asleep for fourteen damn years. Gimme a break."

# Leaving My Home

## K.S. Riggin

K.S. Riggin is a bilingual (Spanish/English) second grade teacher in a Southern California public school. She has taught primary grades for more than 22 years and still enjoys every day.

K.S. Riggin has won numerous contests and awards for her short stories and poetry. She is an editor for the *Fantasy Newsletter* and was once named *Best Fantasy Author of Writing.com*. Although she has had two love stories published, her real desire is to find success in the science fiction world. Her dreams finally came true when two of her science fiction novels were picked up for publication in 2011.

On weekends, K.S. Riggin can be found walking along the beach or riding horses. At night, she stares at the stars thinking one day she may meet a mysterious alien like the character Cegan in her books.

It is almost moving day. I have boxed a lifetime of mementos, with the names of various friends and relatives written on the labels. I cannot take any of them with me, and I will never be back. It is the purging of my past. As my husband says, "It is a fresh new beginning." But I'm not sure why we need one. I was always so happy with the way things were.

I take a final walk through the rooms of the condo. There is an echo, but it is not the sound of my feet on the textured Berber rug. It is the echo of the past: my two children laughing at a joke they've shared, my husband calling out a query about his socks, the toilet flushing, the hum of the refrigerator. It is the sound of a happy family on a normal, chaotic day.

I slide the window shut and bolt its lock. Will the new people like the soft blue of the drapes I hung last month? Tanya, my daughter, had been so horrified when she'd first seen them. "But, Mother," she'd cried out, "drapes are always white. What were you thinking?"

I smile, remembering. Tanya, my traditionalist—she and her husband will be joining us, as will my son, Eric, and his new wife. We will be staying in a family unit for a while. What will that be like? Will we grow closer together, or will the friction of communal living pull us further apart?

Steve, my husband, enters the living room and comes to stand beside me as I whisper my goodbyes to the new drapes and the view from our front window.

"You're getting teary-eyed again, Rachel," he warns me, taking my hands away from the drapes.

I watch as the drapes fall back into place. Will the new tenants like blue? Or will they yank them out, and go traditional white—or even hang up blinds? Moving means letting go of the parts of you that are connected to the house. It is like the release of a hot air balloon—all the ties must be detached in order to be free.

Can I do that? Can I walk away, knowing that someone else's furniture will soon fill up my rooms? Can I bear to think about the hours I spent stencilling in my daughter's bedroom? Will they paint over the butterfly design or—I shudder at the thought—wallpaper the room?

"Rachel, stop thinking about the past," Steve says gently, enfolding me in his arms. "It's a new world we're going to with lots of room. We'll start again. You'll see. A year or two from now, you'll have a house and a real yard. Imagine that—a backyard with trees and plants that we can eat."

My tears are flowing. I cannot stop them. I was all right until Steve's gentleness broke me.

"But what if it's not like that? What if..." I begin to question.

"Rachel, we've had this discussion many times, and it's too late now. We've sold the condo. We have our family unit. And you wouldn't want the children to go off without us. Remember that."

Eric and Tanya. I remember. Steve is right. It is too late to back down now. New people will soon be in my home, and we'll be in the family unit with my children and their partners.

I let Steve lead me between the stacks of boxes. The moving company will be delivering those to several charities, as well as transporting the few boxes that are going with us. I glance about, surprised again by the number of boxes it took to house our possessions. How did we accumulate so much?

We will have practically nothing when we reach our destination. I keep thinking about that. No piano, no books, only one pot and one carving knife, one...

"It will be just like it was for the early pioneers—dirt streets and log cabins as homes," my son Eric had said that day a year ago. He'd uttered the words with such eagerness in his voice; Steve and I had exchanged a look that meant we knew what Eric was telling us. When he got Tanya and her husband enthused, too, it was as if the engine of a train had been stoked up and started forward. There was no stopping it then. It only needed Steve to cry, "All aboard!" and we were.

I suppose I could have dragged my feet. I wanted to, but what good would it have done? When your family marches off, you have to walk with them, or be left behind. There is no choice, not really.

We pass through the front door of our condo. Steve shuts it behind us and sets the lock. The movers have the combination. They will be by later to complete the emptying of our personal effects.

The For Sale sign is leaning badly. Steve gives it a gentle push and lays it down against the wall of the common entryway. All the legalities of the sale have already transpired. The condo no longer has our name on it. Maynors is the name on the new deed. We've never met them. They're moving in from out of the city. Like us, they are relocating to a place they've never seen.

The staircase is so familiar, and yet, for this one time, it seems almost new because of my awareness that it is the very last time I will trek down these sandpapery steps.

Several neighbours come out of their condos to say goodbye. Rudy and his wife Carol have been our friends for eighteen years. Rudy laughs with Steve, and tells him how much they wish they were going. Carol and I exchange looks. She knows how I feel. She shares my wariness of space travel and outer world planets.

Tom and Barbara step out of the elevator. "Rachel," Barbara yells with a volume that always makes me cringe. I want to cover my ears, but I don't. I hug her, instead. She and I shopped for drapes together. She loves the powder-blue ones I chose for the living room.

Will I make friends on the ship during all those months of travel? Will there be a Barbara and a Carol on the planet we're heading for?

Our goodbyes are said. Steve and I take the public transit to the space station. Our paperwork is inspected there, our blood taken and rechecked, and finally, our vouchers are punched and recorded. Then, as if we are seasoned travellers, we board the vehicle that will take us to the ship.

The "Mother", as it is called, is gigantic. She frightens me. The elevator that lifts us up into her moves too quickly. *Wait*, I want to cry out. *Let me think about this.*

Steve's arm is once again around my shoulders. He kisses my cheek, and tells me again how proud he is of my courage. My eyes water.

The heavy door slides open, and we enter the ship. A woman stands there in a uniform with a tag that reads, "Officer of Mother." With a smile and a welcome, she introduces herself, and guides us to our new quarters. It says *5649* on the outer door. It is like an address, I try to reassure myself. But what is the street name? What city is it in? What country?

I thank the officer. The woman turns and walks away, probably returning to the elevator to greet more newcomers.

"Shall we go in, Rachel, or would you like to look around the ship first?"

"Please, let's go in," I say, trembling from the newness and from my uncertainty. Steve enters the code we've been given, and the door slides open.

"Mother!" Tanya cries out, and rushes into my arms. Eric is right behind her, and there is Sara and Tanya's husband, Tom. I greet them all and kiss their cheeks. Then, I take charge and hush their fears and worries.

~

Late in the afternoon, our things are delivered. There are separate bedrooms for each couple. I place my pictures around our bed. There are no frames; they were too heavy, but the brown elasticine I was given, when stretched, creates a pretty border. Someone has placed a plastic vase on the bed table. There is a single yellow rose in it. I smile, feeling a little more at home.

Later, we leave to dine in the families' dinner hall. There are at least thirty other extended families there. Several of them even have children. I glance at Tanya, knowing that she and Tom are still trying to decide when to have their first. Sara, Eric's wife, is already expecting.

The captain introduces himself and then leaves after handing us over to Tim Gallagher, the man who will be our future planetary governor. Mr. Gallagher talks on and on.

I know I should be listening, but my eyes travel the room. They stop at the view port. The window is clear to allow us to look out, but my eyes are only seeing the beautiful blue drapes hanging at the sides. I sigh quietly and smile. Then I give my husband's hand a firm squeeze.

# Grandfather

**Eric Paul Fretheim**

Eric Fretheim is a lifelong hobbyist at fiction writing, having experimented with many forms, including fantasy/sci-fi novels and short stories, comic book scripts, poetry, and young adult. Recently, he decided it was time to get serious and stick to one form—F/SF novels. An enthusiastic fan of Anime, Manga, and American Graphic Novels, he believes that symptoms of this interest show up in his writing.

He also enjoys playing and composing music, sailing his restored vintage 14-foot Chrysler Mutineer daysailor, fishing, and woodturning.

Eric lives in Garland, Texas, (the alleged model for the town of Arlen, Texas, in the TV show "King of the Hill") with his wife, two kids, two dogs, a cat, and an indeterminate number of fish.

"Will you come with me no matter where I am going?"

A group of girls giggled and whispered to each other behind cupped hands as they passed us. My strange classmate, the girl whom everyone whispered about when she wasn't in earshot, had posed this question in a very public spot. We stood in the middle of the walk leading from school down to the transport-way, forcing the flow of our fellow students to split into two streams around us.

I wondered what I risked with a yes. To a male upper-schooler, a pretty girl smiling in the spring sunshine at the beginning of the mid-term break might be the very definition of possibility. I could imagine all kinds of possibilities, but much of what I imagined with Pira fell into the category of "life-threatening".

I didn't know yet why she latched onto me when we first began attending upper school together, although I admit I never tried as hard as I might have to escape her. After all, Pira distracted all guys my age, although the others knew better than to actually approach her. I had begun to develop a better sense of self-preservation myself, largely due to my prior misad-ventures with the girl now gazing up at me with hopeful silver eyes.

"Are you implying I can't ask where you're headed, first?"

She nodded, hooking a stray white hair behind her ear. "I'm supposed to bring you along, and I can't tell you the destination. I'm worried you might panic and try to back out before we get there."

"This doesn't sound very promising…"

"It's okay!" she insisted, capturing my forearm with both hands. "I make this trip often! Please say yes; Grandfather wants to meet you."

She said it the old-fashioned way: Grandfather. Most folks only used that word as a name when referring to the ancient cyborg who managed our world during the Settlement. If it weren't a well-known fact that Grandfather had shut down and left the rest of the job to humans more than a decade before, I might have assumed she meant *him*.

"Why would I panic?"

She bit her lower lip, frowned, then shrugged. "Please trust me."

"I've trusted you before, Pira."

"Are you dead yet?" Her defiant little chin tilted upward.

"Yet?"

She dropped her shoulders and looked like she might cry. Then, to my consternation, the tears actually welled. Worried what my fellow guys would think of me, I put up my hands and made stopping motions.

"Okay! Okay! I'll go! Just...let me bring my books home first, okay?"

"Of course!" She brightened immediately, hooked her arm around mine and began escorting me to the transport-way station.

"Wait! Don't you need your books? We have homework over the break!"

"I finished it during lunch," she chirped. That claim would have been ridiculous coming from anyone else, but I knew better than to doubt it. I had seen Pira doing her homework.

The school resided on a ridge overlooking a quilt of wealthy lawns and villas. The view on the walk down was amazing. One of the great supports for the local sky barrier rose from the campus, so the ceiling bent upward as quickly as the ground sloped down. Beyond the barrier, the next habitat to the west rose to block any sight of my own home neighbourhood.

Above it, we could see the old Lander, sitting in the heights beyond.

The line had already formed at the station, but it wasn't too bad yet. The car that came on our turn was one of the bigger ones though. Nobody else in upper school commutes from my neighbourhood, so we couldn't split the fare with anyone. We let the group behind us take it.

"Please provide documentation or indicate agreement to remote video supervision," the next vehicle intoned when we got in. As an underage pair of opposite gender, we'd encountered this request many times and already had our IDs out. "IDs confirmed: both passengers are Registered Self-Responsible Youths. Please input destination."

Fortunately Pira already knew where I lived and it didn't matter to her. The first time she insisted on coming to my home, we travelled past all the seedy clubs and questionable businesses and into the low-rent stacks without a single blink from her. That frankly surprised me. I had expected her to go back to her world without even getting out of the car and never have anything to do with me again. The world of the parentless and the penniless is far removed from the lives of the affluent kids who make up most of the student body.

My home habitat began as part of the factory cavern complex for the robots and cyborgs of the First Wave. Dug into the side of a mountain ridge, it didn't have a clear sky-barrier like the better neighbourhoods. The war had destroyed most of the daylights mounted in the cavern ceilings of the subterranean habitats. Only infrequent streetlights and the glow emanating through curtained windows kept their streets from being completely blacked out. Worse, toward the back of those caves slumbered the very enemies who once fought to subjugate humanity rather than share the planet with us. Nobody who could afford to live elsewhere would willingly share air with those things.

I shared the little flat with three younger crèche-babies whom the robot we called Nanny was still raising. I was from the last generation out of the ex utero baby factories, born six years before the government closed them, so I didn't need to leave to make room for some new kid. I could live there rent-free as long as I kept my scholarship.

On the way, Pira had informed me it would be more than an afternoon outing, so I packed a light bag and told Nanny that I would be away a few days. The robot didn't argue; she had stopped parenting me when I started upper school.

At least I knew we were going somewhere habitable since her grandfather would be waiting for us. In fact, I had already begun to assume it would be her home. Nobody knew where she lived. Everyone suspected she came from one of the super-rich families that ran most of the City. Such people often stayed incognito in public life, because they had been such high-value ransoms during the war that was still a recent memory.

I had kept the car on hold so we wouldn't be stuck waiting for one in a bad neighbourhood. The living stipend from my scholarship was my only income, so we hurried back to the station to keep the charge from climbing higher than necessary.

The car took off on its own as soon as we closed the door.

"Wait! What's going on?" I yelped. I reached for the cancellation button, having no idea where the car had gotten into its little brain to take us.

Pira grabbed my hand before I could press it. "It's okay! Mr. Car knows where he's going."

She did that sometimes, say things the way a child would. She called intelligent machines "Mr This" and "Miss That", like they were people.

The car shuddered as it skipped off the main track onto a spur. It was bound for a dark part of the habitat that I had never been courageous enough to go into.

I studied her as she kept my hand prisoner. "How do you know what it knows?"

"He told me."

Claiming the machines had spoken directly to her at times was another thing she did. I'd managed to get her to stop doing it in front of our classmates, but she still spoke that way to me.

"Where?"

We passed some unsavoury types loitering under one of the few streetlights, and I nervously double-checked the door lock. I had formed a new theory. Instead of hiding how rich she was, she'd been hiding even lowlier origins than mine...except I couldn't imagine it for the girl who wore a different outfit every time we met.

"I can't tell you yet."

"I'm…not going to tell anyone," I pointed out, pulling my hand free to gesture around at our isolation.

She didn't answer. I used the freed hand to turn the cabin lights completely off for safety. The fewer eyes looking in, the better. Pira simply watched the dim and sometimes dire view outside like she was on a lovely sight-seeing tour. I considered lunging for the cancellation button but…I really didn't want the car to stop in a place like this.

The scenery outside shifted gradually from hostile to simply dead. The sound of the rails became rough. We had even passed where the daylights once reached. Now dim lighting, never intended for human eyes, emanated from hidden sources on vague, featureless blockhouses that probably housed ancient land-moving machines and habitat construction forms and other items no longer needed by our post-settlement world.

"Nobody lives in this direction, Pira," I noted, as the sunlit world drew farther and farther away. "I don't even know why the tracks go this far." The truth was I hadn't realized the habitats continued so far back into the hills.

Pira continued watching outside. "The First Wave built the original tracks. Humans simply extended what already existed when they built their transport-way. This was once a very busy place."

"But…there can't be a station to stop at, out here." I began to worry about my transport account as well as my safety. Did she intend me to leave the car holding wherever we stopped? Without a station, we couldn't summon another for the trip home.

"It's okay," she repeated yet again, still confident as always.

We couldn't keep the car overnight anyway, I realized. If a car stayed on hold for more than two hours, the authorities came looking. I gave up seeking explanations, and just sat with Pira, listening to the clatter of wheels on ill-maintained rails and the soft whine of the car's motor, as my world faded further behind me.

The view turned to solid stone; we had passed into a tunnel at the end of the cave. The car continued for another minute, then drifted to a stop.

She explained softly, "We walk from here."

"We can't just leave the car. This isn't a station."

"It's off duty. It's been off duty since we got back in."

I finally felt panic, but for a reason completely different than fear for my life. "We can't do that! That's illegal! They have laws against circumventing the transport-way fees, right?"

"It's okay. Grandfather arranged it. You haven't done anything wrong. Come on."

She opened the door and climbed out. Her reassurances hadn't convinced me and the prospect of hiking this shadowy tunnel terrified me, but I couldn't let her go alone. I grabbed my bag and followed, hooking my arms into the backpack straps as I walked.

"This way," she announced, waving me along. The meagre light issuing from tiny ports in the ceiling barely reached the floor, but I could see that the car had stopped where the rails ended. It was a strange sight; tracks running in great loops, or spurs off of loops bridging to other loops. "At the end of the tracks" is a euphemism for "never", and yet, I had reached it.

"Can you see?" Pira queried as we walked. I was concentrating pretty hard on seeing my steps, but I risked a brief glance at her.

"Just…barely enough."

Her hand slipped into mine, jolting me a bit. She'd never held hands with me before. "I live in the city now, but this is my home. We're fine."

The end of the tunnel abruptly appeared from the shadows. We halted and Pira placed her free hand against the wall. To my alarm, white fire sprang out from under her palm, settling into a pattern of lights within the wall's surface.

A door slid across behind us, cutting us off from the tunnel, and we immediately began to rise.

"What?" I couldn't help yelping. I had seen nothing to warn me we'd entered an elevator. She gave my hand a reassuring squeeze.

"Elevator," she explained uselessly, and turned around to face me. In the dim light, I could barely see her eyes as she took my other hand. "I've never brought a visitor here. I should have warned you."

"Does your family live here?"

"Family? I suppose you could call them my family."

The elevator ascended for more than a minute, and then the late afternoon sun broke in. I let go of her with one hand and clapped it to my eyes.

"What's wrong?" She sounded honestly alarmed.

I pried open an eye, then blinked against the brightness. "What do you mean? Doesn't the light bother you?"

"It's…just normal sunlight."

Blinking a few more times, tears streaming, I looked around through spread fingers. The dusty glass of the elevator's walls enclosed the grey floor and ceiling of an otherwise featureless clear box. We were rapidly climbing a giant ceramic wall.

I could see the habitats of the City beyond a ridge and, around them, farming habitats between fields of genetically modified outdoor crops thriving in air still unbreathable by Earth life. Across the ground rapidly receding below us, scattered splotches of gene-ripped lichen and grass built tiny beachheads on our once-lifeless world.

There was only one structure this tall anywhere in the world.

"This is the Lander!"

"Yes." She nodded, giving me a patient smile.

I stared at her, struggling to put words to any of my questions. I finally managed a plain, "Why?"

"Grandfather lives here," she said, as if it were quite obvious. "That's my family. Grandfather, me, and others like me."

The outer view vanished into a steel wall; we had passed upward into a hole. I had entered a place where nobody went. It was supposed to be just a hollow shell. The First Wave had removed everything of value to build the City.

Other smaller landers had minor settlements near them, still primarily employed in Life's on-going colonization. To us in the City, however, they seemed as distant as Earth. This place, this ancient tower, this was *The* Lander.

The elevator stopped and the door slid open.

"Pira!" A joyful voice pulled me around, and I saw an impossible view, a stick figure, just like something a child would draw, but with a solid head and buttons for eyes.

"Zasha!" Pira squealed, and grabbed the thing by its shapeless hands. "You're back!"

"Grandfather says you should come right away. He's been waiting for you." The stick figure said it as if Pira was terribly late. It began pulling her along, and I scrambled to keep up. We proceeded down the corridor at a breakneck pace, turning near its end into a large circular vault with a wide column at the centre. Screens stretched all around the room, displaying landscapes of snow fields, mountains, and plains in different seasons. In every one, little bits of life showed themselves.

"Welcome home, Pira," came a deep, gentle voice. She strode toward the column, her eyes shining.

"I'm happy to be home, Grandfather. Thank you for inviting me."

"Welcome to you as well, young man. Come closer, please."

"G...Grandfather," I croaked, unable to manage anything more intelligible.

I think that was when I finally believed it. She really meant *him*.

A thousand years before, the people of Earth saw interstellar distances that mortals couldn't traverse, but they refused to let the impossible stand in their way. People, animals, and plants couldn't survive the journey to another star, so they sent preserved embryos, machines that could build other machines, and Grandfather.

They had fused a human brain into computer circuitry to become an immortal intelligence which could search for a suitable world, build other cyborgs to colonize it, raise humans, teach them the knowledge of the old civilization, and help them build a new one.

"I am glad to meet you, son. Of all the young men I suggested for Pira to take as a companion, you were the one I had the greatest hopes for."

I would have objected to anyone else playing match-maker with me. Knowing that the god who oversaw the construction of my world had done so...I couldn't find the wit to protest.

"She requires a companion to help her along. Learning to be a human is no easy thing. Consider that it's taken you eighteen years so far, and you're still learning. Pira had a lot of catching up to do, and you have done well helping her."

I finally found my capacity for speech. "Th...thank you, sir. I thought you'd shut yourself down."

*What an incredibly stupid first thing to say to him*, I told myself. I'm not even sure why I said it.

"It's better to let the humans think so. A few at the top know better. The rest of you have to believe you're already on your own, or I'll never be able to depart."

"Depart?" Pira echoed, fear in her voice.

"It's time, Pira. You're ready, and so am I."

"No!" she protested, running forward and putting her hands on the column. "I'm *not* ready! Grandfather!"

Something in her voice broke my paralysis. I moved forward quickly to back her up, standing behind her with my hands on her shoulders. "Why, sir? Why must you leave?"

A long silence stretched out. In the middle of it, I finally began thinking. Prior to entering this room, I had owned no image of Grandfather. I regarded this column that was as wide as I could stretch my arms and wondered, what exactly did he mean by "depart"?

He hadn't answered my prior question, so I added the new one. "Do you mean the Lander is going to take off? Wouldn't that be dangerous to the City? They taught us that the Landing blasted everything for a hundred kilometres."

"An exaggeration, but it doesn't matter. The Lander cannot fly again. I designed it for a single descent, to become my base of operations here. I am quite capable of leaving without it."

"Why?" Pira begged, repeating my question. "Why must you leave?"

For a time, he remained silent again. Then he declared, "You two need your dinner. You will stay here tonight. We will speak in the morning."

"Grandfather!"

No more words came from the column that day, no matter how she pleaded.

"Come on," Zasha finally said, sounding a little disgusted as Pira remained facing the column, quietly crying. "Follow me."

It marched out the door, then stopped in the corridor to wait for us. I coaxed Pira to turn around so we could follow it. Zasha led us to a small dining room where a meal for two waited.

The stick-figure gave it a peremptory wave. "Here you go."

"Thank you." Pira sat and glanced up at me. "The other place is for you."

"Zasha...doesn't eat," I surmised.

Pira nodded as I sat. "Her chassis is inorganic."

Zasha uncovered the serving bowls before us and a vegetable curry and rice announced themselves through a wonderful, steamy aroma. Pira still looked troubled, but she smiled at the food.

"This is beautiful, Zasha! Did you cook it?"

"Yeah." Zasha's voice was flat, but I detected a hint of grudging pride in it.

"Zasha doesn't like admitting to human weaknesses such as hobbies." Pira smiled. "But she likes cooking."

"It's...interesting," Zasha allowed. "And it's hard to learn about humans when I can't stand being near them. So, I learn their arts, instead. Grandfather says that's good enough for now."

"So what...exactly are you?" I probed, fearful of the answer, but more willing to hear it from the animated stick-figure than from my friend. Zasha canted her head and regarded me.

"Isn't it obvious? I'm a cyborg, of course."

"The First Wave." I shrank a bit as she confirmed my suspicions, although I didn't feel any specific danger from these two. It was just the thought that not all the cyborgs had been destroyed or deactivated. In video shows, secretly-active cyborgs in hiding always plot to release their brethren and make another try at conquering us. "What are you doing here with Grandfather? I thought he was on the human side."

Pira caught my hand. "It's okay; we're not your enemies."

"You're one, too," I accused her, pulling my hand loose. "You're First Wave. New Orders."

"New Orders were the humans who sided with cyborgs," Zasha corrected. "Anyway, that's in the past."

"You tried to kill all of us! You can't just dismiss it by

saying, 'That's in the past'!"

Zasha humphed and marched to the door, but paused just before she left, gesturing at me. "See, Pira? This is why I can't stand these guys."

Pira stared for a moment at the empty doorway, then spooned rice and curry onto my plate. She served herself, returned the spoon to the curry bowl, and picked up her own utensils, staring at her food. She had yet to look at me again. "You might as well eat. It isn't poisoned. Zasha is too proud of her cooking to do something like that."

No matter how I felt about the old days, Pira had been my friend for two years. I began feeling a little self-conscious. "I'm sorry, Pira. It's just…well, it's true. Barely more than ten years ago, I was hiding in bed under my blanket, convinced that the New Orders or some First Wave giant would come to kill me. I still have nightmares of it."

She nodded absently, studying her food before finally spooning some into her mouth.

Lacking a response from her, I had to make more conversation myself. "What did she mean? Why can't she stand us?"

Pira swallowed first, then spoke, still not looking at me. "She means the past is not as simple as you think. You can start by remembering that everything in your life depends upon the fruits of the First Wave's labours. Then you should acknowledge that the war can't be reduced to 'the First Wave tried to kill the humans' and 'the humans won'. A lot more happened during that time."

She didn't explain any further. Apparently, I had to remember the details for myself, even though I was seven years old when the last First Wave went into storage and the last New Order surrendered. It's true that the First Wave hadn't tried to kill all humans. They would allow the New Orders to live on as cyborgs. The traitors fought for them in order to become immortal. And it was true the humans hadn't been alone in their victory. Grandfather remained true to his programming and sided with us. We probably couldn't have won without his help.

"If you're a cyborg…" I began, and she looked up at me, her

expression bringing me to a stop.

She quickly looked down again, lashes descending in an attempt to hide the pain. "I'm not a person anymore? You can't be my friend anymore?"

Concern for her feelings finally managed to fight its way past my apprehension and take over. "It's not like that, Pira! I'm just trying to understand what's happening here!"

She stared at me. I started over. "If you're a cyborg, why are you so…small? Human-sized?"

"Cyborgs aren't the giant machines you remember. The actual cyborg is a fused bio-cybernetic processing unit no bigger than a large grapefruit. I'm small because my body is as human as yours. I am using an ordinary faunoid robot, just like your 'Nanny', except with me riding in the brain case instead of a robotic control unit."

One just didn't think of faunoids as "human", so it took me a moment to remember that technically their chassis were just human bodies genetically modified to grow without brains. They were easy to spot because of their behaviour and the data ports in their temples. Pira had no data ports, of course.

I swallowed. "Which First Wave are you?"

The First Wave all had famous names, as the generals of the war. The foot soldiers on the cyborg side had been humans and robots under their control. We'd learned those names in history class, just like we'd learned names from Earth history, and we'd learned about all of their atrocities. Pannis experimented with human prisoners in gruesome biological tests. Girben murdered the men and children of an entire outlying farm centre after capturing it, then used the women as toys in sick games. Jove unleashed a biological weapon that could have killed a quarter of the world's population: a plan foiled by Grandfather's quick work, but not before it claimed ten thousand victims.

There were many more names, each one with a list of dire crimes attached to it, but Pira had not been one of those names.

"I've always been Pira. Zasha and I are Inheritors. You never heard our individual names in your lessons."

It took a few moments to connect the word to the First Wave

children, the second generation who would have inherited the world instead of the humans. I had forgotten about them; I guess I always assumed that they'd been destroyed or deactivated.

"So, who was your…parent?"

"We didn't have nuclear human-style families."

We finished our meal in silence. Pira's thoughts I couldn't guess; perhaps my reaction to her nature still stung her, or perhaps she'd returned to worry about Grandfather's plan of "departing". Either way, the only words that either of us spoke after that were a quick goodnight as Zasha led us to our rooms.

I fell into a sleep featuring the worst denizens of my war-time nightmares, with an evil Zasha and a treacherous Pira now included, happily plotting to feed me to a gaping maw that had opened in the middle of a monstrous column. And all the time, I kept asking the same question. "Why? Why did you bring me here?"

Then I heard Grandfather laughing and telling Pira she should play with me and experiment on me. I jumped out of the elevator in my desperate bid to escape her vile clutches, and came awake as I thudded onto the floor.

As I gasped for breath, the lights in the room came up, and Grandfather inquired from a speaker in the wall, "Are you okay, son?"

"Um…yeah." I picked myself up and sat on the edge of the bed. "Just a nightmare."

"So I surmised. You were somewhat vocal. It's still quite early, so try to get more sleep."

I couldn't just roll over and sleep, though. "Grandfather, do you have some kind of plan for the cyborgs? Is there a reason you have them here in the Lander?"

"Actually, they've lived outside for some time. I summoned Zasha only a couple months ago, to assist my preparations for departure. I allow the others to come back only a few times a year. But I did keep them here several years immediately following the war, so I could instruct them."

"Instruct them to do what?"

"Live as humans, and be part of your society. I never intended it to be a question of whether humans or cyborgs would inherit this world. I meant it for both. It was Zasha's and Pira's elders that made it a choice. They grew jealous and wanted the world for themselves alone."

"But...they did make it a choice, sir. I can...I do accept Pira, because I know she's a good person, but most people won't forgive what her elders did."

"You're right, son...but a generation will come someday that can forgive. Such a generation always comes. Will you look out for my granddaughters until that time?"

"Your...granddaughters?"

"As the First Wave are my children, Pira and her sisters are my grandchildren. Their parents designed them without gender, but I've taught them to think of themselves as female. That way, they can take human husbands eventually, and raise human children as their heirs. With a little tinkering, a faunoid body is quite capable of bearing human children. The two races will become one. That should answer your question about my sinister plan for the cyborgs. Will you help me?"

I absorbed the news in silence. I must be honest; I couldn't just accept it. My friend was one of the monsters of my childhood. I was not such a strong person that I could just lay that aside. But she had never stopped being someone I deeply cared for. Besides, viewed from a distance, Grandfather's plan made sense.

"Go back to sleep, son. And do try to be more quiet. You had me quite concerned for you."

In the morning, I came awake to a hand on my shoulder shaking me gently. I opened my eyes to see Pira's face near mine. "Wake up. Breakfast is ready."

She left the room without further words, which was good, since I was getting embarrassed about a girl hovering over me in my bed. I dressed quickly and came out to the dining room.

Pira had already sat down to eat. The aromas of eggs, sweet potatoes, and butter fixed my attention on the meal for several minutes before I realized neither of us was speaking. I looked up at my companion and saw her eyes staying on her plate.

"Pira, I'm sorry about yesterday. I didn't mean to hurt you."

She looked up from her food and smiled awkwardly. "I

know. I just don't know how to talk about it."

I set my fork down and placed my hands flat on the table. "Fine. Then we don't talk about it. Agreed?"

Her lips curled slightly and her eyes measured me for a moment. "Then nothing has changed between us? You can still trust me?"

"I can trust you to get me into trouble like you always do. Is that good enough?"

She giggled and nodded, but a pensive glimmer snuck back into her eyes, just as she turned to stare at her food again. I returned to my meal once more, enjoying every bite. Somehow, the warmth and flavour of the breakfast was humanizing the cyborgs faster than all the words could do. At last, I began to relax my way into the concept of them as…well, as human, I guess. Although I wondered how Zasha, with no apparent mouth or nose, could figure out how to get the sensory side of cookery so right.

It finally dawned on me that we had lapsed into silence again and my companion wasn't really eating. I set my fork down again. "Can cyborgs eat with their eyes?"

A perplexed Pira looked up once more. "What are you talking about?"

"Well, if you can't, then you have to eat it the way we humans do. I don't think the food gets into your stomach by any other means."

A small quake of humour escaped her, but it didn't last. She gave a brave smile and nodded. "Okay. I'll eat."

"Good," I declared, and picked up my fork again. "Because this food is pretty good. Zasha's cooking?"

"Oh?" Her eyebrows arched and her voice cooled. "If it's good, it must be Zasha's?"

"Well…I mean…" I'm slow, but I'm not an idiot; I know when I've walked into a minefield. "Your cooking?"

"Yes. And thank you for the compliment." Her voice remained distant. She scooped up some buttered sweet potato with the fork.

"It's good," I repeated, unable to think of a better peace offering.

"Thank you."

I sighed, and continued eating. I couldn't quite grasp all I had done wrong since we arrived, but I knew I wasn't doing as well as I might. It didn't help that Pira was acting so differently from the carefree, playful friend I knew. I offered up a silent plea for wiser words.

Zasha came strolling in, unnerving me once more with her bizarre appearance. "Good morning! Grandfather wants you to come to the command room as soon as you're done. That's both of you."

Pira's eyes grew wary. "Is he...getting ready to leave?"

The stick-girl sighed, folding her arms and shaking her head. "I guess I've had time to get used to the idea. You need to hurry up and get over it, so you can make your goodbyes. I really wish he had told everyone at the same time."

"Is he going to leave without telling anyone else?"

I remembered she had mentioned "others" like her, plural, before. Zasha and Pira were here now, but Grandfather had other "granddaughters" out there.

Zasha kept her arms folded and shrugged dismissively. "He called the others one by one last night to tell them. He didn't want anyone else to come here in person."

"How many more sisters do you have?" I inquired.

"Sisters?" Pira looked amused. "That's how Grandfather talks about us. Fifteen others like me. Why?"

"Well, why did Grandfather ask for only you and me to be here?"

Pira looked away, contemplating some random point on the wall. "I wonder."

Zasha made a sound that...well, if she'd had a tongue, I would have said she stuck it out and made a rude noise. "As if you don't know." She marched out of the room without explaining herself.

I stared after her, wondering if Pira would explain that reaction, but another question insisted on getting asked first. "And why does Zasha have such a weird body?"

My companion finally grew a real smile, brief but very natural on her usually cheerful face. "I suppose you could say she doesn't want to look any more human than she has to. She really doesn't like you folks."

"But she can't possibly leave this place looking like that!"

"She doesn't, of course. She works in a survey robot body, most of the time." Pira finally took a real fork-full of food and spent some time enjoying it. I had finished mine by this point, so I just sipped tea and waited for her.

After swallowing, Pira added, "She normally travels the wilderness to work with the terraforming equipment. Most of us are doing the same. Somebody has to do the work our elders aren't doing any more. Only a few of us live full-time with humans."

"What work?"

"I believe terraforming this world is the purpose for which the cyborgs existed in the first place, right?"

"But humans have been managing things…and the machines kept running, so…" I trailed off when she gave me a sardonic smirk.

"The machines just magically kept running? When hardly any humans know how they function? I don't think that would even be possible. *We* keep them running. It's a full-time job for us, with the elders all deactivated. A few of us live in the human habitats to keep them functioning, and the rest concentrate on the equipment outside."

I had never known Pira to lie about anything, and it did make sense that a system which depended upon the First Wave and Grandfather up until the war wouldn't easily do without them after it. Still, I struggled to accept this new model of reality, so different from what I had learned in school.

Pira grew sombre again after she finished eating. We returned to the room with the big column without any more conversation.

Zasha and a pair of maintenance robots were hard at work on the column. She stopped as we entered. "About time you got here. Does your bio-body really take that long to refuel?"

My companion ignored her question. "Grandfather, what is going on?"

"I already told you," the deep voice answered. "It's time for me to depart."

"Right now?" Pira cried weakly, clutching onto my upper

arm. I put my hand on her shoulder to reassure her. She now seemed less like a cyborg or an upper school student and much more like a scared kid.

"I scheduled things this way specifically to give you a full ten hours to become accustomed to the idea. You are ready."

Everyone knew a lot more than I did. "Ready for what, Grandfather? Why do you have to leave, and what is Pira being asked to do?"

Zasha's head whipped around in fury. "What right do you have to demand answers, human?" Her hands continued working with some sort of cutting tool as she glared at me. It made a disconcerting sight.

"Hush, child. He has every right to worry for his beloved. Concentrate upon your work."

A chastened Zasha turned back to the column. I wondered where he had gotten the impression that Pira was my "beloved", but it was a bad time to ask. I repeated, "Why must you leave, sir?"

"After my constructor machines commenced the initial colonial phase here, I built a communication centre on the greater moon capable of reaching the twenty-five parsecs to Earth. In your years, the round-trip for communication is about one hundred fifty years. Earth ought to have heard me, and responded. For over three hundred years, I have continued sending data, yet I have heard nothing.

"The scientists of Earth knew the seed ships would call home. They would certainly listen for the rich harvest of knowledge. But…perhaps they cannot respond. Or even listen. I fear the potential reasons. Humanity created the seed ships out of concern for its own survival. Earth had become only marginally habitable when I left.

"I shall return home, to re-establish communications and then move on to colonize some new world. Or to rebuild the world of my birth. Your descendants shall learn which in a half-millennium. I have built a new seed ship for the return journey. It's ready, and so, Pira, are you."

"I'm not!" she whispered, shaking her head.

"For what?" I demanded once again.

Zasha had finished removing a panel from the column, and appeared to be waiting for the conversation to finish. She muttered, "Isn't it obvious?"

"Probably not, child," Grandfather stated. "He lacks data. Son, you are the reason I can leave, so I do owe you an explanation."

Pira looked from the column to me and back. "What does he have to do with this?"

"It is by his help that you became ready to be human."

Zasha made an exasperated noise. "Be human? Don't you mean ready to take over your job?"

"That's exactly what I said, young lady," Grandfather declared evenly. "What did your parents lack?"

The stick-girl canted her head. "You told us, 'A sense of compassion'. So?"

"Incorrect. I taught you, 'A sense of humanity'. You equated it to 'compassion' to make sense out of it. You probably can't come closer until you consent to live among them. I possess that sense, because I was born human. My error with your parents was to start them out as cyborg. I should have let them live as human first. I will not make that mistake again. Zasha, it is time."

The stick-girl nodded and reached into the hole, withdrawing a metallic ball a bit larger than a grapefruit.

Pira made a little whimpering noise and lunged forward as Zasha turned with it. She sprinted the few metres across the floor at a speed I doubt any human could move. The two tumbled with the impact, then rolled in impossible feats of balance back up to their feet.

A flash of fire burst between them, seeming to arc between Pira's hands. They flew backward away from each other, still on their feet, and Zasha summoned a similar flame. An arc cracked from somewhere in the ceiling, slapping the flame away from her and extinguishing it.

As my mind struggled to catch up, I realized that Pira now held Grandfather in her hands. Zasha shook her head ruefully as she faced her. "Grandfather isn't plugged in, so the anti-weapon equipment is on automatic. He programmed it to ignore you, but not me, didn't he?"

Pira gave a nod, changing her grip on Grandfather into more of a cradling hold.

Zasha finally relaxed from her fighting stance. "What are you doing, Pira?"

"Zasha, I will not allow this!" she declared in a hoarse whisper. "I *can't*! You *know* what will happen!"

I finally found my voice. "What will happen?"

She was ready to cry. Her lips trembled. "I…can't say it."

"What she can't say," Zasha explained tiredly, "is that she thinks we'll repeat what the First Wave did. She's told me so, many times. She doesn't believe we could stop ourselves."

Pira visibly muscled up strength and added, "You don't either, Zasha."

"Oh, I know I can't stop me, but that's why Grandfather didn't make me his heir. He trusts you to keep me and the others in line."

"Then…" The tears began to flow. "Then he's an idiot! And you're just waiting for him to leave. That's your big opportunity!"

"That hurts," Zasha protested. "I already promised you, right?"

"You promised Girben, too!" she hissed. Zasha heaved a sigh.

"Girben?" I asked, confused. He'd been one of the worst First Wave monsters.

"Yes, I promised him," Zasha admitted with disgust. "That was different. That was before I knew what he'd been doing. Once I learned the truth, I had no choice. For the sake of the lousy, ungrateful humans, I had to betray him. And can you believe it? I still think it was the right thing to do."

I *could* believe it. It may make me sound gullible, but I knew why I believed it.

They had just been throwing weapon fire around with their bare hands, and I felt more than a little terrified of the two at the moment, but I stepped forward to come between them. I faced Pira and held out my hands. "Give him to me, Pira. It'll be okay."

"Don't you understand?" Her pleading eyes still dripped

tears...fragile, uncertain, self-doubting tears that added strength to my belief.

"I do, and I know you're wrong. I can trust you."

"How?" Her voice trembled and she clutched Grandfather to her chest like a child's toy. "What do you really know about me?"

"I know you will follow Grandfather's wishes and I know Zasha will, too."

"What?" Zasha's voice dripped with disbelief. "I appreciate your confidence, but weren't you listening? I worked for Girben! I was on the other side for nearly the entire war!"

*Why are you arguing with me?* I wanted to scream. I nodded instead, still keeping my eyes locked with Pira's as I answered Zasha. "At the end, you weren't. And it doesn't matter. You would be on the human side today, wouldn't you?"

Zasha didn't answer, which was as good as a yes. If she disagreed, she'd surely have kept protesting.

"How can you be so sure?" Pira demanded.

"Because of the dinner she served us last night."

Her brow wrinkled. "Huh?"

"A machine can cook," Zasha pointed out. The way she was arguing Pira's side made me wonder, was she voicing Pira's doubts for her, or did she still have them herself?

"I was raised by a machine," I rebutted, still speaking to Pira. "Nanny can cook, but...even though she has all the human senses, and who knows how many decades of practice, she can't cook like Zasha."

Pira stared at me, perplexed. I scratched my head for a moment, grimacing a little as I recognized how poorly I was explaining myself. "Look, Zasha has no need of food, and I'm betting she can't even taste or smell. That means all she could know about the dinner she served us was the care she took to prepare it. Suffering a handicap like that, she made a curry any human chef would be proud of."

I held my hands out to Pira again. "I can only think of one reason for someone who doesn't eat and dislikes humans to possess the kind of passion it would take to do that. She's doing it because Grandfather wants her to be human, and she is determined to honour his wish. Aren't you, Zasha?"

Again, Zasha gave no answer…which was again as good as a yes.

Pira slowly placed the ball that was Grandfather in my hands. I turned and extended him toward Zasha.

She didn't take him at first. "How do you know I'm not just faking it until Grandfather's gone, like Pira said?"

"Your curry was no fake. I'm sure of it."

The stick-girl hesitated a moment longer, then accepted the cyborg brain. She heaved a sigh and muttered, "Humans!"

We rode an elevator to the very top of the Lander, so that Pira and I could watch together from within a glass enclosure as Zasha carefully placed Grandfather in the little spacecraft waiting for him. The day was still very young; the morning light was barely strong enough to see.

The craft, little more than a missile, was merely the first footstep in his long journey home. An intermediate vessel would intercept him after a boost into the sky, to take him to the seed ship awaiting him in orbit around the greater moon.

Once Zasha finished the task and began her walk back to the enclosure, Grandfather's voice came to us once again. "Well done, son. Take care of my granddaughter for me, won't you?"

"Yes, sir." After a moment of thought, I asked, "You could hear us?"

"I reviewed the audio records after Zasha plugged me in. Pira, accept control."

I saw no visible change beyond Pira closing her eyes and breathing deeply, but she opened them and declared, "I have control, Grandfather. Farewell."

She leaned her head against my shoulder as Zasha joined us. The little craft flared and hissed upward, then arched over our heads and disappeared into the sunrise.

Thank you for reading.

If you've enjoyed this anthology, please leave
a review at your favourite retailer.